It Started With Memories

A PORTHGARRION STORY

by

Suzie Peters

Copyright © Suzie Peters, 2022.

The right of Suzie Peters as the Author of the Work has been asserted by her in accordance with the Copyright, Designs and Patents Act, 1988.

First Published in 2022
by GWL Publishing
an imprint of Great War Literature Publishing LLP

Produced in United Kingdom

Apart from any use permitted under UK copyright law, this publication may only be reproduced, stored or transmitted, in any form, or by any means, with prior permission in writing of the publishers or, in the case of reprographic production, in accordance with the terms of licences issued by the Copyright Licensing Agency.

All characters in this publication, with the exception of any obvious historical characters, are fictitious and any resemblance to real persons, either living or dead, is purely coincidental.

ISBN 978-1-915109-19-4 Paperback Edition

GWL Publishing
2 Little Breach
Chichester
PO19 5TX

www.gwlpublishing.co.uk

Dedication

For S.

Chapter One

Nicki

A funeral at any time is awful… but just before Christmas, it seems so much worse.

The shops are filled with toys and gifts, and an excess of perfume, and the streets are lit with sparkling lights and the wonder of children's faces. The sounds of carols and annoying Christmas tunes from thirty, or sometimes fifty years ago drift across the air. It's a time of love and happiness… for families.

It's not a time to bury your mother.

But we don't get to choose the circumstances of such things, do we?

A damp, overcast afternoon in the middle of December certainly isn't what I'd have chosen for Mum, and as I watch her coffin being lowered into the ground, I let out a sob. I've been expecting this day for such a long time, but now it's here, I'm overwhelmed by the realisation that I'm alone in the world. I'm forty-one years old, and I have no-one.

"Oh, come here, love." Shirley's unusually hushed voice is a mark of respect, not just for my mother, but for the surroundings.

She puts her arm around me, but as much as I want to relish the comfort, I can't. She's my mum's neighbour, and someone who I've enjoyed a chat with over the last four years, but she's not my mum. I don't push her away, though. That would be rude. I let her hug me for a while, until it feels appropriate to pull back, and then I smile at her and murmur a polite, "Thank you."

She smiles back, although it doesn't touch her pale brown eyes, her effort at good cheer clearly as half-hearted as my own, and then she nods towards the car park.

"Shall we go?"

I want to ask for a few minutes to myself, but she's done so much for me already, I don't feel as though I can impose upon her any further. I nod my head and, with a last glance at the hole in the ground where my mother now lies, Shirley and I make our way to the edge of the path, where her husband, Gerald is waiting to accompany us back to the car park.

They're roughly the same age, in their mid-sixties, and like many couples who've been married for as long as they have, they bear certain similarities. They're both a little overweight, and although Gerald is taller than his wife, it's not by much. Their hair has greyed, but it was once a mid-brown, in both cases, and they are constantly kind and dependable.

Gerald smiles and falls into step behind us, walking with us back to their car, where he opens the doors and waits for both of us to get in, before he climbs in behind the wheel.

I came to the church in the funeral car, with Shirley by my side. Gerald had to drive their Honda here, so we'd have a way of getting home again, although he said he didn't mind. I don't blame him, either. There's something about funeral cars… about the way people stare at them, and at their occupants. It makes you feel uncomfortable… as though the day isn't bad enough already, and you need an audience for your grief.

The church is only a short drive from Mum's house, and luckily I'm sitting in the back, so I don't feel obliged to make conversation. I can stare out of the window at the narrow streets of Mevagissey; my home for the last four years… although I don't think it will be for much longer.

Gerald parks on the driveway outside the bungalow he and Shirley share, but we don't go inside. The wake – if it can be called that – is being held in my mother's home, so we all traipse out onto the road, along the path, and up my mother's driveway, by-passing my five-year-old Mini. I let us in, pleased now that I left the heating on. It relieves some of that cold, damp feeling that seems to have been following me around all day.

I take Shirley's coat and put it, together with my own, on my bed, before I come back out. Shirley's rolling up her sleeves and she gives me another of those sympathetic smiles.

"Come on," she says. "They'll be here any minute."

I follow her through to the kitchen, where the plates of sandwiches and sausage rolls she brought around earlier today are sitting on the work surface, all covered with cling film. She's also supplied me with extra crockery, and while I fill the kettle, the cold water tap running slowly, like it always does, she lays out cups and saucers on a large tray. I gaze out of the kitchen window at the desolate garden, Mum's precious roses pruned to skeletal twigs, the last of the autumn leaves still peppering the lawn, and I try my hardest to hold back my tears.

"I thought they'd never leave." Gerald comes back into the living room, having shut the front door on the last of the guests.

Shirley nods her head and picks up a stray teacup from the side table. "That's the problem with funerals. People tend to hang on, thinking they're helping by keeping you company, but in reality, it's at times like this you'd rather be by yourself." There's a moment's silence and I look up from my seat in the corner of the sofa to see the two of them exchange a glance. "Speaking of which," she says, "we should probably be off."

"No… please…" I'm suddenly terrified by the prospect of being truly alone, even though I've been living here by myself for the last ten days, and she puts down the cup and comes to sit beside me. "I mean, if you've got something you need to do, then…"

"No, my dear," she says in the kindliest of voices. "We can stay for as long as you need us."

"I'll put the kettle on, shall I?" Gerald offers and I smile up at him, grateful to both of them.

"It's awful, isn't it?" Shirley says once he's gone. "Having such a big gap between a death and a funeral. I mean, ten days isn't that long, I suppose, but it's long enough to think about getting used to the person being gone, only for the funeral to bring it all back again."

"I know. I was just thinking about that." Or more precisely, about how lonely I feel now this final act of death has been completed.

"Have you made any plans yet?"

I turn to face her, knowing she's asking out of concern, not nosiness. "I'm going to sell the bungalow." She raises her eyebrows, although she doesn't say anything. "I want to move back to Bath."

"I see." She nods her head.

"I enjoyed living there… being surrounded by history and losing myself in a city. Hopefully, the proceeds from the sale of this place will give me the chance to buy somewhere of my own."

"That's what your mum would have wanted."

I know she's speaking the truth there. Mum and I discussed it often enough in the years since I gave up my rented flat on the outskirts of Bath and moved here to look after her.

"Did I hear you say you're going to sell up?" Gerald says, coming back in with the tea.

"Yes." I look up into his smiling face and take a cup from him, leaving him to pass another to Shirley before he takes a seat with his own. "I think I'll wait until after Christmas, though. It would be a waste of time to put it on the market now."

"Absolutely," he says. "Never a good time to sell. People are too preoccupied with other things."

"Will you fix the place up at all?" Shirley asks, and we all look around at the living room. I know she's not being rude, but I think the best way to describe this space is to say that it's functional. We had to make it that way to accommodate Mum's walking frame and her recliner chair, which has to sit a long way out from the wall. Even so, this room looks fairly 'normal' compared to Mum's bedroom, and the bathroom, which were both completely refurbished after her first stroke, to allow for the restrictions of only having the full use of one side of her body.

"No. I know I could have it ripped apart again to make it more appealing for a family buyer, but I'd rather drop the price and let someone else have the hassle of living with builders in the house."

"I don't blame you." Shirley rolls her eyes. "I've never forgotten the chaos of our extension."

"Hmm… never again." Gerald shakes his head. "Three days without water, windows that didn't fit, a leaky roof, and uneven flooring… it was a nightmare."

I wasn't living here at the time, but I remember Mum telling me all about the work Shirley and Gerald had done not long after they moved in next door. The stories were enough to put anyone off.

"There's no mortgage on this place, and there's some money left from Dad's life insurance, so even if I have to sell for less than the market value, I should still have plenty to buy myself a flat, or maybe a small house."

"Will you go back to teaching?" Gerald asks.

"Probably. It's all I know." And I can't think for the life of me what else I'd do.

They nod their heads in unison, which is something else I've noticed they do quite a lot.

"Well, if you need any help, you know where we are." Shirley reaches over, giving my hand a squeeze as she's talking, and it's all I can do not to burst into tears.

We've washed up, cleared away, and taken all the crockery back round to Shirley and Gerald's house. She suggested I could stay with them for dinner, but I declined. I felt like I'd taken up enough of their day as it was… and I had to face the reality of an empty house eventually.

As I say, it's been like this since Mum passed away, but oddly, it feels so much more final now, probably because what I'm really facing is an empty life, rather than an empty house. Planning the funeral has kept me busy… stopped me thinking. But that's all done now, and I walk back in the door, pushing it closed behind me, and lean against it, listening to the 'tick-tock' of the hall clock, the slight rattle the bathroom window always makes, and the low hum of the fridge-freezer. They're the everyday sounds of life… but there's no life here now. Not for me. This isn't my home. It's not where I grew up, so I have no attachment to it, other than the woman who's no longer here… whose presence I miss more than I thought possible.

"Pull yourself together," I mutter out loud, standing up straight and squaring my shoulders before my emotions get the better of me… again.

I wander into the living room and glance around, although I can't face staying in here. There are too many reminders of Mum.

I close the door and go into the dining room instead. We used to eat in the kitchen more than in here, so there aren't as many memories. It's chilly, but I don't mind, and I pull my cardigan around myself. I feel a little aimless. I'm not hungry and it's too early to think about bed, so I go over to the writing desk in the corner of the room, opening it and sitting down in the leather chair that used to be in my father's study. He didn't need one when he took early retirement and they moved here, but he kept the desk and chair, simply because he liked them. He was an accountant by trade, and I smile to myself, wondering what he'd think of my plans… whether he'd agree with what I've got in mind, or if he'd tell me to spend a little money making the house look more presentable. Not that I'm going to, but I can't help wondering what he'd say.

I've already been through a lot of the paperwork in here, on the advice of Mum's solicitor, just to make sure everything was in order. It's stacked in neat piles… one for the bank, one for utility bills, one for insurance…

There really isn't much left to do, except go through her personal letters and photographs. My mum was someone who wrote letters… back when she could write, before the stroke stole that from her. She didn't even own a computer, and had no idea about e-mails or doing anything online until I moved here. I smile, recalling her confusion when I first gave her my laptop, and we set her up with an e-mail address… and then her excitement, when her old schoolfriend Jocelyn, who lives in Australia, replied to her very first message. It used to take her hours to type them, but she enjoyed it, and although she sometimes moaned about it not being the same as writing a letter, it was an excellent compromise.

And life was full of compromises.

I suck in a breath, wondering if I'm ready for this. I could leave it all for another day, but out of morbid curiosity, I pull out one of three photograph albums and open it, my breath catching in my throat when I look down at images of myself as a child in the back garden of our home in Porthgarrion. My father is standing behind me, his brown hair swept back from his handsome, smiling face. He's dressed casually, so it must have been taken at the weekend. I look like I was about five years old, my long dark hair tied up in bunches, wearing a bright pink t-shirt and denim shorts... ever the tom-boy at that age. Turning the page, I smile, tears welling in my eyes as I come across another picture of myself... although this one dates from several years later. I think I'd have been fourteen when this one was taken, and I'd left my tom-boy days behind. My hair hangs in waves over my shoulders, which I seem to remember hoping would make me look older. That always felt necessary to me, being as I was so much shorter than everyone around me. I'm wearing jeans and a white t-shirt, worn tucked-in but baggy, with a sunflower on the front. Sunflowers were all the rage at the time, as were belts with enormous buckles, like the one I can see just beneath my t-shirt. I'm not in the garden, but standing by the harbour wall. Beside me is Rory Quick, a good five or six inches taller than me, even then, dark-haired and serious-looking, in what appear to be grey jeans and a black t-shirt. Beyond him is Suzannah Grigg, beautiful as ever, her long blonde hair tied up in a ponytail. She was taller than me, but I recall many an afternoon spent in either her bedroom or mine, during which she'd bemoan her more boyish figure.

"I wish I wasn't so flat-chested." She'd usually be pushing up her breasts as she said that, trying to make them appear more generous, while staring at herself in the mirror. I'd be lying on the bed, reading a magazine, or messing around with my hair.

"I'm sure you won't always be."

I'd invariably say something like that, just like she'd always tell me my bum didn't look big in my jeans. It was what best friends were for.

And I was right. She wasn't always flat-chested... although her best asset was always her legs, and in this photograph, she's wearing a bright yellow dress that's perfectly decent, but is short enough to show them off to perfection... along with the tan she'd no doubt been working on for most of that summer.

I sigh, finally letting my eyes rest on the fourth member of our group, a smile touching at my lips. Ed Moyle is grinning mischievously at the camera, his sun-streaked blond hair as much of a mess as ever. He's wearing stonewashed jeans, a white t-shirt and a baggy check shirt and I let my finger trace over his perfect face, lingering on his lips, as I feel that familiar ache in my chest.

There was something about Ed, even from my earliest memories of him. He and Rory were renowned for getting into mischief, although Ed was usually the ringleader. Rory was the more serious of the two, and Ed was the one who was constantly fooling around. At least it seemed that way. But he had a quieter side, too... a softer side. He didn't show it very often, but when he did, it was memorable... or it was to me, anyway. I've never forgotten that time, probably only a year or two after this photograph was taken, when I fell while we were walking along the harbour. It was my own fault. I was so busy looking at him, I tripped over my own feet and fell like a sack of potatoes. I felt like such an idiot, but I also cut my hand on a piece of glass that was lying on the path. The pain was excruciating, and while Rory ran for the doctor and Suzannah went to find my mum, Ed sat me back against the harbour wall before yanking off his t-shirt and clamping it over the wound. He held it tight, reassuring me I'd be okay. I leant on him, quite intentionally. He didn't seem to object, and it took my mind off the pain.

Then there was that time when we were all walking down Church Lane together. We were on our way back from college, and had just got off the bus. Suzannah lived in one of the side streets, and we'd already said 'goodbye' to her. Normally, Ed would have gone back to the pub, but he was spending the afternoon and evening with Rory, and the three of us carried on together. We were laughing about something, and as we turned onto the harbour, a car came from behind us, taking the corner far too quickly, and mounting the pavement. I was closest to the edge, and Ed grabbed me, pulling me to safety. Rory wrote down the car's registration number and ran back to the police station to speak to his father, while Ed kept hold of me… not tightly in his arms, with any degree of affection, but enough to make me feel safe, which was what I needed. I recall thanking him, just before Rory came back out, and wishing the episode had meant as much to him as it had meant to me.

I look down at the photograph again, and sigh, remembering that feeling, and wishing I could have it back… wishing I could have it all back. We may have been little more than children when this picture was taken but I knew, even then, that I loved him. I've never stopped in all these years, even though I know it's pointless. Of course, he never knew about that, just like I never knew that, within a few short years, my friendship with all of them would take a back seat to their romances.

Rory got together with a girl called Joanne. She wasn't part of our group and I didn't like her very much. I certainly didn't think she was good enough for Rory, but her arrival on the scene wasn't the reason for my eventual drifting into the wilderness. That was because of Ed and Suzannah. You see, it's one thing for the man you love not to notice you romantically… but to watch him fall in love with your best friend, that's something else altogether. And it was too much for me.

Chapter Two

Ed

I push my bowl to one side and pick up my cup, finishing the last of my tea. A glance at the clock on the kitchen wall tells me I've only got a few minutes before I need to get downstairs again, and I sit back, letting out a long sigh.

Half an hour goes nowhere, although I've got no-one to blame but myself for not having any time. It was my decision to lengthen the opening hours, and it felt like a good idea. I reasoned if I was working longer, I'd have less time to think… less time to dwell. I forgot I'd also have less time to eat, to rest, to have a life of my own.

Okay, so I haven't had a life to speak of for the last seven years, but the principle remains the same. With the pub being open from eleven in the morning until ten-thirty at night, I don't remember when I last did something as simple as cook a meal. I don't starve… obviously. I eat from the pub menu, but it's not the same as cooking for myself, or better still, cooking for someone else.

Still… I'm not going to think about that now.

I get up and put my bowl and cup into the dishwasher, and then make my way downstairs, groaning slightly when I hear another Christmas song playing on the sound system. It's not that loud… little more than background noise, really, but it's enough to drive you insane when you've heard the same piece of music twenty times in a day… and when you know Christmas is still ten days away, so it feels like there's no end in sight.

A wave of heat hits me as I pass the door to the pub kitchen, but that's not my destination and I carry on down the corridor, coming out behind the bar and squinting slightly. Ordinarily, the squinting isn't necessary, especially not at this time of night, but at the moment the pub is decked with so many fairy lights I feel as though I should hand out sunglasses at the door.

Fairy lights around the bar, the windows and the fireplace aren't the limit of the festive decorations. There's an enormous tree in the corner, festooned with yet more lights that flash intermittently, which I'm hoping is intentional and not a wiring problem, caused by an overload on the circuit. As if the lights weren't enough, the tree is mostly hidden by more tinsel than should be permitted in the twenty-first century.

I shake my head, making a conscious decision not to be a humbug, even though Christmas does nothing for me anymore… it hasn't since Suzannah died. It used to be fun. That's to say, she used to make it fun, like she did with everything else, but I can't seem to raise the enthusiasm anymore. Like most other things in my life, it's so much 'less' without her, and it's a struggle to paint the smile on my face as I step forward for another evening shift.

The door opens and I glance up, my smile becoming more genuine as I see Sergeant Rory Quick enter the premises. I call him 'Sergeant' because he's still in uniform, but otherwise he'd just be Rory… my oldest friend.

"We don't usually see you in here at this time of night," I say as he walks up to the bar and perches on a stool, his shoulders shuddering slightly as he gets used to the warmth in here from the blazing log fire. Outside, it's just dipped below freezing, so the difference must be more than noticeable.

"I'm surprised you can see anything with all these lights." He looks around the pub, raising his eyebrows.

"Don't blame me… Leanne did it." I nod down the bar, towards the elfin young woman who's currently pulling a pint, and making an outstanding job of it.

He orders a red wine and settles back on the stool a little, watching me pour it. "How long has she been with you now?"

"Since the end of August."

"And that hasn't been long enough for her to work out that this level of frivolity isn't really your style?"

"Evidently not."

I pass the glass across to him and he hands me a ten-pound note, waiting while I fetch his change.

"You've still got Fiona and Nancy, though, haven't you?" he asks.

"Yes. But I need them waiting on tables, not working behind the bar, although Fiona can pull a pint when she has to."

He smiles. "Where's she from?"

"Leanne?"

"Yes. I know where Fiona and Nancy live."

I chuckle. "I'm sure you do, but I love how you know Leanne's not from here."

"Of course I do. What kind of policeman would I be if I didn't know something like that?"

There's something comforting about Rory's knowledge of this place and the people who live here. It's reassuring.

"She's from Mawgan Porth. That's where her family live, anyway. I can't guarantee she was born and bred there."

He glances along the bar again and smiles. "She's good with the customers," he says.

13

"She's good in general… if you discount her obsession with fairy lights."

Rory laughs. "Haven't you taken on a young lad now as well?"

"Yes. That would be Reece. He started at the beginning of the month. Don't get me wrong, Leanne is brilliant behind the bar, but she's not great with the heavier work."

"That's not surprising. There's nothing of her."

I have to agree with him. Leanne might be about five foot six, but she's very slim. She's also very pretty and looks a lot younger than her twenty-four years… to the extent that I asked her to prove her age before I employed her, even though she assured me she'd worked in several pubs before.

"Reece might be the same age as Leanne but he has no experience of working in a bar," I explain. "He finished uni and then went travelling and stayed in Australia and New Zealand for a while."

"It's all right for some." Rory smiles.

"Hmm… He came back earlier this year, but hasn't been able to find any work, so I'm training him up, although it's taking longer than I'd expected."

"Oh? Why's that? Is he a slow learner, or something?"

"No… although he can be quite shy. But the real problem is, we're so busy, I don't have much time to devote to him. Still, he's great with the cellar work, which is a godsend."

"Are you getting too old for it all, then?" Rory says with a smile twitching at his lips.

"If I am, then so are you."

At that moment, the door opens and I look up to see Reece entering the pub. He sticks out, because he's quite tall, with reddish-brown hair, and usually wears brightly coloured clothes, which belie his timid nature.

"Evening, boss," he says with a wave, his eyes wandering over to Leanne and staying there.

"Evening, Reece."

He ignores my reply, and I turn my attention back to Rory.

"Is that him?" he says.

"Yes. About half an hour early for his shift, as it happens."

"He's keen."

"No. He's smitten."

Rory frowns. "With whom?"

"Leanne."

"And how does Leanne feel about that?"

"Oh, she's smitten too… and as he only comes from St. Mawgan…"

"They can give each other a lift to work," Rory says, finishing my sentence.

"I don't think things have progressed to that level yet."

"But they will," he says. "Give it time."

I roll my eyes. "Young love…"

"Hey… it's not restricted to the young, you know?"

"Speaking of love, and people who are significantly younger than us… how's Laura?"

He narrows his eyes, although he's smiling. But that's quite normal when he's talking about his wife. "She's great," he says. "Although she's had to work late tonight. She and her boss are having a meeting about Christmas."

"It's almost as big a deal for the hotel as the summer holidays."

"Yes, it is." He takes a sip of wine, looking a little despondent.

"I know you miss her, but I'm sure you can get through one evening by yourself."

"I wish it was just one evening," he says, shaking his head. "But I have a feeling things are going to get worse before they get better."

"Why's that? Christmas will be over soon." Thank heavens. Personally I can't wait for the New Year and a return to something more 'normal'.

"I know, but the hotel has plans to become a wedding venue."

"Really? I hadn't heard anything about that." It makes sense, when I think about it, though. Apart from the church, there aren't many options for weddings near the village. Not only that, but the hotel is a popular choice for wedding receptions. It's where Laura and Rory held theirs, back in the spring, so branching out into weddings is a natural progression.

"It's early days yet, and there are quite a few hurdles they have to jump over. Laura's handling it all, so even when she does finish work on time, she's been bringing home forms to complete, and files to read."

"And does that bother you?"

He frowns at me, like he doesn't understand my question. "Of course not. Laura loves her job… and she's really good at it. If she wasn't, Stephen Goddard wouldn't have trusted her to deal with this whole wedding venue thing by herself."

I can't help smiling. I've known Rory all his life… all through is first marriage, and I don't remember him ever showing that much pride in Joanne. Although that's not surprising, based on what he told me back in the spring, when he finally revealed that he'd been a little economical with the truth over his first wife's reasons for leaving him. Joanne walked out about six years ago, and at the time, Rory said it was because she'd needed to 'find herself'. To be honest, I wasn't that surprised. Joanne was always flighty, and it was just the kind of thing she would have said. Except it wasn't true. It transpires she had an affair with one of Rory's colleagues, and the two of them ran away together. I don't blame him for keeping that to himself. In his shoes, I'd probably have done the same thing. He did it because he felt embarrassed, like he hadn't been enough… and while I don't believe that, I can understand his reticence to talk about it. I can't see there being any such problems with Laura, though. The two of them are so in love, it's sickening. It's also clear that, even though he was married to Joanne for over fifteen years, he can't have loved her… not like he loves Laura. He never used to show his affections to Joanne in the way he does to Laura. He always kept himself to himself before, but now his feelings are obvious for anyone to see.

"So, I'll have to put up with seeing a lot more of you, will I? If Laura's working all these extra hours."

"I can leave, you know." He smiles. "To be honest, I've only come in because I needed a little Dutch courage."

"You did? What for? Or shouldn't I ask?"

"It's nothing to do with Laura," he says, shaking his head. "At least, not directly."

"Is it a secret?"

"No… it's just that we're going round to Tom and Gemma's later."

"And you need a drink first? Is this because you're going to be discussing the wedding?"

"In a manner of speaking. I'm going to talk to Gemma about inviting Joanne."

I'm more than a little shocked. "To the wedding?"

"Of course to the wedding." He sighs. "I'm pretty sure Gemma's going to say 'no', but Laura wanted me to ask."

"Laura did?"

"Yes. You don't think I'd have come up with such a daft idea by myself, do you?"

"No, but I'm surprised Laura would want Joanne there."

"I'm pretty damn shocked, too. She brought it up while we were on our honeymoon."

They've only been back for about a month, having postponed it until things quietened down in the village. They waited for the holidaymakers to return home after the summer, and for the Bonfire Night festivities, which Rory and I always organise, after which Rory felt he could leave the upholding of law and order in

17

someone else's hands for ten days while he and Laura flew off to Portugal.

"That doesn't sound very romantic."

"It wasn't, but if you want me to be honest, I think she's testing me."

"Do you need testing?"

"No, but I guess it's hard for Laura, what with this being my second marriage…" His voice fades.

"It's her second marriage too."

"I know. But she was only with Wes for a brief time, and I've met the guy. I've seen what a loser he is, and I know what he did to Laura. If I had any insecurities about them, which I don't, they'd be history. She doesn't have that advantage."

"You mean she feels insecure about you and Joanne?"

He tips his head to one side and then the other. "I didn't think so before, but now I'm not so sure. As far as she's concerned, I was married to Joanne for a long time, we had a child together, and the only reason we broke up was because Joanne had an affair with another man and left me for him."

"But surely Laura knows how much you love her… I mean, I know you said you never really told Joanne how you felt, but surely…"

He holds up his hand. "I tell Laura all the time. But you have to remember, her ex ground her down, he took away her self-confidence, and belittled her at every opportunity. No matter what I say, she still sometimes goes through bouts of self-doubt."

"And this is one of those times?"

"Yes… I think so."

"How is Joanne coming to the wedding going to help?"

"It's not about Joanne actually being there. Like I said, I'm pretty sure Gemma won't want to ask her, anyway. She hasn't heard from her mother since she left, and I can't see why she'd want Joanne present on her special day."

"Then why suggest it?"

"To show Laura that it doesn't bother me either way… that I'm happy to put it to Gemma and let her decide."

"I see… I think." He smiles. "You two are okay, aren't you?"

"Of course we are." He seems surprised by my question. "That's the whole point. I'm willing to do this, if it makes Laura feel better… because part of the process is getting her to realise I'd never have done anything like it for Joanne."

I nod my head. "Then why do you need the Dutch courage?"

"Because I'm going to have to open up in front of Tom… and Gemma." He rolls his eyes. "And there are limits." I laugh, and he joins in. He waits while I pull a pint for another customer, and when I return, he says, "You'll have to come and see the house now it's finished. You won't recognise the place." I guess my momentary absence has made him realise he doesn't want to 'open up' too much more in front of me, either. But that's Rory for you.

"I should have been before now."

They've had builders in since not long after their marriage, and have knocked the whole of the downstairs into one open-plan space, installing a new kitchen and having a conservatory added to the back. I think it was finished just before they went on their honeymoon. Or it may have been the week after they got back. I can't remember now, but either way, I haven't had time to take a look yet.

"Why don't you come over after the New Year… when all the craziness has died down?"

"I might just do that."

It's a relief to get into bed… but then, I think that every night at the moment. The noise levels in the pub are ludicrous, but at least it drowns out the dreadful Christmas songs. Sometimes I wonder how we ever had live music. I'm not sure you'd hear a

19

military band if it was playing down there some nights, let alone a solitary singer. We used to have them though… when Suzannah was alive.

She might not have wanted to move here and take over the pub. She might have argued with me loud and long about my plans to develop the place, but once all the work was done and I'd got the pub how I wanted it to be, she became more involved. Live music was one of her suggestions, as was a quiz night. They were both great successes, and I only stopped them when she died… unable to raise the enthusiasm anymore.

I turn over, staring at her side of the bed… or what was her side of the bed, and I struggle to remember what she looked like when she used to lie there. It's become harder of late. I can't recall the exact shade of her hair, or the colour of her eyes… and as for her voice, that's long gone. She's like a wraith, a shadowy figure in the distance… ever present, but hazy now, and always out of reach.

Sometimes I wonder if that's a sign; if I can't hear or see her so clearly anymore because something is telling me it's time to move on. Except every time I think that, the guilt washes over me in waves, and I drown, just a little more in the tide of missing her so much, I can still taste it.

Chapter Three

Nicki

Maybe it was finding the photographs, or the memories they brought back. I can't be sure now. Or maybe it was the feeling I got when I put them away again, that I needed to lay those ghosts to rest…

Or perhaps it was a desire not to spend Christmas by myself at my mother's house, remembering so many other Christmases spent with her… and Dad. I would have been by myself too. Shirley and Gerald are going to stay at their daughter's place in Sidmouth from Christmas Eve until the day after Boxing Day, so maybe there was a subconscious wish to avoid the ultimate loneliness.

Whatever the reason, the result is that, with less than a week to go until Christmas, I'm driving to Porthgarrion. Now I'm on my way, though, I'm not sure it was such a good idea. It felt like it when I went online and booked myself into a suite at the Seaview Hotel. I could have taken a room. There was one available, but I felt like a little luxury… and hang the expense. As I put my credit card details into their website, I contemplated days and days of pampering… no cooking, no making beds, no cleaning... no staring at the blank space where the Christmas tree usually sits. I haven't bothered to put it up this year. It felt inappropriate before the funeral, and once I'd booked the hotel, there seemed little point.

I've got no idea what I'm going to do while I'm away, but I've packed my Kindle and, providing the weather stays fair, I'm looking forward to walking on the cliffs and around the harbour.

Of course, there's every chance I'll see Ed and Suzannah while I'm there, and maybe that's the reason I'm having second thoughts. It might have been over twenty years since I left the village, but I did so with a broken heart. One that's never really mended.

I wonder, will the years have made them more similar, like Shirley and Gerald? I always thought Ed and Suzannah were kindred spirits in the first place, so I'm not sure what difference the passage of time will have made. They had the same colouring, the same sense of humour and outlook on life. As couples go, they were perfectly suited to each other, and I know they'll have been happy together. I don't envy them that... not really. I wanted happiness for Ed, more than anything. Suzannah too. She was my best friend, after all. If I'm being completely honest with myself, I suppose that's why I need to go back... so I can put my broken heart behind me and hopefully move on with my life. Mum's death has made me realise how alone I am... and that I don't like it. Pining for a man who only ever saw me as a friend isn't helping, and no matter how hard it is, I need to leave him – and my memories of him – in the past.

What I'm not so certain about is whether this is the best way to achieve that. With every passing mile, I recall past humiliations... like that cold winter's evening when I stood outside the pub where Ed lived with his mum and dad, and cried my undying love for him. There's nothing very humiliating about that… unless you're caught doing it… by the village policeman. Fortunately, Rory Quick's dad was a lovely man. He didn't comment on what I was doing there, he just offered to walk me home. He didn't lecture me about young love, or there being plenty more fish in the sea, and when we got to my garden gate, he just told me to go indoors and get warm, and then he gave me the kindest of smiles. It was the sort of smile that showed he understood.

I still feel embarrassed, even now, although I console myself that I won't be doing anything like that again. I'm older and wiser now… well, I'm older, anyway. This holiday is making me question my wisdom.

Before I know it, there's a sign for Porthgarrion, and I indicate, turning off the main road into the village. I slow down and smile as I think about the fact that I've never actually driven around here before. I didn't pass my test until after I left Porthgarrion, so I've got no experience of its narrow roads, although they're not too dissimilar to those of Mevagissey.

My parents' former home was in Garden Close and I pass the turning on my left, thinking that I'll take a wander down there while I'm here and have a look at our old house, just for old time's sake. I slow down even more, taking a wide turn into the hotel entrance to avoid hitting the wall, and wondering if it would have been easier to come at it from the harbour instead, although it's a bit late to be worrying about that now. There's a small car park at the front and I pull up in one of three available spaces, checking the clock on the dashboard. It's two-thirty, which is half an hour earlier than the check-in time that was noted on the website, and the confirmation e-mail they sent me. Should I sit here? Or maybe go for a walk?

"Oh, to hell with it."

I get out, pulling my suitcase from the boot, and carry it into the foyer, where I stop for a moment and look around. It's more sumptuous than I'd imagined, with a thick red carpet underfoot, and lots of polished wood on display. Some pretty flowers adorn the table in the centre of the room, and there's a wide staircase at the back, with a shiny brass balustrade. Next to that is an enormous Christmas tree, decorated with white lights and red baubles, and I take a deep breath, feeling pleased now that I came here. It's lovely.

The reception desk is to my left and I wander over, to be welcomed by a pretty red-headed lady, who smiles her greeting at me.

"Good afternoon. Can I help you?"

Her name tag says 'Laura' and I smile back. "Hi. I'm afraid I'm a little early…"

"You've got a reservation?"

"Yes. My name is Nicole Woodward. I know I'm not supposed to be here until three, but I allowed too much time for making the journey, and…"

"Oh, don't worry about that." She waves away my excuses, just as another woman appears, scurrying back to the desk. She's older, with dark brown hair and a name tag that says 'Hazel'.

"Sorry about that," she says. "Do you want me to take over?"

"No, it's fine," Laura replies, tapping a couple of times on the keyboard in front of her and then looking up at me. "You're in the Harbour View Suite."

"What an original name," I say with a smile, and she chuckles.

"I'll show you up."

"Thank you."

She turns, taking a key from one of many hooks behind the desk and steps out, revealing that she's wearing a fitted black suit and high heels that would kill me if I had to wear them all day long, although they look good on her. She leads the way over to the stairs and I follow, pausing with her at the bottom. "That's the dining room," she says, pointing to a door in the corner. "Dinner is served from six-thirty."

"Do I need to reserve a table?"

"No… you're here on the dinner, bed, and breakfast package, so your table is pre-booked."

"Oh, okay."

She starts climbing. "My name is Laura Quick, by the way. I'm the assistant manager here. If you need anything, let me know, although I'm only on duty until three. After that, you can always call down to reception and speak to Hazel, or the Deputy Manager takes over from me. He's quite new, but very friendly. His name is Kieran."

I'm not sure I'm going to remember all that information, but that's not surprising. I'm still reeling from hearing her full name.

"Did you say your surname was Quick?"

"Yes." She turns and looks at me as we reach the top of the stairs and she opens a door to our left, leading into a long corridor. We both pass through and start walking again.

"You're not related to Rory Quick, are you?"

I'd find it impossible to believe she wasn't, although I can't think how. Rory certainly didn't have any sisters, and I'm not aware of him having any cousins either, unless she's very distant.

"Yes," she says, with a broad smile. "He's my husband."

I nod my head, doing my best to hide my surprise. If Laura is married to Rory, what on earth happened to Joanne? They might not have been married when I left Porthgarrion, but they were definitely engaged. Their wedding was all planned, although I can't remember the exact date it was due to take place. I just know it wasn't long after Ed and Suzannah's.

I take a moment to study Laura. She couldn't be more different to Joanne, who was kind of mousey, and had a boyish figure, which is another way of saying she was a stick-insect.

Laura's auburn hair, wide smile and sparkling green eyes hint at someone with a sense of humour… someone who could bring Rory out of his shell. She doesn't look more than thirty, though, so the age-gap between them must be at least eleven or twelve years. Not that I'm judging… I'm just surprised.

I'm also surprised that Rory didn't marry Joanne. But maybe he saw through her in time. I hope so, for his sake. I always thought he could have done better, not that I can claim to have known her very well – certainly not as well as I knew Suzannah – but she always struck me as selfish. She was also one of those people who wants what everyone else has got. I remember, when Ed and Suzannah announced they were getting engaged, she suddenly started talking about her engagement to Rory, even though I'm not sure he'd actually asked her. When Ed and Suzannah revealed the date of their wedding, Joanne told everyone that she and Rory would be getting married just a few weeks later. She couldn't let Ed and Suzannah have their moment. She had to try and steal their thunder… or that's how it felt to me.

Laura stops by the last door on the right. It has the name 'Harbour View Suite' engraved on a wooden plaque in the centre panel, and she puts the key in the lock, turning it, before handing it to me and opening the door.

"Do you know Rory then?" she asks.

"Yes, I do… or I did. Many years ago."

I decide not to ask about Joanne, in case Laura knows nothing of her husband's former romance… if it can be called that. The Rory I remember could never have been called a great romantic. But I think that suited Joanne.

I step into the room and let out a long sigh. "Oh… this is lovely."

She smiles. "It is rather nice, isn't it?"

I look around, taking in the enormous room, which is dominated by a raised four-poster bed, covered in fresh white linen and a dark blue throw, which matches the carpet. On the far side, by the windows, is the living area, which comprises a lighter blue sofa and a low coffee table, adorned with magazines. Slightly off to one side is a small dining table and two chairs. There's a television mounted on the wall, and in the corner of the room is an open door.

"That leads through to the dressing area and bathroom," Laura says, noticing the direction of my gaze.

"How luxurious." I leave my suitcase by the bed and wander over to the window, looking out across the harbour, my eyes instantly falling on the Harbour Lights pub. "Does Ed Moyle still live here?" The words leave my lips, unbidden, and I feel myself blush.

"Yes. He owns the pub." I turn to find Laura's head is tilted to one side, and she's frowning slightly. "I'm sorry… are you from Porthgarrion?"

"Yes. I was born here. I moved away over twenty years ago, though."

"I doubt you'll find much has changed." Laura laughs and so do I.

"Is Rory still a policeman?"

"He's a sergeant," she says, and I can hear the pride in her voice.

"Following in his father's footsteps."

"Yes. You'll have to make a point of catching up with him and Ed while you're here. I'm sure they'd love to see you."

That might be true of Rory, but I'm not so sure about Ed. Although I don't know why he wouldn't be pleased to see me. As far as he was concerned, I was a friend… nothing more, nothing less. The problem with us seeing each other is mine, not his.

Laura explains that, although my table has been reserved for dinner and breakfast, I can phone down to reception and order room service, if I prefer, and she shows me the menu. Then she leaves, wishing me an enjoyable stay.

Once I'm alone, I sit on the edge of the bed, wondering about her suggestion... not about catching up with Rory, but about going to see Ed.

Should I?

Obviously it would mean seeing him with Suzannah, but that's what I came here for... to lay that ghost to rest. And I need to get it over with.

Although I might unpack and have dinner first...

Chapter Four

Ed

One of the advantages of keeping busy and having less time to think is that I don't have to focus too much on the time of year. Okay, so the fairy lights and Christmas tree are a bit of a give-away, but I haven't bothered to decorate the flat this year. I always find Christmas quite hard. It reminds me of that first year without Suzannah. She'd only died a couple of months beforehand, and I struggled through the festive season, barely functioning without her. I'd like to say things have become easier over the years, but that would be an exaggeration. The reality is, I've just learned to function better on my own… that's all.

I don't yet know what I'll be doing over Christmas, other than working… obviously. I don't open the pub on Christmas Day and normally I'd spend it with Dan and my mother. She usually comes over here… or she has done since Suzannah died, and I suppose this year, that means it'll just be the two of us, because I haven't heard from Dan in ages. I don't expect him to come home, either. He didn't even make it back during the summer, which he usually does. Instead, he sent me a rare text message in August, by which time I'd already worked out for myself that he wasn't coming home. He didn't give a reason for his absence, but told me about a big surfing competition he'd been invited to attend in December… in Hawaii. The information he gave was scant, but I knew it must be big, otherwise I don't think he'd have bothered to tell me… unless that was just his way of letting me know he wouldn't be home for Christmas. I can't be sure. Anyway, the point was, he'd been invited to take part, and it sounded quite prestigious, so I replied, congratulating him. It was a reminder that I know almost nothing of the life he lives now, and I'm starting to question why I spent so much money having the attic here converted into a self-contained apartment for him. He hasn't been home since it was completed, and there's a part of me wondering if he'll ever come back again. He seems to enjoy his life on the surfing circuit, and has done for several years now, only coming home for a few months in the summer to teach at the local surf school, and earn enough money to tide him over. Like I say, this year, he didn't even manage that, and it's crossed my mind on more than one occasion that there might be a girl involved… not that I've asked. It's another side of Dan's life I know nothing about…

"Can I have another red wine, and a gin and tonic?" Michael Cole puts two glasses down on the bar, and I smile at him. He's quite tall, probably around my height, with short, dark hair. I didn't serve him when he first arrived, earlier this evening. Leanne did. But I know he's here with his twin sister, Melissa. They're not inseparable by any means, but I think their dad's illness has brought them closer. He was diagnosed with dementia a few years back, although his health had been failing for a long while before his diagnosis. He lives in a nursing home now, and from what I've heard, has no recollection of anything, including his own children… which has to be hard.

"How's business?" I ask him as I reach for a clean gin glass and add a few ice cubes.

He and Melissa own the gift shop on the harbour and have done for years, ever since they took it over from their ailing father. It wasn't a gift shop then; it was a toy shop, but I think they're making more of a go of it, now they've branched out. Their range includes small hardware items, and even gardening supplies. It helps to keep them going through the winter.

"Pretty good," he says with a smile. "But I suppose, if we can't make money at this time of year, we probably shouldn't be in business."

"Same here."

The door opens and I'm aware of the chilly breeze that filters into the pub, along with the new arrival, and I glance up.

The woman who's just entered is by herself. That alone is unusual at this time of year. She's also tiny, and wrapped up against the cold, in a thick jacket, with a scarf around her neck, and as she undoes it, I'm struck by two things. The first is how beautiful she is. The second is that I'm sure I've seen her before. I can't place her, though, and Michael's slight cough brings me back to reality.

"Sorry," I mutter and finish preparing his drinks.

He pays by card, tapping it against the machine, and then thanking me before he picks up the glasses and wanders back to the table he's sharing with Melissa, close to the roaring fire.

The woman who's just come in walks straight up to the bar, right up to me, undoing her jacket and then taking it off. In doing so, she reveals herself and although I don't mean to, I find my eyes wandering to her full bosom, narrow waist and rounded hips. She's like the perfect little package, all wrapped up in tight stonewashed jeans and a pale pink sweater, and I feel myself blush as my eyes alight on her smiling face once more. I've got no idea whether she noticed my admiration, but that's not the point here. The point is, I haven't looked at a woman like that in years... not since Suzannah died, and I'm not sure how comfortable I feel about it. Even so, now isn't the time to dwell, especially as the woman is staring at me expectantly, which is even more confusing than my reaction to her. Why doesn't she just ask for a drink?

"Hello, Ed." My stomach lurches, my chest tightening. I'd know that slightly husky voice anywhere. It's one of the sexiest sounds in the world. It always was, and it's like all the intervening years just fade away. I'm eighteen years old, all over again, and suddenly, admiring her doesn't seem wrong at all. It seems perfectly natural. I used to do it all the time, back when I was torn between infatuation with the most beautiful girl in the village, and loyalty to my best friend. Loyalty won, but that doesn't mean I've forgotten.

"I can't believe it's you. Who'd have thought? Nicki Woodward, back in Porthgarrion, after all these years." What's more unbelievable than her presence here, is that she looks even better than she did then. I wouldn't have thought that possible, but the irrefutable evidence is standing right before me. She was beautiful twenty years ago, but she's beyond that now. I can't see a trace of grey in her dark brown hair, and while she used to wear it loose around her shoulders, it's a little shorter now, and tucked behind her ears. That's a good thing, because it means I can see even more of her bewitching face. Her eyes are dark and sparkling… although to be fair, I need to allow for the glaring fairy lights, and her skin is glowing, with not a wrinkle in sight, not even when she smiles. I can't say the same for myself.

"I'm amazed you recognised me." She hops up onto a stool, still smiling, and I smile back, although I can't help feeling a little awkward. I know how much I liked her all those years ago, but she thinks we were just friends. She has no idea I wanted so much more.

"Can I get you something to drink?"

"Hmm… a small red wine, please."

I turn, reaching for a glass, and notice my hand is shaking slightly as I pour the wine. *Pull yourself together, man.* I take a breath and attempt to regain some control, before turning back to her and pushing the glass across the bar.

"It's on the house," I say, as she reaches into her handbag.

"You don't have to do that."

"For old time's sake."

Why did I say that? There are no 'old times' between us. Except, I suppose, we were friends. We were good friends, and if I needed an excuse to buy her a drink, that's more than adequate.

She raises the glass and says, "Cheers," putting it to her lips and taking a sip.

"So… what's brought you back to Porthgarrion?" I ask, just to make conversation.

She puts down the glass and purses her lips, blinking once or twice. "My mum just died, and…"

"Oh, God… Nicki. I'm so sorry. I—"

She waves her hand in front of her face, and I stop talking. I feel bad now, watching her struggle with her emotions. It's a feeling I know far too well, and I wish there was something more I could do. I could go around to her side of the bar and give her a hug… but would that be too familiar? We don't know each other anymore, after all. The passing years have changed us… well, they've changed me. I wait, and she takes a breath, swallowing hard.

"Sorry about that," she says.

"Don't apologise. I know how hard it is." *Better than most.*

"It's just that she only died a couple of weeks ago, and…"

"That recently?"

"Yes."

"How's your dad coping?"

She frowns. "My dad?" Her face clears. "Oh… I suppose you don't know. Dad died years ago… probably only about eighteen months after he and mum moved away from Porthgarrion."

I remember that. It was just months after Nicki left, and I shake my head, feeling guilty. "I'm sorry, Nicki."

"Why? You had no way of knowing."

I manage a smile. "What happened to him?"

"In the irony of ironies, having saved all their lives, and decided to take early retirement so they could make the most of things while they were still young enough, he had a massive heart attack."

"How old was he?"

"Fifty-seven."

I sigh, unable to help myself. "And your mum?"

"His death hit her hard. She'd only just turned fifty. But I think what made it worse was that she'd left her friends behind when they moved away from here. I wondered for a while if she'd move back, but they'd bought the bungalow because Dad liked the garden. It was going to be his project, and she set her mind on doing it herself, the way he'd have wanted it done."

"Hmm… they never had much of a garden here, did they?"

"No, although Dad still liked to potter."

I can see the sadness in her eyes and I lean over the bar, just slightly. "I'm sorry, Nicki."

She shakes her head. "Dad's death was a long time ago now, and as for Mum's… it was hardly unexpected."

"Had she been ill then?"

"Not ill as such, but she had a stroke four years ago. It was a bad one, and I've been caring for her ever since. I always knew it was just a matter of time."

"I know that feeling."

"You do?"

"Yes. My dad had a stroke too. It's what forced him to give up the pub."

"Is he still alive?"

I shake my head. "No. He survived for about three years. We all thought he was doing okay, but then he had another massive stroke, right out of the blue."

She reaches out, her hand halfway across the bar, and while I could take it, I don't. "I'm sorry, Ed," she murmurs. "Does your mum still live here?"

"No. After his first stroke, they moved to Padstow, and Mum lives there now."

"She didn't want to move back after he died?"

"No. She'd had long enough to make friends over there, and I think there were too many memories here. I could understand that. I could understand why they left, too… but sometimes it could be difficult."

"In what way?"

"Padstow might only be half an hour away, but whenever she called, because Dad had fallen, or because – I don't know – she couldn't manage something by herself, I'd have to drop everything and go rushing over there, and leave Suz… Suzannah running this place by herself."

That's odd. I haven't struggled to say Suzannah's name for ages. For a while, I couldn't say her name at all… not without breaking down. Then, I used to stumble over it, like I just did. But I haven't done that for a long time. So why now?

"Why didn't they stay here?" she asks, either not noticing my difficulties, or choosing to ignore them.

"My dad found it hard to accept that he couldn't work anymore. He might have been older than Mum, but he wasn't ancient, and the day before his stroke, he'd done a full shift in here as usual. It's quite physical work, too, but he never shied away from it."

"I'm sure," she says and for a second or two, her eyes drop, roaming over my chest and arms, before they dart up to my face again and I notice a slight blush on her cheeks. "What happened? On the day he had his stroke, I mean."

"Mum woke up and noticed one side of his face had fallen. She didn't realise what was happening, but she knew something was wrong, so she called an ambulance… and then phoned me. I met her at the hospital, by which time they'd already sent him for an emergency scan, which revealed a brainstem stroke."

She frowns. "Those are usually… serious, aren't they?"

I notice her hesitation, but I guess she was just trying to find another word for fatal. 'Serious' feels okay to me, though. It all felt pretty damned 'serious' at the time.

"They said Mum had saved his life. If she hadn't acted so quickly, things could have been very different. As it was, he lost the use of his right side. Literally, in the blink of an eye, he went from being a strong, fit, healthy man, to someone who couldn't feed, or wash, or clothe himself without help."

"He had physiotherapy, though?"

"Oh, yes. He stayed in the hospital for weeks, having all kinds of rehab, and then once he was released, someone came to see him at home. They helped him get limited movement back in his hand, but that was about it. He was certainly never going to stand behind the bar and pull a pint again. That affected him mentally. He got angry about the smallest things, so Mum decided it was better to move him away from here… to somewhere different, where he didn't have the same memories."

Nicki nods her head. "And that's when you and Suzannah took over the pub?"

"Well, we took it over before they moved. It was clear Dad wouldn't be able to work again, and someone had to step in.

Mum couldn't have done it, even if she'd wanted to – which she didn't. Dad needed her too much, and working here is more than a full-time job… it's a way of life."

"You wanted to do it, though, didn't you?"

"Yes, I did. Although it wasn't an easy decision. It was as unexpected for us as it was for Mum and Dad. I was working for a brewery, earning well, with fairly steady hours. We were renting a house on the edge of the village, but had saved quite a bit towards buying somewhere. Dan was still a baby, and…"

"Dan?" She raises her eyebrows, looking surprised.

"Yes. My son."

Her eyes widen, and she sits back slightly. "I didn't realise you had children."

"Just the one."

"How old is he?"

"Twenty-one."

She frowns. "Gosh. He must have been born very soon after your wedding. I'm surprised Mum and Dad didn't know about him."

"I think they moved away before we made the pregnancy public knowledge. We kept it quiet for quite a long time in a vain attempt to stop the gossip-mongers."

"Who, I'm guessing made the assumption that Suzannah was already pregnant when you got married?"

I nod my head, chuckling. "They certainly did."

She smiles. "Can I assume she wasn't?"

"You can. I'm not saying we remained completely innocent until after we'd got married, because we didn't. But we were careful… at least until after the wedding."

She stares at me for a second or two and then smiles. "So Dan was a honeymoon baby?"

"Yes, he was."

Her smile widens, although it doesn't touch her eyes, which I find interesting. "I can just imagine Suzannah as a mum."

I struggle a little, swallowing down my emotions, as my memories get in the way. "Hmm… she took to it like a duck to water. My job paid well enough that she didn't have to worry about working, and she relished being a stay-at-home mum. The last thing she wanted was to move in here and raise our son above a pub." That wasn't the only reason for Suzannah's reticence, but it was the one she gave me at the time.

I glance around while Nicki takes another sip of wine, and although I now know how great the cost was in coming here, I also know this is where I belong… and no amount of guilt over past mistakes is going to change that.

Chapter Five

Nicki

Judging from the look on his face when he realised who I was, Ed didn't know I was back in the village… and I'll admit that came as a bit of a surprise.

Knowing what Porthgarrion is like, I'd half expected that Laura would have gone home and told Rory of my presence at the hotel, and that he'd have called Ed. But evidently not.

Ed's hardly changed a bit. Okay, so maybe he looks a little older, but don't we all? And I'd say it's maturity, rather than age. When he smiles, there are tiny lines around his eyes that crinkle up. They speak of years of laughter, and love, and happiness… although I don't want to think about that. His smile is just the same as it always was. It still lights up his handsome face and makes my heart sing. I have to say, I remember him as having a more athletic build, but now he definitely falls into the muscular category, his shirt fitting tight across his chest and arms. He said his job was quite physical, though, so I suppose that accounts for it. I just hope he didn't notice me admiring him… not that I could help myself. He's worth admiring. He always was.

He's just as tall as I remember, with eyes that are the colour of a perfect summer sky, and I look up into them, still struggling to come to terms with what can never be, as I glance at the doorway behind him, wondering if Suzannah might walk through it at any minute. I know she'd greet me warmly, as I would her, and we'd laugh and chat, just like we always did. I was good at hiding how I felt back then… and hopefully I still am, because nothing's changed. My heart still flutters every time Ed looks at me, and my stomach keeps flipping over at the sound of his deep, soothing voice. No matter what my intentions might have been, it seems those ghosts aren't ready to be laid to rest. Not yet.

I wonder if perhaps seeing them together might help. It'll hurt, I don't doubt that. But maybe it'll make me realise, once and for all, that this is pointless.

I take a sip of wine, just to distract myself, and when I look up, he rubs his hand across his chin. My eyes are drawn to his wedding ring. *Great.* Yet another reminder that, while my heart might be his, his heart belongs to Suzannah. Just like it always did.

"What happened to your mum?" he asks, glancing down the bar to make sure no-one needs serving, before his eyes settle on mine again. "Was it the same as with my dad?"

"Not really. She was living alone when she had her first stroke, so no-one knew anything about it until her neighbour realised the milk hadn't been taken in. Shirley raised the alarm, and the police came, along with an ambulance and the fire brigade, and between them, they broke into Mum's house and found her lying on the bedroom floor."

"God… how long had she been there?"

"We don't really know, and she's never been able to remember.. She was in her nightdress, evidently, but that didn't help. She said something about going to the bathroom, but that could mean anything. It's possible she got ready for bed the night before and was on her way to the bathroom to brush her teeth, or she might have got up to go to the bathroom in the early hours of the morning. Either way, she'd been there for a while. The delay in treating her meant she was left with quite severe paralysis and speech problems."

"We were lucky that way... Dad's speech was never affected."

I nod my head. "Mum never fully recovered hers. She struggled to find words all the time, and slurred over certain letters."

"What about the physical side?" he asks.

"She was improving, with lots of physical therapy, but then she had another stroke. That was about fifteen months after the first one."

"Oh, Nicki. I'm so sorry."

I shake my head, struggling with my unshed tears again. "Don't be kind to me."

He pauses and sighs, and then looks away before he says, "I know. Kindness can be the hardest thing to handle sometimes, can't it?"

"Yes, it can."

Judging from his expression, he seems to understand that better than most, although his loss was a long while ago now. Still, I suppose it's not a feeling you forget in a hurry.

"How did she fare after the second stroke?" he asks.

"Better than I'd feared. When I was sitting in the hospital with her, I was worried she might end up bed-ridden. I wasn't sure how I was going to cope with that by myself, and was working out if we'd need to get a carer to come in and help... but it turned out I was worrying about nothing. She recovered quite well in the end. I think the worst part after that was the fatigue. Sometimes just getting her up and dressed in the morning would be enough to wipe her out until lunchtime."

"Yeah, Dad could be the same. He had good days and bad days with it."

"So did Mum, although after the second stroke it was significantly worse."

"Was she still your mum, though?"

"How do you mean?"

He tilts his head to one side, like he's thinking... or remembering. "Dad's personality changed after his stroke. It's not that unusual from what I've heard, but I know Mum found it hard. She said to me once he wasn't the same man she'd married, and I thought that was really sad."

"It must have been heart breaking for her."

"It was."

"At least I didn't have to go through that. Mum was still exactly the same as she'd always been... just less able. I'm sure she found it frustrating that she couldn't do things, but she used to laugh about it."

"She never got angry?"

"Not that she showed me, no."

I can't help but remember some of the fun we had, even through the darker times of the last four years, and my eyes sting, yet again, at the loss I'm still struggling to come to terms with.

"Would you like to change the subject?" he says.

"Yes, please."

He smiles and nods his head before leaning forward slightly. "I often used to wonder... what made you leave the village so suddenly? I know we'd all drifted apart a bit, but it seemed like you were here one minute and gone the next."

I might have wanted a change of subject, but I wish he hadn't asked me that. Anything but that. I can hardly tell him the truth...

"I—I wanted to get away, to see what the world had to offer." I wonder if that sounds as pathetic to him as it does to me.

"And you couldn't tell any of us? You couldn't let us know your plans?"

"I didn't really have any plans. It wasn't that organised."

"That doesn't sound like you… to be so spontaneous."

I laugh. "Thanks. You'll be calling me boring next."

"I didn't mean it like that. But out of the four of us, I'd have said Suz… Suzannah and I were the more impetuous, and you and Rory were the more… structured."

That's the second time he's stumbled over Suzannah's name, although I can't work out why.

"Structured doesn't sound a great deal better than boring," I say, and he smiles again.

"Either way, I'm surprised." So am I… but then I'm making this up, so I'm entitled to be. "How far did you get?" he asks.

"Not very. I made it to Bath." That at least is the truth, and he laughs, throwing his head back, which makes all my nerve endings tingle. God, I love him so much… and this is hopeless. Why did I come here? Why did I think I could put him, or the memory of him, behind me?

"What did you find in Bath to hold your attention?"

"A university."

He tilts his head again, clearly confused. "You went to university?"

"I hate the fact that you're surprised by that."

"I—I'm not. But when we all left college, you never seemed that interested."

"I wasn't." Back then, the only thing that held my interest was Ed, and even though he'd just started seeing Suzannah, I still held on to a dim hope that it wouldn't last… that he might notice me one day and realise the error of his ways. He didn't, of course, but I took a job in the local supermarket, just so I could stay here, and keep those hopes alive.

"So, what did you end up doing?"

"I became a teacher."

"Of what?"

"Children." He laughs again and I join in. "I taught them history."

"Ahh… always your favourite subject."

"I'm surprised you remembered." He opens his mouth, but then closes it again and grabs a cloth from behind the bar, using it to wipe over the shiny wooden surface, before he looks up at me again. "I even made it to head of department."

"Why are you talking in the past tense?" He puts the cloth down again, focusing on me, in a way that would probably make me feel uncomfortable, if I was talking to anyone other than Ed.

"I gave it up to care for my mother."

He nods his head. "And what are you going to do now?"

"I've got absolutely no idea. In the immediate future, I'm spending Christmas here… obviously. And then I've decided to put my mother's house up for sale. As for the longer term, who knows? I might go back into teaching again, or I might decide to travel the world."

"That sounds like fun."

It does actually. My preferred choice would be to stay here forever and live a life with him. But that's never going to happen, and although I threw that remark out as just something to say, the prospect of travelling for a while seems appealing, now I come to think about it. I could take a few months, see something of the world, and then come back and decide what to do. They're always crying out for teachers, so waiting a while won't hurt… and hopefully Mum's house will have sold by then, and I can buy a place of my own.

Of course, if I should find somewhere abroad, where I felt like putting down roots, I could always do that. There's nothing to keep me in England anymore, and now I've seen Ed again, I think it might be better to put some distance between us, because my feelings for him are still dangerously intense, and I don't think any amount of time is going to help. So maybe distance is the answer.

"Where are you staying?" he asks, snapping me back to reality.

"At the hotel."

He smiles. "Have you met Laura?"

"You mean Rory's wife? Yes, I have. She showed me to my room. She... She's not what I expected at all."

"What does that mean?"

"The last time I was here, he was engaged to Joanne, and no-one in their right mind could say there's any similarity between Laura and Joanne. Laura's so much prettier... and younger."

"You're not jealous, are you?" he says with a smile and a glint in his eye.

"Jealous? Why would I be jealous?"

"Because you used to have a soft-spot for Rory, of course."

"I think you must be mistaking me for someone else."

He shakes his head. "No. It was common knowledge. Everyone knew you fancied Rory."

"Everyone except me." And Rory's dad. He knew the truth. He'd heard me crying my love for Ed. But I guess he must have kept that to himself. If he'd told Rory, then I have no doubt he'd have told Ed, and this conversation wouldn't be happening. "I'm not saying Rory wasn't a really nice guy, but he wasn't my type."

"Are you sure?"

"I'm positive." I'm staring at the man who was my type, who filled my dreams back then, and still does now.

He pushes his fingers back through his thick hair, frowning, just as a man puts a pint glass down on the bar at the far end and makes enough noise about it to catch Ed's eye. He looks away and then turns back to me again.

"I won't be a minute."

I nod my head and watch him walk away, trying very hard not to moan out loud. He still looks good in jeans. If anything, I think he looks better, and I suck in a breath, letting it out slowly, and wish I had the courage to tell him how I really feel. I wish I could tell him I've never had a 'soft-spot' for anyone in my life, but that I've been in love with him for as long as I can remember. Except telling him that would be wrong. He's married. He's married to the woman who used to be my best friend, and they have a son together. My confession would only embarrass us both, and for that reason alone, it's best kept to myself.

I glance around the pub, trying to remember what it used to look like, although I'm struggling. I wasn't a regular visitor to this place, even when I lived here, but I'm sure there weren't as many tables as this.

Ed comes back, walking quite slowly, and looks down at me.

"Didn't there used to be a pool table over there?" I ask, pointing to the corner of the room.

"Yes, there did. But you have to remember, Mum and Dad didn't serve food when they had the licence, so it was about keeping people in here drinking for as long as possible. There was a dartboard over there…" He points to the other side of the bar. "And there were a few tables dotted around, but nothing as formal as this."

"You decided to serve food when you took over?"

"Yes. It was the first thing we did. It's the best way to maximise profits."

"Was there a kitchen here, then?" I don't remember it, if there was.

"Not really. There was just a room behind the bar here. It was used for the dishwashers, and gave Mum and Dad somewhere to store supplies. We converted it into a proper commercial kitchen. The chef will tell you it's nowhere near big enough, but short of building an extension, it's going to have to do."

"And you took out the pool table and dart board?"

"Yes. If we were going to serve food, we needed somewhere for people to sit. We ploughed all our savings into having the work done in the kitchen, and adding a terrace at the back."

"There's a terrace?"

"Yes. It's really popular in the summer."

"I can imagine."

"It was…" He stops talking suddenly and looks down at the space between us.

"It was what?"

"It was something Suzannah and I argued about. She didn't want to spend the money."

"And you did?"

"Obviously. If we were going to make a go of this place, having all the work done was our only option."

There's a pained expression on his face, which makes me uncomfortable. I presume it's the memory of arguing with Suzannah, and I guess that just goes to show what a rare occurrence that is in their otherwise perfect lives. I glance around the room to take my mind off my own bitterness.

"Well, it certainly looks like you made a go of it."

"Yes, we did."

"So… no regrets?"

He stares at me for a second or two. "No. No regrets."

Two men further down the bar attract his attention. Between them, they're carrying four empty pint glasses and Ed waves a finger of acknowledgment at the men before leaning closer to me.

"This shouldn't take too long."

I nod my head as he turns away, only this time I don't watch him.

This is feeling like a terrible idea now. Not that I know why I ever thought it was a good one. My only saving grace is that

Suzannah hasn't put in an appearance, although she's been here in spirit, if not in person.

The last hour or so has reminded me I'm nothing to Ed… except perhaps a distant memory of friendship. Suzannah is his everything. She always was and always will be, and that's how it should be. That's why he went out with her and not me. That's why he asked her to marry him… it's why they built a life, worked through their disagreements… and why they had a child together.

I shouldn't be here. This was a mistake. It wasn't perhaps as humiliating as being caught outside the pub by Rory Quick's dad, but it comes a close second.

I reach into my bag, finding a ten-pound note in my purse, and I leave it under my wine glass. I haven't even finished the wine, but I don't feel happy taking the drink from him anymore. A glance towards the end of the bar shows he's still busy pulling pints and chatting to the two men, so I jump off of the stool and make my way over to the door. I don't look back, I just open it and step outside.

It's freezing, and I quickly pull on my jacket, doing it up and wrapping my scarf around my neck as I gaze across the harbour. There are Christmas lights in the shop windows and hanging from the street lamps, and I can't help remembering similar scenes from my youth… back when I had hope… or I thought I did.

The lights blur and mingle as I think about all the time I spent pining for Ed, wishing he'd notice me, praying he'd choose me.

God… what a waste.

I plunge my hands into my pockets, ignoring my tears, and start the slow walk back to the hotel. I've got nothing to rush for, and although it's cold, I'm not ready to face the reality of my loneliness yet. At least out here I can re-live distant memories… and pretend it doesn't still hurt to know I'm not enough.

Chapter Six

Ed

The taller of the two men pays by card, while the other starts carrying their beers back to the table they're sharing with two other men. They're all in their mid-thirties, I'd say, and they've just told me they're staying at the campsite. They're not mad enough to be camping at this time of year, but have booked two log cabins between them, which they assure me are really warm

"You're not spending Christmas with your families?" I ask, feeling intrigued as the man puts his debit card away in his wallet and I notice the wedding ring on his left hand.

"We will be. We're going home in a couple of days, but honestly… what with screaming kids, shopping, wrapping presents, the in-laws coming to visit… I ask you, who needs the hassle of getting ready for Christmas? That's what wives are for."

He chuckles, taking a sip from one of the pints, before he picks up the other one, and gives me a wink and a nod, returning to his friends. If I'd ever taken that attitude with Suzannah, she'd have skinned me alive… and rightly so. It was bad enough that I had to work all the hours I did – and still do – but there's no way I'd have taken her for granted like that. At least, I hope I didn't.

Oh, who am I kidding? I didn't need my conversation with Nicki, or with that man, to confirm I didn't always treat Suzannah as well as she deserved. I loved her more than life, but I could have done better by her. There's no getting away from the fact that I could have given her more say in whether we took over this place, and what we did once we had. I discussed it all at length with Mum, going into great detail about taking over the licence and what was involved, and how we'd manage living in the flat upstairs. That was right back at the beginning, when Mum was still living here, Dad was still in the hospital, and I was running this place, but continuing to live in the house I'd shared with Suzannah since our marriage. I'd given up my job already, but Mum kept telling me it wouldn't work… that the arrangement was impractical, and she'd have to find somewhere else to live. Suzannah didn't like the idea of change. If I had to run the pub, then fine, but she didn't want to move. I agreed with Mum. Living here was always going to be easier, and much more practical, and when Dad came out of hospital and it became clear that he needed to be somewhere else, the problem was solved for us. Through all of that, though, I don't remember any great discussions with Suzannah. I remember her saying what she thought, me telling her what was happening and the arguments that followed. Although that was nothing compared to the rows we had about converting the kitchen. I suppose, looking back, I was quite arrogant about that. I'd done the research and made the decision that we needed to serve food if we were going to make a profit, and I thought Suzannah would agree with me and back me up. It never occurred to me that she wouldn't… that she'd want to hang on to our savings for a 'rainy day'. As far as I was concerned, we'd been saving for a house, not a change in the weather, and we didn't need a house anymore, so what was the point? Suzannah didn't see it that way. The money was ours and she didn't want to invest it in the pub.

"But the pub's our home now. We'd be investing in our future."

She gave me a look then that said she didn't believe me… which I chose to interpret as she didn't believe *in* me. She didn't believe I could make it work… or that was how it felt, and I said as much.

"That's not what I meant, Ed, and you know it. But if this is what you really want…"

She sounded resigned, and I knew she'd agree, which she did. Now, looking back, it feels like such a hollow victory… won at too great a cost, although I didn't find that out for many more years.

They were happy years. I know they were. Back then, we didn't open the pub all day. We worked together a lot of the time, too, especially once Dan started school, and we found plenty of time to be alone… just the two of us. Suzannah often made a point of telling me how much she liked that, and how lucky she felt compared to other wives, whose husbands were out at work all day long.

Even now, though, I still struggle to forgive myself for what I took from her.

I suck in a breath, taking my time before I turn around to face Nicki. That's partly because I'm finding the memories of Suzannah too much to cope with, which I guess might be why I've stumbled over her name so much. It's also because I'm still coming to terms with the revelation that Nicki didn't have a soft-spot for Rory. I wasn't alone in thinking that. I might have exaggerated when I told her that 'everyone' believed it, but my parents certainly did, and so did Suzannah. It was their conviction that Nicki fancied Rory and no-one else, that convinced me to leave well alone… except it seems we were all mistaken.

I don't remember her ever going out with anyone else, though… not throughout school, and college, and the few years afterwards before she left the village so unexpectedly. That said, once Rory started seeing Joanne and Suzannah and I became inseparable, we saw less of Nicki. Like I said to her earlier, we drifted apart, and I always felt bad about that. The four of us had been really close friends for such a long time, but it was like she didn't fit anymore. Or was it that we were so wrapped up in our love lives, we excluded her? God… I hope not. I hope that wasn't how it felt.

I turn, wondering if I'm brave enough to ask her the question, my heart sinking when I see her seat is now empty.

She's probably gone to the ladies', although she'd have had to come right past me if she had, and I didn't notice her. My theory is blown out of the water when I see the ten-pound note under her glass. She's paid for her drink and left? What the hell is that about?

I don't know whether to be angry or disappointed… or to stick with confused, because I don't understand why she's gone. Or why she felt the need to leave the money.

"Leanne?" I grab the ten-pound note from underneath the glass and put it in my pocket as I turn, raising my voice, and Leanne looks at me, even as she's bending to reach for a bottled lager.

"Yes?"

"Watch this place for a minute, will you?"

She nods her head and I dash down the corridor, grabbing my keys, and go out of the back door. I suck in a breath as the freezing air hits my lungs, but I ignore it and make my way around to the front of the pub.

Fortunately, the harbour is lit up like Christmas, which is no great surprise, and I can see Nicki walking along the wall, moving away from the pub. She's going slowly and I call out to her, noting the slight break in her stride, before she continues, speeding up slightly, or so it seems to me.

What does that mean? She must have heard me, surely. So, should I go after her, or accept that she doesn't want to talk to me?

I put my hands in my pockets and feel the ten-pound note languishing there, making the decision for me. I'm not going to leave this. Something's wrong and I want to know what.

I set off, picking up my pace, partly because it's cold but mainly because I want to catch up with Nicki before she gets back to the hotel. By the time I reach her, she's opposite the florist's and although I think about grabbing her arm and pulling her around to face me, I don't. Touching her feels wrong, on so many levels. Instead, I say her name and she jumps, stopping in her tracks. She obviously wasn't expecting me to be right behind her.

"Nicki?" I say again, a little more softly, and she turns.

I look down into her beautiful face and in the sparkling Christmas lights I can see tears in her eyes and a dampness on her cheeks.

"What's wrong?" I ask. Something clearly is, and I'm surprised by how much that, and the sight of her tears, hurts me.

"Nothing."

"Do you know how much I hate it when people do that?"

"Do what?" She frowns, tilting her head slightly.

"Say there's nothing wrong, when there so obviously is." Suzannah did it all the time, and it cost us both dearly. "Did I upset you? Was it something I said?"

"No." She looks down at my chest and somehow I don't believe her, although I can hardly accuse her of lying, even if this very obvious evasion is no different from saying there's nothing wrong, despite her tears.

"In that case, why did you leave the money for your drink, and then walk out without saying goodbye?"

"I left the money because I didn't feel it was right to take a drink from you."

"Sorry?" I step a little closer to her and pull the ten-pound note from my pocket. "You didn't think it was right for me to buy you a drink? Why on earth not?"

"I'd rather not say."

I don't know what that means, and she clearly doesn't want to elaborate. "It was just a small glass of wine, and that doesn't cost this much." I hold out the ten-pound note to her. She raises her head and stares at me. "Take it, Nicki… unless you're trying to offend me." She sucks in a breath and takes the note, shoving it in her jacket pocket. She goes to turn away, but I grab her arm, less worried about right and wrong now, and more concerned about her motives.

"Wait a second. Tell me why you didn't say goodbye."

"I didn't realise I had to."

That hurts… even more than her refusing to let me buy her a drink.

"What did I miss? Aren't we friends anymore?" I wave my arm in the vague direction of the pub. "I thought we were getting along okay… like old times. But if I did something…"

"You didn't miss anything, Ed, and you didn't do anything wrong either… okay?"

I can see the hurt in her eyes, just as a tear overflows and falls onto her cheek.

"Then why are you crying?"

"Does it matter?"

"Yes."

She shakes her head. "Well, it shouldn't." She looks down at my chest again. "You're only wearing a shirt. You must be freezing."

"I hadn't noticed, and before you tell me to go back to the pub, I'm not going anywhere until you tell me what's wrong." In my head, I quickly run through the conversation we were having immediately before she left. We were talking about the pub, and how Suzannah and I had argued about spending our money on getting the work done. I can't see why that would have upset Nicki… so what else can it be? Before we talked about the pub, I think we had that brief conversation about Rory…

Can that be it? She might have said she didn't have feelings for him, but maybe she did and was just denying it to save face.

"Is this about Rory?" I ask, and she looks up at me, her brow furrowing.

"Rory?"

"Yes. I heard what you said about him not being your type, but were you bluffing? Did I open up an old wound? Because if I did, I'm sorry. I didn't mean to make you…"

"This has nothing to do with Rory." There's a firmness in her voice, which I can't doubt, even though her eyes are overflowing with tears. "It was never about Rory."

"In that case, I don't understand…"

"No, you don't, do you? I know you think I wanted Rory, but I didn't, Ed… I—I wanted you."

Her voice catches as she says those last few words, a sob leaving her lips, and she turns, running along the harbour towards the hotel. Part of me wants to follow. Part of me knows I should. I feel responsible, even though I didn't realise… didn't have a clue. The problem is, I can't move. I'm rooted to the spot, staring after her, barely able to breathe.

I know I heard her right, despite the emotion in her voice. 'I wanted you.' That was what she said. She wanted me… just like I wanted her. And while so much has happened in the intervening years, that those days ought to feel like ancient history, they don't. They feel like yesterday.

"No… stop it."

I can't think like that. It's wrong.

I close my eyes and try to put a picture of Suzannah in my head. As usual, it's a struggle. She's just a mirage, a shadow from the past, distant, faded and unattainable. I need to see her more than ever, to give some substance to our love, but she's not there, and all I'm left with is that familiar feeling of loneliness and guilt.

Nicki's disappeared into Bell Road and I can't see the point in standing here anymore. Besides, I'm freezing. So, I turn and wander back to the pub, going around the back, so I make less of an entrance. I take a moment, putting my keys on the hook by the stairs and walk through to the bar, which is considerably quieter than when I left.

"Sorry about that." I wander over to Leanne, who looks up at me.

"Is everything all right?"

No. "It's fine." I smile at her and gather up some glasses from the bar while she goes off to clear a few tables.

I let Leanne go home as soon as the last customer had left. Aside from being grateful that she covered for me earlier, I need some time by myself… although I'm not sure what good it's doing me. I still can't think straight, and I'm actually relieved when my phone rings, and I see Rory's name on the screen. It might be late, but I don't care, and I answer straight away.

"Sorry to call at this time," he says, before I've even said 'hello'.

"That's okay. I'm just closing up."

"I thought you would be. I wasn't in the mood for going to bed yet, and I've got something to tell you."

"I don't think men who've only been married for a few months are supposed to confess to not being in the mood for bed."

"I meant, I'm not tired."

"My answer remains the same. At this early stage of your marriage, not being tired is no excuse not to go to bed."

"Oh, be quiet, will you? I called for a reason."

"Which is?"

"I've just found out that Nicki Woodward's back."

"I know."

There's a second or two of silence and then he says, "You do?"

"Yes. She came to the pub this evening."

"Well... I feel completely behind the times now."

"That's because you are. Can I assume you heard the news from Laura?"

"You can. But how did you know that?"

"Because Nicki told me they'd met when she checked into the hotel. I'm just surprised it's taken her until this time of night to tell you... unless you've been otherwise occupied, of course."

"I have," he says, the tone of his voice changing, and I sit up on one of the stools.

"What's happened?"

"I had to attend an accident on the main road," he says. "It was a fatal."

"Oh, God..."

"It wasn't anyone we know, but at this time of year..." His voice fades and he lets out a long sigh.

"Are you okay?"

"I don't think you ever get used to seeing things like that, but I'll be fine."

"Were you by yourself, or was Tom with you?"

"I wasn't alone. There were other emergency responders there, too. But I decided against calling Tom when I saw how bad it was."

"He's from London, Rory. I'm sure he's seen it all before."

"He probably has. But he's going to be my son-in-law in a few weeks' time."

"And you want to protect him?"

He doesn't say a word, but I know I'm right. It's the sort of thing Rory would do.

"I take it you've told Laura?"

"Of course. She was trying to distract me by telling me about Nicki, but we'll talk it through some more later… or tomorrow."

"I'm glad you met her. She's good for you."

"She is." He coughs and I wonder if he really is as 'fine' as he's trying to pretend. "How was Nicki?" he asks, his voice a little brighter, although whether that's pretence too, I can't tell.

"She was… fine." I hesitate over the word, unsure whether to tell him the truth, even if it would be a sanitised version. There's no way I'm going to tell him she left here in tears, or anything to do with our conversation on the harbour. Rory and I have talked about Nicki before. He's aware that I used to like her, and that I wanted to ask her out, but didn't… because I believed she liked him, and wanted to go out with him instead. I know I was wrong now, but I don't feel comfortable saying that out loud. I'm not happy with where that admission takes me, or how it makes me feel.

"What does 'fine' mean?" he says, and I can hear the frown in his voice.

"It means… she was a blast from the past." In so many ways.

"She reminded you of Suzannah?"

I can't deny that. Almost everything about Nicki reminded me of Suzannah… just not in the way Rory means.

"Yes," I say, because it's easier than telling the truth.

"Do you need me to come down there?" I shake my head, even though he can't see me. He's the best friend a man could hope for, and he's been there every step of the way since Suzannah died, but this is something I have to work out for myself… because it's not just about Suzannah.

"No. I'm okay. And besides, I think you've got enough problems of your own. After what you've seen tonight, I think you need some time with Laura."

"I do, but if you…"

"I'll be okay, Rory. Honestly."

"As long as you're sure."

I'm not sure about anything at the moment, but I tell him I am. I wouldn't know what to say to him, and besides, his place isn't here with me. It's at home, dealing with his own demons.

We end the call and I lower the phone, glancing around the bar and deciding the rest of the clearing up can wait until the morning. I'm not in the mood.

I check the door's locked and switch off the lights... all of them, and then wander through to the back of the pub, climbing up the stairs and going straight into my bedroom.

Normally, at the end of a busy evening, I'll have a cup of coffee, and maybe watch the television for a while, but I don't feel like doing any of that tonight.

I close the door, shutting myself in, and without switching on the light, I sit down on the edge of the bed, and then lie back and stare up at the ceiling, letting thoughts of Nicki flood through my head.

There are so many memories... too many to hold on to, as they flit through my brain, and I have to smile as I recall her surprise that I'd remembered her love of history. I nearly blurted out then that I'd never forgotten anything about her... but I stopped myself, just in time. I'm never likely to forget how much she enjoyed history, though. How could I, when I used to spend so much time watching her read? It was one of my favourite things to do when we were teenagers. She used to get this furrow, just above her nose, when she was concentrating, and I used to want to kiss it... all the time.

That's not my only recollection, though. I remember her laugh. It used to make me smile, especially when her nose wrinkled. Her voice always captivated me, too, with its low, sultry tone. That hasn't changed in the slightest... and nor has the habit she's got of making jeans look too sexy to be true.

When we were younger, her mum used to make ice lollies out of fruit juice, and we'd sometimes go round there after school, or during the holidays and sit in the back garden, away from the tourists, and eat them. I can vividly remember how that pastime changed over the years. When we were children, I just enjoyed the ice lolly, especially when it was made from slightly tart apple juice. That was always my favourite. But as we got older and became teenagers, I grew less and less interested in the lolly itself, and more focused on watching the way Nicki licked hers. I know it sounds ludicrous, but I used to feel jealous of those ice lollies. I used to watch the way she'd wrap her lips around the tip and suck it, and then let her tongue slide from bottom to top, licking up the drips.

God… did I want to be that ice lolly…

I remember other times too… like when she cut her hand on a piece of glass. We'd been walking along the harbour, and I don't know how, but Nicki fell over. I'd been talking to her about something – I can't remember what – and the next thing I knew she was crumpled on the floor. She went to get up, and then noticed her hand was bleeding badly, and when I crouched down to look, there was a piece of glass sticking out. Rory told me not to touch it, and ran off to get the doctor, while Suzannah decided Nicki's mum should be told what had happened, and went to find her, leaving the two of us alone. Instinct took over, and after I'd checked she wasn't hurt anywhere else, I picked her up and moved her across the pavement, sitting her against the harbour wall. Then I pulled off my t-shirt, using it to stem the flow of blood. I sat beside her and she leant in to me, and although I was concerned about her, all I can remember thinking was how nice that felt… and that I hoped the doctor and her mum didn't hurry to get there.

I'm not sure how old we were when that happened, but I know we were at college when I first got to hold her in my arms. That was unintentional, but memorable, nevertheless. It happened one evening, when we were all walking back into the village, having caught the bus home. Suzannah had already left us, and I was going to Rory's house for the evening, so we could pretend to be working on a project, while actually trying to outscore each other at whatever PlayStation game was currently occupying most of our time. I remember we were laughing as we came out onto the harbour, just as an idiot in a BMW Z8 came haring down the hill from behind us and took the corner far too tight. I heard him coming before I saw him and a sixth sense told me to grab Nicki, which I did, pulling her out of the way, just as the car mounted the kerb where she'd been standing. Rory pulled a pen from his bag and wrote the car's registration number on his hand, running back to the police station to tell his dad what had happened, and I was left alone – yet again – with Nicki. I still had hold of her, and I desperately wanted to pull her closer, to keep her safe. I didn't, because I thought she wanted Rory, not me, and even though I now know I was wrong about that, it doesn't change how I felt at the time. Saving her felt like second nature to me, so I hated her thanking me. I wanted to ask her why she couldn't want me, and not Rory... except I wasn't brave enough. And more than anything, I wanted to wrap her up... to protect her, because there's something about Nicki that's always made me feel like that.

I cover my face with my hands. I failed to protect her tonight... dismally. What's wrong with me? I should have followed her back to her hotel... made sure she got there safely. I can only blame shock for my inability to behave like a gentleman. But how was I to know she liked me all along? I can still see her face when she said that. She was in agony. There was no disguising it, and I know the look in her eyes and the tears flowing from them are going to haunt me.

The thing is, as much as I feel responsible – and I do – I never meant to cause her so much pain. Not then and not now. I had no idea she felt like that. If I'd known back then, I'd have...

What would I have done?

Would I have acted differently?

Of course I would. If I hadn't been hampered by loyalty to Rory, I'd have asked Nicki out. I wanted to, more than anything. But if I'd done that, there's every chance we'd have stayed together. I think Nicki's a 'staying together' kind of person... and so am I. So that means I'd never have married Suzannah... never have had Dan... never have lived the life we had.

"Oh, God..."

Guilt overwhelms me, pain consumes me, confusion gnaws at me, and I turn onto my side, curling up, defending myself against them... and failing.

"Suze... please." I need to see her face, to hear her voice... to know that what we had was as good as I remember. "We were happy, weren't we?"

I close my eyes, but she still won't come to me, and instead, all I can see is the tortured look on Nicki's face, knowing I put it there... that I'm responsible for hurting her. I've made a lot of mistakes in my life, but hurting Nicki is starting to feel like one of the worst.

Chapter Seven

Nicki

Climbing out of the shower, I turn off the water, and wish I could feel refreshed. I don't. I feel just as exhausted as when I got out of bed twenty minutes ago… probably because I've had hardly any sleep.

That's not an enormous surprise, considering what happened last night, and that I made a fool of myself in front of Ed. I didn't mean to tell him how I felt about him, but he kept going on about Rory, and in the end I just blurted it out… frustration getting the better of me. That's no excuse, though… not when he's happily married. I'm supposed to be here to put the past behind me, not reawaken it.

I brush my teeth and dry my hair, trying not to remember the shocked expression on his face, when I told him I'd wanted him, not Rory. If I'd planned to tell him, I might have been able to work out what kind of reaction to expect, but I hadn't, and I suppose shock was a little disappointing, if I'm being honest. Embarrassment might have been better. It would have been nicer still if he'd felt flattered. Except he wasn't. Why would he be? I imagine the last thing he either wanted or expected was my declaration of love… even if I didn't mention the word itself. Thank God.

I get dressed, putting on the same jeans as I wore yesterday, and a slightly thicker top. I've already opened the curtains, and it looks cold outside, but I think I'll go for a walk to clear the cobwebs and hopefully wake myself up.

"Is everything okay?"

I look up to find Laura standing beside me, glancing at my untouched breakfast.

"Yes. Everything's fine, thanks."

I don't know why I bothered coming into the dining room. I'm not hungry and all I've done is nudge my bacon and eggs around the plate.

"Can I get you something else?"

"No." I put down my knife and fork, pushing the plate away. "I'm not hungry."

"I can get you some fresh toast, if you'd like?"

"No, really… I'm fine."

I get up and she steps aside, giving me some space.

"Rory told me you went to see Ed last night," she says, continuing the conversation as I push my chair under the table. I turn and glance up at her.

"Nothing changes here, does it? You still can't sneeze without someone you barely know handing you a tissue."

"I'm sorry. Did I say the wrong thing?"

"No, it's not your fault. You'd think I'd be used to this place." I smile, even though it's an effort. "I just thought I'd go to the pub for a drink, and ended up chatting with Ed for a while, that's all."

I know that wasn't 'all', but I'm not in the mood for elaborating, and I don't know her well enough to confide the truth.

"I'm sure it was nice to catch up."

I nod my head, although 'nice' isn't the word I'd choose to describe our evening.

"I thought I might go for a walk." I step away.

"Wrap up warm, won't you? It's freezing out there."

I smile my acknowledgement and turn away, heading for the door and then the stairs, bolting up them and straight to my room, where I duck inside, closing the door behind me.

I suppose I should give thanks for the small mercy that Laura didn't seem to know the content of my conversation with Ed last night. He must have kept that to himself, which is something. Although whether he'll have told Suzannah is another matter. Is that the kind of thing a husband would tell his wife? Or would he keep it a secret? Does he have any secrets from Suzannah? Somehow I doubt it. And that means I'm going to have to face her at some point. Porthgarrion is far too small a village for me not to run into her, even if I avoid the pub, which I have every intention of doing for the remainder of my stay. That being the case, I suppose I'd better start working on my apologies, on my reassurances that my feelings for her husband are in the past, even if they're not.

I pick up my coat from the sofa where I left it last night and shrug it on, wrapping my scarf around my neck. I'm wishing I'd never come here now, but I can't stay cooped up in my hotel room for the next week and a half, can I? I'll have to face the music eventually… although I can't help hoping that, by going out this early, I'll be avoiding any potential confrontations, at least for today.

Laura was right, it's icy cold, and I fasten my jacket, pulling my scarf a little higher as I head out of Bell Road and onto the harbour. The wind is coming off of the sea and I smile slightly as I remember the times we used to complain about the frozen winter winds when we were children. Of course, we used to complain about the heat in summer, too… seemingly never happy. Except we were. Despite my unrequited love for Ed, and the misery that seemed to surround that, I always think of Porthgarrion with happiness, the memories rose-tinted by the passage of time.

The sun is shining and I look out onto the harbour, taking a deep breath, and soaking in the view. I've always loved the way the sun sparkles on the water, like millions of precious gems, swaying with the tide, bewitching… beguiling…

I walk straight into a man coming the other way and step back, my eyes raking up over thick-soled boots, dark blue jeans and a heavy, navy-coloured coat. I think they're called pea coats, but I'm not sure… although that hardly seems important now. "Sorry. I didn't mean…"

"Excuse me. I should have…"

My head darts up at the sound of the familiar voice, straight into Ed's eyes. *So much for avoiding confrontations.*

"Sorry," I say again. "That was my fault. I wasn't looking where I was going."

"Neither was I. And it wasn't your fault. It was mine." He steps a little closer, frowning. "Are you okay?"

He's staring right at me, his eyes boring into mine and for just a second or two, I wonder if he means am I okay because we just bumped into each other, or am I okay because I ran away from him last night, crying my eyes out.

"I'm fine." I decide it's best to lie, regardless. Bumping into him was the last thing I needed, and after last night, I'm not sure I'll ever be 'okay' again. 'Okay' feels like alien territory… and so does this. He's still staring and an awkward silence stretches… interminably. Before it gets too unbearable, I step to one side to move around him, and he seems to startle out of his trance, letting me. I take two or three paces, wondering why I couldn't have timed my outing a little better. If I'd left the hotel ten minutes earlier, or later, I'd probably have missed him altogether.

"Nicki?" I feel my shoulders drop as he calls my name. Can I ignore him? I tried it last night, and he came after me. I'm not sure I could cope if he did that in broad daylight. It was bad enough under the cover of darkness, when there was no-one around to see. I turn, but don't move, and he steps closer. "Can I ask you something?"

"I suppose so." I'd prefer to say 'no', but that would be rude.

He looks out at the harbour for a few moments and then takes a deep breath, before he turns back to me again, confusion written all over his face. "Why did you leave the village?"

I don't know what I'd been expecting him to ask, but that wasn't it. "I told you last night, I wanted to see something of the world."

He narrows his eyes, nodding his head slowly. "I know what you told me, but you also said you only made it to Bath. So you didn't exactly try, did you?"

"I explained that. I got there and decided to go to university."

"Right. But that's not really the point."

"Then what is?"

"The timing of your departure. What was it that made you leave here exactly a week before I married Suzannah? Seeing the world is all well and good, if that's your thing. Getting to Bath and deciding to go to uni is fine, if that was what you wanted from life. But why then? Why couldn't you have waited until after the wedding? It was only a matter of days… so why couldn't you hang on?"

I glare up at him, marvelling at his insensitivity. How can he ask me that? "Weren't you listening last night? Didn't you hear what I said? You think I wanted to stay here and watch my best friend marry you? I wanted to be happy for you both… I really did. But I couldn't. I couldn't bear to see you starting your life together... the life I knew I'd never have." I step aside again, but this time he gets in my way, blocking my path. "Please, Ed... haven't you humiliated me enough?"

"I'm not trying to humiliate you, and if that's how it feels, then I'm sorry." I look up into his eyes and see the torment behind them. This isn't any easier for him than it is for me. "I didn't realise how you felt... not until last night."

"What difference does it make?"

He shrugs his shoulders. "Now? I don't know. Back then, it would have made all the difference in the world, if I'd realised."

What's he saying? I don't understand. "Why?"

"Isn't it obvious?"

"Not to me, no."

He takes a step closer, so we're almost touching, and I struggle to breathe. "I liked you too."

It's as though all my dreams have come true. The words I've longed to hear him say have finally been uttered. But even as I let them roll around my head, I know they're all wrong, and judging from the look on his face, so does he. "You can't say that to me."

"Why not?"

"Because you can't. It's not fair... on any of us. It's only going to make things difficult, and that's not why I came here."

"Why did you? Why are you here? Is it just to do with your mother? Or is there something else?"

"I don't know." I do, although it won't help either of us if I tell him now. "But I think it's best if I go."

I try to dodge around him, to go back to the hotel, but he grabs my arm, holding on to me. "Go where?" I look down at his hand, resting on my arm, and he releases me. "Tell me where you're going."

"Home... insofar as I have one. I shouldn't be here. It was a stupid idea."

"So you're just going to leave?"

"Yes. I'll check out of the hotel and go back to Mum's place. I don't want my presence here or anything I've said to cause trouble between you and Suzannah."

"You don't have to worry about that. Nothing you've said could cause any problems between us."

That's like a stab to my heart. Considering he said he wasn't trying to humiliate me, he's doing a magnificent job. "Thanks, Ed… that didn't hurt at all."

I step away from him again, desperate to escape, but he reaches out, pulling me back, and even though I try to yank my arm away, he keeps hold of it.

"Stop trying to get away, and let me explain, will you?"

"Explain what? What is it you want to tell me? That even though you say you liked me when we were younger, you love Suzannah more? I already know that. I don't need to have it explained. Why do you think I left, Ed? It was torture seeing the two of you together back then, and I've got no desire to go through it all again. It's better if…"

"You won't have to go through it all again."

"How do you work that out? I can't just bury my feelings to suit you."

"I know you can't, and I'm not asking you to. I'm trying to tell you that you don't need to worry about seeing me with Suzannah, or about causing trouble between us… because Suzannah's d—dead."

He struggles to say the word, almost as much as I struggle to hear it, and take it in. "She's… oh, God… Ed…"

It's too much, especially coming on top of Mum's death, and without warning, I burst into tears.

"Oh, Nicki… come here."

Ed pulls me into his arms, my head resting against his chest, and he holds me. There's nothing romantic or sexual about this.

It's just one friend comforting another, although I'm not sure it's the right way around and I lean back, looking up at his face, his handsome features blurred by my tears.

"Sorry. I shouldn't be crying over you."

"Why not? She was your best friend."

She was also the woman I've been jealous of for over half my life… and I had no idea she was dead. I pull away, putting some space between us, and he lets me.

"I shouldn't have said all those things, Ed… about you and her."

"It's okay. You weren't to know."

He turns and moves over to the harbour wall, leaning against it, and I follow him. We both gaze out to sea for a moment or two, lost in thoughts, memories… regrets. I know I've said I couldn't have borne to see them together, but I wish I'd come back here sooner. I wish I'd been a better friend.

"When did she die? If you don't mind me asking."

"It was seven years ago… just after Halloween. She had a heart attack."

"A heart attack? But how? She'd only have been thirty-four." We were all the same age, so it's easy to work out how ludicrously young Suzannah would have been.

"I know. She was too young to die. I kept telling myself that, and I used to spend hours going back over those last few days and weeks, wondering if I missed anything."

"I'm sure you didn't."

He shrugs his shoulders. "There was nothing out of the ordinary. She'd been a bit under the weather, but it wasn't anything serious… or we didn't think so. She told me on the morning she died, that if she still felt bad after the weekend, she'd make an appointment to see the doctor." His voice cracks and he coughs. "We never got to the weekend, though… Dan got home from school and found her at the bottom of the stairs."

"He found her?"

"Yes. She was surrounded by broken teacups, with an upturned tray by her feet, and he ran out of the pub, bumping straight into Rory, who was on patrol."

"That was fortunate… for Dan, I mean."

He turns to me and manages a half smile. "Yes, it was. At least Dan wasn't on his own."

"Where were you?"

"I'd gone to Padstow to see Mum, but Rory called and told me to come home. He didn't say why, just that I needed to go to his place. I—I knew something was wrong, but to be honest, I assumed it was something to do with Dan… not Suzannah. When I got back and he told me what had happened, I… I…"

I reach over and rest my hand on his arm, and we both fall silent, listening to the waves lapping up against the harbour wall, the gulls cawing overhead, and the soft hum of people's conversations as they walk past behind us, while he relives that horrifying moment. I try to imagine it, even though I can't… and I don't really want to. The thought of him being in that much pain is too much for me and my eyes mist over again.

"Please don't cry," he says eventually and I turn to see him staring at me.

"It's hard not to."

"I know, believe me."

"I'm sorry, Ed. Suzannah was the love of your life. To lose her like that…"

He sucks in a breath and lets it out slowly. "It was the worst thing that's ever happened to me. I think I aged ten years overnight." I can't believe I thought the lines around his eyes were brought about by laughter. The truth is a very different story. "I blamed myself for a long time, too."

"Why? What could you have done?"

"I kept thinking I should have made her go to the doctor's sooner, rather than let her put it off… that if I had, it might have saved her life."

"Would it though?"

"Probably not. The post mortem showed a tear in one of her arteries. It's not a common cause for heart attacks, but it's not that unusual among younger women. They told me that, even if she had gone to see the GP, it's something that's often missed and probably would have been misdiagnosed."

"So, why did you blame yourself?"

"Because I had to blame someone."

I can hear the pain in his voice, even now, all these years later.

"How did Dan cope?" I ask, trying a temporary diversion of sorts, for both our sakes.

"Better than I did. I think that's why he lives his life at nine hundred miles an hour… because he knows how quickly it can be snatched away."

"You know how lucky you were, don't you?"

He turns, frowning. "Lucky?"

"Yes. You and Suzannah were so in love with each other. Not everyone gets to experience that."

"I know… although I'm not sure I always deserved her."

"I'm sure you did. I'm sure you made her happy, too."

"I hope so." There's just a hint of doubt in his voice, and I can't allow that. I won't allow that.

"You did, Ed. I left because I couldn't bear to see the happiness you gave her, when I wanted it for myself. If I'd been able to discern the slightest chink in her love for you, or yours for her, do you honestly think I could have walked away?" He frowns at me, uncertain. "If I'd thought I stood a chance, I'd never have gone, but as it was…"

"I'm sorry. I never meant to hurt you."

"I know. It's not like you knew how I felt."

"No. I didn't have a clue."

"And it's in the past now." It's not, but what else can I say? Telling him that my feelings haven't changed won't help, will it? Not when he's still so mired in grief, seven years after Suzannah's death. I think it'll only make him feel guilty... and that's the last thing I want.

He coughs and leans in a little closer, lowering his voice to a whisper. "Did you find love with someone else?"

"Love? No. Marriage? Yes."

His brow furrows. "Can you have one without the other?"

"Evidently."

Chapter Eight

Ed

I've still got the bar to tidy up after last night, but having barely slept, I thought a walk along the harbour would help clear my head.

I never thought I'd bump into Nicki… quite literally. But I suppose that's what happens when you're not watching where you're going. I don't know what she was doing, but I was staring out to sea, thinking about yesterday evening… Nicki's words still spinning in my head. 'I wanted you'. That was what she'd said, and I kept hearing it, over and over, replaying the scene, and still wondering how I could have got it all so wrong when we were younger.

That's why I wasn't paying attention, and how I came to bump into her. We both apologised, before we'd even realised who we were talking to, I think. But once I'd registered it was her, and taken in her skin-tight jeans, her scarf wrapped high around her neck and the way her cheeks were pinked by the cold sea breeze, I was mesmerised. My instinct was to ask her if she was okay. She said she was, but I wasn't sure she'd understood what I meant. I didn't think I'd hurt her; the bump wasn't that significant. But she'd run away from me last night in floods of tears, and I wanted to know – no, I *needed* to know – that she was all right. I didn't feel like I could ask again, though, and I didn't get the chance. She tried to dodge around me, and although I was too bewitched to stop her straight away, I came to my senses in time to call her back.

I wondered if she was going to ignore me, but she didn't. She stopped, and I knew then that I wanted answers. Her saying she'd wanted me all those years ago wasn't enough. I had to know why… and how… and what it all meant.

I didn't mean to humiliate her, although I think I did. That was just inexperience and desperation talking. Inexperience with women and emotions… and a desperation to understand how she felt… and to tell her how I'd felt too. It seemed important to be honest about that; to let her know she hadn't been alone.

Of course, that led to me telling her about Suzannah's death… although perhaps not in the way I would have chosen. I didn't want her to leave, so I blurted it out, rather than breaking it to her gently, remembering when her face crumpled and her tears fell, that she'd been Suzannah's best friend, and that grief isn't always a solitary emotion, even if it often feels that way.

For only the second time in our lives, I held her. It was nothing like that first time, when I'd just pulled her back from the danger of that speeding car, and she'd thanked me for saving her. In this instance, it was the right thing to do, to comfort her, and let her cry it out, but I won't deny that when she pulled away, my arms felt empty without her… and I felt lost.

She apologised, although that was the last thing I wanted to hear. But then I was overwhelmed with guilt again, and I wandered over to the harbour wall, to put some space between us. Nicki followed me, which I was relieved about. I hadn't wanted to put her off… I just needed to put a distance between my grief and my feelings for her… not that they're going anywhere.

She's still beside me now, and although we've talked about Suzannah's death, about how that felt, about the blame I attached to myself… the thing I'm haunted by most of all is nothing to do with grief, or regret. It's Nicki's declaration that she'd never have left Porthgarrion if she hadn't believed me to be truly in love with Suzannah. I was in love. I'm not going to deny that. But I can't help wondering what Nicki's words mean. Was she in love, too? With me? Did her feelings stretch that far? Was it more than 'wanting'?

I let out a sigh. Does it even matter? She's just said it was in the past, so however she felt back then, she clearly doesn't now… and that's my question answered, isn't it?

I wonder whether that's because her heart belongs to another man now, and am surprised by the stabbing pain in my chest. I cough to try and clear it, and then lean in closer, only managing a whisper, when I ask, "Did you find love with someone else?"

"Love? No. Marriage? Yes."

I feel my brow furrow. "Can you have one without the other?"

"Evidently."

"Hmm… I suppose. Look at Rory."

It's her turn to frown now. "What are you talking about? Are you trying to say he doesn't love Laura, because…"

I hold up my hand to stop her talking, and she does. "No, I'm not talking about Laura. I'm talking about Joanne."

"You mean, he married her?" I can see the surprise in her eyes.

"Yes. But surely you knew about that, didn't you?"

"I knew their wedding was planned for a few weeks after yours, but I didn't realise he'd gone ahead with it… not after meeting Laura."

"Yeah, he went ahead with it. I'm not sure Joanne gave him much choice in the matter."

"No. And I see what you mean… he was never in love with her, was he? Any more than she was in love with him."

I turn to face her properly. "How did you know that?"

"It was obvious… at least to anyone who wasn't so wrapped up in their own relationship, they were blind to everything else." There's a slight twitch at the corner of her mouth, like the beginnings of a smile.

"Can I take it you're referring to me?"

"Of course. You weren't aware of anything other than Suzannah." I smile myself, but don't comment, because while that might have been true by the time of my marriage, it hadn't always been that way. "I don't know about you, but I always thought Joanne only wanted to get married to Rory because you and Suzannah had announced your engagement, and she didn't want to be left out. And if that means my claws are showing, I don't care."

I smile more fully than before. "Your assessment might not be far wrong."

"Did they get divorced?"

"Yes… after she left him."

"She did? When?"

"About six years ago now."

"They stayed together for that long?" I can tell she's surprised.

"They did… and they had a daughter, too."

"Really?"

"Yes. She's the same age as Dan… well, a few months younger."

She rolls her eyes. "Knowing Joanne, she probably only got pregnant because Suzannah was."

I chuckle. "I'm not sure about that, but Dan and Gemma were great friends growing up. They still are, even though Dan's hardly ever here, and Gemma's getting married soon."

"She is? That must make Rory feel old."

"Not just Rory. It makes me feel old too."

She pats my arm, looking up into my eyes. "You're not old, Ed. You've hardly changed at all."

I think we both know that's not true, but I smile anyway. "Neither have you." The air stills and we stare at each other for a full minute, until a sudden gust of wind catches her hair, breaking the spell.

"Will Joanne be coming back for the wedding?" she asks.

I shake my head. "I'm not sure yet, but I doubt it. Rory was going to ask Gemma if she wanted her mum there, but he fully expected her to say 'no'." I don't mention Rory's main reason for asking Gemma about her mother. Laura's problems with her ex, and her lack of self-esteem, aren't exactly common knowledge and although he didn't say our conversation was in confidence, I don't feel like I can share it. "It would be understandable. Joanne walked out on Rory… left him and Gemma for another man. As far as I'm aware, neither of them has heard from her since, and she's never been back here."

"Seriously? She just abandoned him? I mean, them?"

"Yes. But why is that such a shock? You said yourself, you didn't think she was ever in love with him."

"No. I always thought theirs was more of a physical attraction… at least on Joanne's side. I never understood what Rory saw in her. At the risk of showing my claws again, he could have done a lot better…" She stops talking and although her cheeks are flushed from the icy wind, I can still discern a blush creeping up them.

"Are you sure you didn't fancy him?"

She tilts her head and bites on her bottom lip. "I'm positive. It's always been you, Ed."

She's definitely talking in the present tense now, even if she put her feelings in the past earlier on. But does that mean anything? Or is it just a turn of phrase?

The silence between us stretches, and she looks away, no doubt because I haven't replied. I'm still drawn to her; I still want her… but Suzannah's ghost-like figure is ever-present, in the back of my mind, making me doubt my own feelings.

"Was it the same in your marriage?" I ask, in an urgent need to change the subject.

She turns back to face me, raising her eyebrows. "How do you mean?"

"You said there was no love, so was it all physical attraction?"

I'm not sure how I feel about that, but the question's out there now, and I can hardly take it back.

"I suppose… to start with. It began as a clandestine affair."

"Why? Was he married?"

"No, but we were both teachers in the same school, and students can be wicked if they find out there's anything going on between members of staff."

"So you saw each other in secret?"

"Yes. I'd been at the school for about three years by then, and he'd just joined."

"I know you taught history, but what was his subject?"

"Geography."

I chuckle. "Do you remember Mr Beddows?" She nods her head, clearly remembering our geography teacher from school. "I hope your husband was nothing like him."

"He's my ex-husband now, and no, he was nothing like Mr Beddows. He must have been at least a hundred years old, and could barely see. Terry was thirty-two when we met, and as far as I'm aware, there was nothing wrong with his eyesight."

"Clearly not."

She turns. "What does that mean?"

"He noticed you, didn't he?"

She blushes. "Yes, he did."

"So, if he was thirty-two, how old were you?"

"Twenty-nine. It was a school with an older staff, and being two of the younger members, we were naturally drawn together."

"And into a clandestine affair?"

She narrows her eyes at me. "Yes, but not straight away. We didn't jump right into bed with each other, if that's what you're implying."

I hold up my hands. "I'm not implying anything."

She stares at me for a moment, like she doesn't quite believe me, and then slowly shakes her head. "After we'd been together for about six months, we decided to get married."

"Why?"

She frowns and shrugs her shoulders. "Why not?"

"Well… I can understand the whole clandestine affair thing, but getting married is a lot more serious, especially after only six months. It's a big step to take."

"It was a big step, but it was also the next step. I think we'd reached a point where our relationship had nowhere else to go. It either ended, or we took it to the next level."

"And you didn't want it to end?" Maybe she felt more for him than she's letting on.

"I didn't want to be alone again. I thought that once we started living together, I might learn to love him."

"You weren't living together?"

"No, but we spent a lot of time in each other's company. We got on well, and we wanted the same things… or we seemed to when we weren't living in each other's pockets, and it was all just hypothetical. There was something very practical about the whole thing. We both had quite small flats, and realised we'd need somewhere bigger to live, so we sold up and bought a three-bedroomed house together."

"With a view to having children one day?" I ask and I swear her face pales. Her eyes seem to darken too, like a shadow's passed behind them, blocking out the light.

"No… not with with a view to having children. I wanted space for my books, and Terry wanted a games room."

"As in PlayStation and X-Box?"

"Yes. I hadn't realised he was into all that until we were moving his things in, but he wasn't fanatical… thank goodness." She sucks in a breath. "Once we'd set our plans in motion, we went and saw the head teacher. It seemed only fair, considering we'd been seeing each other behind his back for so long. We'd obviously hidden our affair very well, because he didn't know we were even involved. We told him we were planning on getting married during the summer holidays, and at the end of term, he made an announcement in the final assembly. There was an enormous cheer, and a few raucous comments, but the general response was good."

"So you got married?"

"Yes. We had a very quiet service in a registry office."

She looks out to sea, the wind catching her hair, and I long to move closer, to put my arms around her and hold her close to me, like I did earlier… even if she's not crying now. She looks like she could use a hug, and I know I could.

"You said he was your ex-husband now… so what happened?"

"It was nothing dramatic. Nobody cheated, or anything like that. But it seemed neither of us was very good at compromising. We argued constantly about really trivial things that probably don't matter so much when you love the person you're with. When you're just glorified house-mates, it's harder to ignore them not putting the milk back in the fridge after they've made themselves a cup of tea, but haven't offered you one, and you quickly tire of them leaving the loo seat up all the time. Like I say, none of it was important, but it caused tension between us. If we'd been in love, I imagine we'd have laughed about it, instead of arguing. But as it was, we fought almost constantly. In the end, our relationship became so wearing I dreaded going home."

"Did he feel the same?"

"I don't really know how he felt. We didn't discuss feelings. But when we split up, he told me he'd have been happier if we'd just carried on as we were before."

"Having a clandestine affair, you mean?"

"Yes. I think he enjoyed the novelty of that more than the mundanity of everyday life with me."

I move closer, even though I still don't put my arms around her. "Hey… don't put yourself down."

"I'm not… not really. The fact of the matter is, we should never have married. It was a huge mistake, and it was doomed to failure right from the beginning."

"You can't say that. It might have stood a chance…"

"No, it wouldn't. That's why I left him." She turns to look at me, her voice filled with conviction.

"You left him?"

"Yes. I had to. There was no point in staying."

"No point in even trying?"

"No."

"Why not?"

"Because he wasn't you, Ed." The words fall out of her mouth even as she clamps it shut, trying to stop them, and I'm once again filled with that mixture of regret, guilt and longing, that I ought to be getting used to by now.

Except I'm not.

I don't know how to handle all these feelings. I want to hold her so much, and kiss her too… and deep down, I probably want a lot more than that. *No… stop it…* I can't let my mind go there. It used to, all the time, when we were younger… and it wasn't just about ice lollies and a vivid imagination. I used to fantasise about Nicki. I used to dream of her, and all the things I longed to do with her… things I never got to do with Suzannah…

I close my eyes and clamp my hands together, squeezing them tight, trying to blot out the regrets, and the guilt, and the longing.

"Are you okay?" Her voice breaks into my nightmare, and I open my eyes again, glancing down at her, just as the church clock strikes ten.

"Yes. But I didn't realise the time. I need to get back. I have to get ready to open up."

"Okay… well, I'll probably see you around." The resignation in her voice is heartbreaking, and as she goes to move away, I grab her arm, pulling her back. She stares up at me, blinking, tears brimming in her eyes.

"Come to the pub tonight?" I hear the words, wondering where they came from. It was my voice uttering them, but why? What earthly good can come of it?

"Why?" she says, like she's read my mind.

Because I can't stop thinking about you, no matter how hard I try. Because I'm in love with you, even if the guilt is tearing me apart. Because I want you to be mine, regardless of the fact that a part of me will always belong to someone else.

"Because I want to see you again."

That much is true, and it doesn't come with any conditions.

"You're sure about that?"

"Yes."

She smiles, her eyes sparkling now. "Okay. I'll come over later on." She takes a step backwards. "Have a good day."

She's so much more cheerful, and as she turns and starts walking away, back towards the hotel, I wonder if I'm being unfair. I wasn't lying when I said I wanted to see her again. I wasn't being untrue to myself when I thought all those other things, either. She's constantly on my mind. I'm in love with her, and I want her to be mine. But that doesn't mean any of it can happen. Have I just led her on into thinking it can, though? I have an awful feeling I might have done.

In which case, what am I going to do this evening? Does she think this is some kind of date? Is that why she was suddenly so much more cheerful?

Of course it is…

But I'm not ready to date. I'm not ready for any of it.

"Oh, God… Suze." I whisper the words under my breath and turn, seeing Tom Hughes out of the corner of my eye. He's wandering down the other side of the road, in his uniform, and holds up a hand, waving to me. I wave back, as a thought occurs, and I pull my phone from my pocket, walking towards the pub as I connect my call.

"Ed?" Rory says. "Are you okay? You don't normally call me during working hours."

"I'm fine. I was just wondering if you had any plans for this evening. You and Laura, that is."

"Not that I'm aware of. Why?"

"I thought you might like to come down to the pub for a pre-Christmas drink."

"That sounds like a good idea. I'll check with Laura when she finishes work, but unless she's arranged something she hasn't told me about, we'll see you later, after dinner."

"You could always have dinner at the pub, you know?"

"We could, but she's left something in the slow-cooker. It's a new recipe she's trying to beguile me with."

"Beguile you? Are you that easily pleased these days?"

"You've never lived with a vegetarian. You wouldn't understand."

I laugh, unable to help myself, and we end the call.

I know I ought to feel guilty, but I'm already so saturated with guilt, I can't take any more. Instead, I just feel relieved… and then ashamed. I asked Nicki to come to the pub tonight. Should I really be looking for excuses not to be alone with her?

Chapter Nine

Nicki

I feel so torn.

Part of me is devastated by the news of Suzannah's death. It might have been seven years ago, but to me it's immediate. It's here and now. I've been labouring under the impression that she was still alive and living in bliss with Ed, when for the last seven years, she's been dead, and he's been alone. It makes me feel like the most inadequate of friends… although I already knew I was that, being as I put my feelings, and my fears of seeing her and Ed so happy together, ahead of hers. I know her death would have broken Ed, too. It was obvious, just from the look in his eyes. The kind of love they shared doesn't end just because one person isn't there anymore, and although I'm perfectly well aware of that, seeing it on his face made it so much more real… and painful.

He still loves her. He always will.

At the same time, though, there's a part of me that can't help wondering if there might be some hope for me… for us. I know I should feel guilty for thinking like that, but I can't help it. After all, he chased me out of the pub last night, didn't he? Obviously,

I didn't know about Suzannah at the time, so I didn't attach the same importance to his actions then as I am now… and maybe I'm over-interpreting, but it seems an odd thing to do for someone who doesn't care.

What's even odder though, is the way he questioned me so hard today. He could have just said 'hello', after we'd both finished apologising to each other, and then walked on. But he didn't. He kept on asking and asking about why I'd left the village when I did. I remember him saying that he hadn't realised how I felt until last night, and when I asked what difference it made, his reply threw me. He said that now, he didn't know, but back then it would have made all the difference in the world. At the time, I was focusing on what came next – on him saying that he'd liked me too, and how inappropriate that felt, considering I believed him to still be married to Suzannah. But now, I'm wondering what he meant by his earlier remark… about not knowing what difference it makes now. Was that a good thing for him to have said? I can't work it out. What I do know is that it felt good to be held in his arms, even briefly. It felt good to see the concern in his eyes and hear it in his voice… but then he didn't deny Suzannah was the love of his life, did he? Does that mean he'll never be able to love again? It's not as though I'd expect him to stop loving Suzannah… I know that's too much to ask. I'd just like it if he could find a space in his heart for me.

I wonder why he asked to see me tonight. He didn't give me a reason, even though I asked. All he said was that he wanted to see me again, but his eyes spoke of something deeper than friendship. And he must know I want more than that. It's not as though I've made a secret of how I feel. I told him my marriage ended, as far as I was concerned, because Terry wasn't him. I might have said it was in the past, but that was only to make him feel better, because he was beating himself up over hurting me…

and surely that's indicative in itself, isn't it? If he didn't care, why would he be worried about hurting me at all?

I'm going round in circles, I know I am… and it's not getting me anywhere. I suppose the only thing I can do is to go to the pub tonight and see what happens.

I get back to the hotel, relieved that Laura is on the telephone at the reception desk. I'm not in the mood for conversation, and I make my way up to my room, letting myself in and closing the door.

I lean back against it, sighing out a long breath, a smile twitching at my lips as I remember how it felt to be held in Ed's arms, after all this time.

Is it wrong to hope? Is it wrong of me to wish? Can it be wrong to want happiness?

I've spent the afternoon in my room, curled up on the sofa, reading. I'm currently enjoying a series of detective novels, set in the Second World War, in a rural village. The murders are a little gruesome, but there's a romantic side-story, which lightens the mood and stops it from becoming too grisly. I'm so engrossed, trying to work out who the murderer is, that I haven't noticed the time, and it's only when I shift position, that I realise it's dark and that my back-lit Kindle is providing the only light in the room. I reach over and turn on the lamp on the side table, its soft glow illuminating the surrounding area, and I glance at the time on my Kindle, letting out a slight gasp, when I realise it's almost six-thirty.

"Where did that day go?"

I get up and stretch my arms above my head, leaving my Kindle on the arm of the sofa and wander into the dressing area, pulling open the wardrobe doors. It feels like a good idea to change before going out tonight, although what I'm going to wear, I don't know. I don't want it to look like I'm trying too hard, but I want to look nice… or as nice as I can, anyway.

I brought a dress with me, but I'd intended to wear it on Christmas Day, and it would probably be a bit much for an evening at the pub. Perhaps I'll just go for my long skirt and a sweater… and maybe my black boots. I pull everything out of the wardrobe and carry it back into the bedroom, laying it down on the bed.

I'm about to pull off my jumper, ready to shower, when I realise I haven't eaten. Obviously, I could eat at the pub, but I don't want to outstay my welcome there. Ed didn't say 'come to dinner', did he? I hesitate, unsure what to do. I'm going to eat here, but should I have dinner before I shower, or afterwards? A glance at the clothes on my bed makes the decision for me. If I get changed first and spill something down myself, I'll only end up having to find something else to wear.

I pull my jumper back down again, straightening it out and, grabbing my handbag, I go out of the room, making my way downstairs to the dining room.

Inside, it's fairly quiet, but I suppose it's still quite early, and I head for the table I sat at last night, taking a seat and picking up the menu. I skip over the starters and focus on the main courses, trying to decide between the baked sea trout, or the roasted cod.

"Can I get you anything to drink?"

The male voice is unobtrusive, and I continue to study the menu as I reply, "I'm not sure. I haven't decided what to eat yet."

"Oh? Can I be of any assistance?"

I look up now and do my best not to gasp at the beautiful man who's staring down at me. He's tall and slim, with dark hair, chocolate brown eyes, and a razor-sharp square jaw. He's wearing a dark grey suit, white shirt and navy blue tie… all utterly immaculate.

"I—I can't decide between the sea trout and the cod." Why am I stammering? I'm forty-one, not fifteen… and he can't be more than thirty.

He smiles and leans in, bending so he can whisper, "The sea trout… definitely. I don't have anything against the cod, but the trout comes with a mussel sauce, which is just sublime."

"Okay." I nod my head.

"A glass of Chablis would go very well."

"I'll take your word for that."

He smiles, revealing perfect, white teeth, and as I close the menu, he takes it from me. "You're in the Harbour View Suite, aren't you?"

"Yes. How did you know?"

"I'm one of the deputy managers. It's my job to know."

I glance at the name tag pinned to his jacket lapel, and see that it says, 'Kieran', recalling that Laura mentioned him when I arrived yesterday. I didn't see him when I dined last night, but I imagine a deputy manager has many duties to fulfil, other than recommending food and wine to confused guests. Whatever his role, he's very good at it, although that doesn't surprise me. If memory serves, Laura said Kieran was new, but friendly, and I'm not going to disagree.

"I'll bring your wine, Miss Woodward."

He knows my name, too? I'm impressed, but before I can say anything else, he turns and walks away.

I glance around the dining room, the square tables covered with white linen cloths, although some have been joined together to accommodate larger parties. There are floor-to-ceiling windows with a view over the hotel's gardens, which are currently decorated with fairy lights wound into the branches of the trees to make it seem more festive, I suppose. In the corner of the room is a gigantic Christmas tree. It's not perhaps as big as the one in the foyer, but it's huge, nonetheless, and is decked with yet more lights, and silver baubles, neatly arranged in order of size, the largest at the bottom and the smallest at the top.

"Your wine…"

I startle at the sound of Kieran's voice and turn to face him again.

"Thank you."

"Were you just admiring my handiwork?"

"Sorry?"

"The tree," he says, nodding towards it.

"You decorated it?"

"Yes."

"You're braver than I am. I wouldn't tackle a tree that big."

"I don't know about brave." His smile widens. "It wasn't quite the same as fighting off a wild bear, or taming a crocodile."

"You've done that lately, have you?"

"Not since moving here, no."

"Well, there isn't much call for crocodile taming in Porthgarrion."

"I'd noticed that," he says, tilting his head. "There's also a distinct lack of wild bears. If you ask me, something needs to be done about it." He glances up, raising his eyebrows and nodding his head, before he looks back at me. "Will you excuse me? Duty calls."

"Of course."

He smiles again and departs, going over to a table on the other side of the room, where a young couple are seated. I watch him for a moment, noting that although he seems friendly enough with them, he doesn't linger, and soon moves away from their table. When he does, he glances over at me again, and I look away, ashamed of being caught staring.

"Your sea trout." The young female voice beside me makes me jump and I sit back in my seat, letting her put the plate down in front of me. The dish looks delicious and once she's gone, I tuck in, savouring the delicate sweetness of the mussel sauce, and how well it compliments the trout.

"Was I right?" Kieran comes over within a few minutes of me finishing my meal.

"You were. The sauce was amazing."

He smiles. "Can I get you anything else?"

"No, thank you. I'm going out for the evening, so I just wanted a light supper."

I go to get up, but he reaches for my chair, pulling it back and helping me to my feet. "I hope you have a lovely time," he says. "And with any luck, I'll see you tomorrow."

I'm not sure how to reply to that, so I just nod my head and make my way from the dining room, smiling. That felt like he was flirting… at least a little, but I wonder whether he'd have bothered, if he'd realised how old I am.

It feels even colder out here than it did last night, and I'm wondering about my choice of clothing. My skirt might be a winter weight, but trousers would definitely have been warmer. I'm also wishing I hadn't bothered to curl my hair. Having taken so much time over it, I was reluctant to put on a hat, except now that feels like vanity getting the better of common sense. My ears are freezing.

I'm relieved when I push open the door to the pub, and feel a welcome rush of warm air greeting me. The noise level seems even greater than it was yesterday evening, and I wonder how Ed and I are going to hear ourselves think, let alone talk. I step further into the room, leaning up a little as I undo my jacket and unwrap my scarf, trying to see where he is, my stomach flipping over as I spot him. He's at the far end of the bar, and for a moment, I'm torn between going straight to him, and staying down at this end, nearer to where I sat last night, and waiting for him to come to me.

"Well… if it isn't Nicki Woodward."

I turn, hearing my name, and can't help smiling as the unmistakable figure of Rory Quick bears down on me.

I hold out my hand and he takes it, although we don't really shake, we just hold hands for a moment or two, until I pull away.

"It's good to see you, Rory." I can't say he hasn't changed, because he has. His hair has greyed at the temples, and while he's still just as tall and handsome as he ever was, he's also a lot happier. I can see it in his eyes.

"You, too. Laura told me you were back."

"Yes… I decided to come for Christmas. My… My mum died, and…"

"Oh, Nicki, I'm sorry."

I nod my head, accepting his sympathies. "It only happened earlier this month, and I couldn't face the festivities by myself."

"That's understandable." He smiles. "Why don't you come and join us?" He tilts his head back towards the bar and I look over his shoulder, seeing Laura sitting there. She's smiling and I smile back. This isn't quite what I had in mind for my evening with Ed, but I can't be rude, and I nod my head, letting Rory lead me over to the bar.

Laura holds out her hand as we approach, and we shake properly, like the comparative strangers we are, before I perch up on the stool beside her.

"I know you two have met," Rory says, talking to Laura. He doesn't sit, but stands right next to her. "Although I'm not sure Nicki explained that she, Ed, Suzannah and I all went to school together."

Laura smiles. "No, she didn't."

"I didn't go into any detail," I explain

Rory moves a little closer. "Have you heard about what happened to Suzannah?" He lowers his voice, so I have to strain to hear him.

"Yes. Ed told me earlier, before he invited me here tonight."

Rory nods, although his brow furrows, and he looks up, just as Ed turns and sees me. I can't fail to spot the odd exchange of glances between them. Rory is frowning now, looking almost angry, while Ed raises his eyebrows, as though feigning innocence, and in that moment, I know he set this up. I know he invited Rory and Laura to be here, so he wouldn't have to be alone with me.

I can feel myself blushing, and am grateful that, despite the multitude of fairy lights, this corner of the bar is dim enough for no-one to notice.

Why would Ed do this to me? Why would he invite me to spend the evening here with him, and then invite someone else, too? Clearly he doesn't want to be with me, but in that case, why ask me here in the first place?

I glance over my shoulder at the door, wondering if I should just leave… except that would probably be even more embarrassing than staying here and fronting this out. I don't have to stay for very long, though. One drink should do it, and then I'll make an excuse and go.

Ed finally makes his way down the bar and stands in front of us. Rory is closest to him, and glares hard at his oldest friend, who ignores him and turns to me, smiling.

"What can I get you?"

"A small red wine, please. And I'm paying for it this time."

"No, you're not," Rory says, pulling his wallet from his back pocket.

I nod my head. "Thank you."

Ed pours my drink, pushing it across the bar, and taking a five-pound note from Rory. I half expect him to ask why I'll accept a drink from Rory and not from him, but he doesn't. He just goes to get Rory's change, returning a few moments later to hand it over. An awkward silence descends, and I take a sip of wine, unable to think of a single thing to say.

"Whereabouts did you used to live?" Laura asks, taking a deep breath, and glancing at Rory, although she's clearly talking to me.

"My parents' home was in Garden Close."

She frowns for a second or two and then her face clears. "That's the little side street off of Bell Road, isn't it?"

"Yes."

She nods her head, sipping at her white wine. "My boss lives in a flat down there."

I put my wine down beside hers. "That can't be right. There are no flats in Garden close."

"There are now," Ed says, and I turn to face him. I still feel angry and disappointed. I wish he'd just been honest with me. If he'd explained he was nervous, or worried, or confused about being alone with me, I'd have suggested inviting Rory and Laura. I wouldn't have minded if Ed needed his friend to help break the ice. Doing it this way is just so underhand, and so degrading.

"Have they knocked down Mum and Dad's house?"

I don't know why, but that thought bothers me. Perhaps because I'm having such a dreadful evening… I'm not sure I can take any more.

"No," he says. "But they knocked down the houses opposite."

"Not that lovely little terrace of cottages?"

"Yes." He nods his head. "And they built a three-storey apartment building instead." He glances at Rory. "It was about seven or eight years ago, wasn't it?"

"It was nearer ten, I think," Rory says. "There was quite a lot of opposition in the village, but the people who owned the houses were keen to sell. The developers were offering a very good price."

"I'm sure they were. But what about the people who lived in the houses on Mum and Dad's side of the road? Didn't they get a say?"

"They got to object at the public meeting the developers held," Ed says. "And then they were completely ignored."

"I feel quite relieved Mum and Dad left when they did. They loved that house."

My voice cracks a little and I reach for my wine, taking a larger gulp. Everything's blurring, and I can't look up at Rory and Laura. If I was just here with Ed, like I'd expected to be, I'd probably be able to look at him, and maybe explain it all, too… but as it is, he didn't want to be with me, so I'm damned if I'm confiding.

Another awkward silence descends. I stare at my glass, unwilling – unable – to raise my head. I don't know what everyone else is doing, but eventually Rory says, "Is Dan coming home for Christmas, or have you lost him to the surfing circuit for good?" and I realise he must be talking to Ed. He didn't tell me his son was a surfer, but he seems to have been selective with his truths, so why would he?

"No. I think he's a lost cause. He's taking part in an important competition in Hawaii."

"How do you know it's important?" Laura asks.

"Because you have to be invited."

I look up now, blinking away my tears. "And he was invited?"

He turns to me, tilting his head, and although there's something in his eyes that looks like sorrow and sympathy, I can't dwell on that. "Yes… at least, that's what he told me when he texted me about it."

"It's been years since I've seen him surf," Rory says.

"Was it something he just picked up naturally?" Laura asks.

"Well, he didn't inherit the talent from his father," Rory jokes, and both he and Ed chuckle, although I struggle to join in.

I wish I'd never come now… not just to the pub, but to Porthgarrion.

I know I said I was coming here to bury my past and lay my ghosts to rest, but Ed brought them back to life… or at least I thought he did. It felt like it, and I was stupid enough to let myself hope.

The problem is, things have changed. Nothing is how I thought it would be, and all my hopes are being crushed, right before my eyes.

Ed doesn't want me, no matter how much I want him. And while it's lovely to see Rory again, and to discover that he's found happiness at last with Laura… I wish I'd stayed away.

Chapter Ten

Ed

Inviting Rory and Laura here tonight felt like a good idea this morning, but now I'm not so sure.

I might have asked them here because I thought I wasn't ready to be alone with Nicki, but seeing her again, I know that's not true. Okay, so I'm still conflicted. I'm still filled with guilt and confusion, but I can't escape the fact that I want to kiss her, and hold her, and tell her how I feel about her. Wanting that and doing it might be two entirely different things, but if I don't at least give us a chance, I'll never find out if I'm capable, will I?

The trouble is, I think I might have upset her. That's probably got nothing to do with Rory and Laura. She can't know I invited them… and they've got as much right to be here as anyone else. No… I imagine it's because I just told her about the changes they made to Garden Close… the road where her parents used to live, and where she grew up. Her grief about her mum is still very close to the surface, and I probably should have allowed for that, and been less flippant about it. I'm sure she had tears in her eyes, and I wanted to give her a hug then, to tell her it gets better… or at least it gets less raw. Because it does. Except I couldn't, could I?

Not with Rory and Laura sitting right next to her... at my invitation.

"Have you never surfed then?" Laura asks, bringing me back to our conversation.

Rory glances at me. He's stopped chuckling, as have I, and I'm relieved to see that at least he's not scowling anymore. He's been looking daggers at me almost since the moment Nicki arrived. "Ed? Surf?" he says, like it's the most ludicrous idea in the world.

"I tried it once," I admit. "It didn't end well."

"Why not?" Laura asks, smiling.

"I fell off the board."

"So? I imagine that happens all the time, doesn't it?"

"Yes. Except I forgot the instructions about how to fall, and in my efforts not to look an idiot in front of Suzannah, I ended up getting hit around the head by the board... and looking even more of an idiot when it knocked me out."

Rory laughs again, clearly remembering the episode. "The surf school had only just opened and Sam – who's the guy that owns the place now – he was working there during his summer holidays. He can't have been more than seventeen, but he was as cool as a cucumber, and he and I dragged Ed out of the water."

"So, you were surfing too, were you?"

"Yes. I was terrible at it... but not quite as terrible as Ed."

Laura smiles and then turns to me again. "I take it you made a full recovery?"

"Oh, yes. I had one hell of a headache, but I was fine. I think Suzannah wanted to beat me senseless for scaring her like that... but then she was about eight months pregnant, so her reaction was understandable."

"This was after your wedding?" Laura says, sounding surprised.

"Yes."

"And you still felt the need to create a good impression?"

"Of course. I don't think that ever goes away. We always want to impress the women we love, don't we?"

I turn to Rory, looking for support. He frowns, glances at Nicki and then says, "Yes... yes, of course," with so little conviction, it's palpable.

I've said the wrong thing, and although the realisation dawns a little too late, I turn to Nicki, reaching across the bar.

"I—I just need the ladies'." There's a catch in her voice, and she jumps down from her stool, rushing away, before I can get another word out.

I can hardly go after her, but I watch her walk away, her head bent, and once more, I'm awash with guilt. Why did I have to make such a big deal about Suzannah... about wanting to impress her? *Because she was your wife... because you loved her... because you still do...*

"Are you trying to cause trouble?" I swing back around at the sound of Rory's voice and stare into his angry face.

"Me?"

"Yes, you."

"Why would I be trying to cause trouble?"

"Because you've always thought Nicki had a thing for me."

Laura turns to face him, twisting on her stool, as she tilts her head slightly. "Oh yes? Is there something you want to tell me?" Her lips are twitching upwards, so I know she's joking, but Rory seems deadly serious still.

"No," he says, looking right at her, and taking her hand in his. "There was never anything between Nicki and me. But Ed's always thought she liked me." He turns to face me again, although he keeps hold of Laura's hand with one of his. "Nicki told us you invited her here tonight, so why did you ask us to come too? Why did you make it sound like you wanted us to come over here for Christmas drinks and not mention the fact that Nicki was going to be here, too? If you weren't looking to cause trouble, I don't see—"

I lean forward, putting my hand on his arm, and he stops talking. "I got it wrong."

"You certainly did. I feel like we've been set up here, and…"

"That's not what I mean." I interrupt him, and he glares at me, raising his eyebrows.

"What do you mean, then?"

"It wasn't you she liked… it was me."

He frowns, tips his head to the right, studying me, and then leans back slightly. "Are you sure about that?"

"Yes. But thanks for the vote of confidence."

He chuckles and I struggle not to sigh out my relief. I've never seen Rory so angry before… not with me, anyway.

"I didn't mean it like that," he says. "I'm not questioning that she liked you, I'm just wondering how you know about it."

"She told me herself, last night, and I'll admit, it came as an enormous shock."

"Why? All jokes aside, I don't see why you'd be surprised."

"Isn't it obvious? This isn't easy for me, Rory. You know how much I liked her, before I got together with Suzannah, and finding out that she felt the same… thinking about what might have been…"

"You can't do that," Laura says, leaning forward slightly and I turn to look down at her. "It's ancient history."

"It doesn't seem like history. It seems like yesterday."

"What does?" Rory asks. "The way you feel about Nicki?"

"Yes. It's all still there. Nothing's changed. But the problem is, what does that say about me and Suzannah?"

"It doesn't say anything about you and Suzannah."

Laura pulls her hand from Rory's and reaches across the bar, placing it on my arm. "Forget the past," she says. "If you like Nicki and she likes you, just go with it."

I shake my head. "I wish it was that easy."

"Why…"

At that moment, Nicki reappears, resuming her seat, and an awkward silence descends… even more awkward than the previous ones. This is my fault. I set this up, after all, and I need to do something about it, even if I'm not ready to open up to Nicki yet.

"I've been meaning to ask," I say, turning to Rory, "what happened the other night, when you went to talk to Gemma about inviting her mother to the wedding?"

We all turn to look at him, and he rolls his eyes.

"Needless to say, Gemma doesn't want her there. In fact, she gave me a lecture on how inappropriate it would be, considering I'm married to Laura now."

Laura smiles, looking a little self-conscious. "We told her it had been my idea, but Gemma was still adamant… there's no way she wants her mother to attend."

"I can understand that," Nicki says, joining in the conversation, much to my relief. "Joanne would only try to steal the limelight, knowing her."

Rory chuckles. "You remember her well, then?"

"Of course. I never liked her, but I remember her."

The silence descends again, and Rory picks up his glass and takes his time having a long sip from it, while Laura looks at me, rather pointedly, as though she expects me to act on her earlier advice to 'go with it'… right here, right now. I stare straight back, making it clear I've got no intention of doing so, and after a few seconds, she turns to Nicki. I wonder, for a fearful moment or two, whether she's going to say something herself… to intercede on my behalf, but she doesn't.

"How are you finding the hotel?" she says.

"It's lovely." Nicki swivels on her seat, looking at her. "The suite is really comfortable. I spent the whole of this afternoon up there reading, and totally lost track of time."

"Nothing changes then," I say without thinking and she turns her head, glancing at me.

"Doesn't it?"

I wonder if we're talking at crossed purposes. I might be thinking about the fact that she always used to have her head in a book, but there's a hurt look behind her eyes which tells me she's not talking about the same thing at all.

She doesn't wait for me to answer her, and in a way, I'm relieved. I'm not sure what I'd have said, anyway. Instead, she looks back at Laura. "I had a lovely dinner tonight, too."

"Oh? What did you have?"

"Sea trout, with a really lovely mussel sauce. It was recommended to me by Kieran."

Laura smiles. "Ahh... Kieran."

"What does 'Ahh... Kieran' mean?" Rory says, with a slight edge to his voice... one I haven't heard before.

"It doesn't mean anything... except that he's a very efficient deputy manager, and so much better at his job than Brian was." She nestles into Rory, tilting her head and looking up at him. "You've got nothing to be jealous of. He's far too young for me."

He leans down and kisses her, surprising me with such a public display of affection. "Anyone under forty is too young for you," he says with a smile.

"In which case it's just as well you're forty-one."

He chuckles, putting his arm around her, and I marvel. I've never seen Rory be so possessive... not that Laura seems to mind. She seems to have the measure of him.

"How old is Kieran then?" I ask. "If he's far too young for you?"

"He's thirty."

"Which makes him the same age as you, doesn't it?"

She shakes her head, trying to look offended, although she's smiling. "No… thank you. I'm only twenty-nine."

"Of course. I was forgetting you were Rory's child bride."

She laughs, and Rory joins in. "I don't think I can be called a child bride when it was my second marriage."

"You were married before?" Nicki asks, getting back into the conversation at last.

"Yes. But the less said about that, the better." Laura smiles at her. "Still, I'm glad you're enjoying your stay."

Nicki's face falls and I wonder if she's going to contradict Laura… if she's not enjoying herself at all.

"Can I get everyone another drink?" Rory says, and Laura nods her head.

"I won't, thanks," Nicki replies. "I—I think I'll head back to the hotel."

"Already?" I reach across the bar, but she pulls back. She's barely been here for an hour, and despite the conflict in my head, and all my doubts, I want to be alone with her. But how can I do that if she isn't going to stay… at least until closing time?

"Yes. I'm tired."

She doesn't look tired. She looks upset, and maybe angry… presumably with me.

"I can get Leanne to cover for me if you want me to walk you back?"

She shakes her head. "I'm fine."

"Please, Nicki…"

"I said, I'm fine." She raises her voice, jumping down from her stool, before she turns to Rory. "It was good seeing you again."

He smiles and nods his head. "It was good seeing you, too. Don't be such a stranger in future."

Nicki doesn't reply, but turns to Laura. "It was nice to meet you properly, too."

Laura stands and steps away from Rory, moving closer to Nicki. "Are you okay? Do you want Rory to see you back to the hotel?"

Nicki shakes her head. "No, thanks. Honestly, I'm fine." I don't believe a word she's saying, but she manages a slight smile. "Goodnight, then." She doesn't look at me again, but moves away, towards the door, and I watch her go, rooted to the spot.

"Well, that was embarrassing." Rory's voice sparks me back to reality and I turn to him, just as Laura slaps him on the arm. "What?" he says. "It was embarrassing. Nicki obviously didn't expect us to be here."

"No, she didn't," I say. "But that's because I was hoping this might seem like a coincidence."

He rolls his eyes. "There was nothing that felt even remotely coincidental about any of that."

I lean on the bar, glancing over at the closed door. "I've hurt her feelings, haven't I?"

Laura and Rory both stare at me, like I'm a prize exhibit… or a prize fool, and then Laura nods her head.

"What do you think?" Rory says, giving words to his wife's expression. "You've just effectively told Nicki that you didn't want to be alone with her. I don't know how anyone wouldn't take that as an insult."

"I didn't mean it that way." Although I can see his point now. How could I have thought she was upset about the flats being built opposite her parents' old house? This is to do with us, and the fact that I've just publicly denied there's even an 'us' to speak of.

"Then why did you invite us?"

"Because after I'd asked her to come here, I regretted it."

Laura shakes her head, sitting up on her stool again. "Then why didn't you contact her and cancel?"

"Because I didn't want to cancel, either. I knew, deep down, I wanted to see her again… and to be alone with her."

"And you thought inviting us was going to help?" Rory frowns at me.

"No, but…"

Laura leans over slightly. "We haven't known each other for very long, Ed… but I have to say, you're not making any sense. You're a bag of contradictions."

"I know I am. You should try being inside my head. Between the guilt, the regrets, the confusion…" I don't mention the longing, the deep need, the desire… I don't know Laura well enough.

"Why do you feel guilty?" Rory asks.

"Because of Suzannah, of course."

"You mean because you like someone else?"

"Yes. It feels disloyal… but I think it's made worse because I liked Nicki before."

He sighs. "Okay… and the regrets? What's that about?"

"How long have you got?"

"All night, if you need it… as long as you're not going to try and persuade me that you regret marrying Suzannah, because I won't believe you."

"No. I don't regret marrying her. But I suppose I regret not knowing how Nicki felt back then…. when I could have done something about it."

"You can do something about it now, can't you?"

"I suppose, but it's complicated. You saw how it was tonight."

"Tonight was only complicated because you made it that way by inviting us and making Nicki feel awkward, and unwanted." He shakes his head. "You need to stop messing her around and decide whether you're ready to see someone else yet. If you're not, no-one's going to judge you… not even Nicki. But you have to be honest with her. You can't let her think there's hope where there is none. That's not fair."

"I know. I didn't mean to hurt her. It's just…"

"Suzannah?"

I nod my head. "It's been seven years. That ought to be long enough, but…"

Rory holds up his hand, and I stop talking. "There's no time limit on grief. You and Suzannah had been together for nearly half your life when she died. No-one expects you to just wipe out all those memories… but can you honestly say Suzannah would have wanted you to be this miserable?"

"Who says I'm miserable?"

"Anyone who knows you." He looks me right in the eye. "You've got a chance to be happy again… and I think you could be really happy with Nicki. Don't blow it over past regrets, and things you can't change."

At that moment, I notice a man further down the bar. It's Sean Clayton, doing his best to attract my attention, without drawing too much to himself. He's a best-selling novelist and the closest thing we have to a celebrity, and while he's not a regular visitor to the pub, he comes in often enough that we know who he is, and that he likes to keep himself to himself.

"E—Excuse me," I murmur to Rory, who nods his head, and I wander down to the other end of the bar.

"Can I have two red wines, please?" Sean puts a twenty-pound note on the bar and I grab two glasses from above my head, looking over his shoulder at the blonde who he came in with about an hour ago, not long after Nicki got here. I've never seen him with the same woman twice, but like I say, he doesn't come in that often… and in any case, who am I to judge? At least the woman he's with looks happy… so he's one up on me.

I pour his drinks, taking the twenty-pound note and handing him back his change without uttering a word, and while I know Sean likes his privacy, even he seems surprised by my silence.

"Is everything okay?" he asks, hesitating as he picks up the two glasses of wine.

"Yes, thanks."

He frowns, but says nothing more and returns to his table, putting down the drinks before the woman places her hand behind his head and pulls him in for a kiss. He lets her, although I notice he doesn't touch her, and I wonder if she realises how detached he is. Whatever her feelings for him, it's clear he doesn't return them.

The thought crosses my mind that someone observing Nicki and myself would probably think the same thing. They'd be wrong, but how would they know? I've done nothing to show her how I feel… nothing to encourage her. And Rory's right; if I'm not careful, I'm going to blow my own happiness, and Nicki's.

I turn back around, seeing Rory and Laura at the opposite end of the bar. Rory's still standing right beside Laura, with his arms around her, and she's looking up at him. They're talking, and then he laughs. I can't see her face, but I can see his, and his eyes are so full of love, I almost don't recognise him. Not once did I see him look at Joanne like that, and for a moment, I'm jealous. I know I've had what they've got, but I want it again… with Nicki.

I wake with a start, my body covered with sweat, and I groan out loud, torn between guilt and the need to cling to the fading images that were so fresh in my mind just seconds ago. I lick my lips, wondering how I can taste her, even though it was just a dream… wondering how I can feel her lips around me still, even though it's all in my imagination.

"Oh, God… Nicki…"

I throw back the covers, ignoring my very obvious arousal, and wander into the bathroom, going straight into the shower and bracing my arms against the wall as I turn on the water, letting it cascade over my head.

I try very hard to plant images of Suzannah into my mind, but she's a blur, and all I can see is Nicki, looking at me, her eyes filled with confusion and sadness, just like she was when she left here last night. She didn't look like that in my dream, but life isn't a dream, is it? And in real life, I know I'm not the man who made her scream with pleasure. I'm the man who made her feel unwanted… even though nothing could be further from the truth.

"How would she know that?" I murmur to myself. Given the way I've behaved towards her, how would she know how much I want her?

I wash quickly, thinking that, if I hurry, I might have time to go to the hotel this morning… to explain. I'm not sure what I'll say, but I have to say something. There's no way I can leave it like this.

I turn off the water, grabbing a towel from the heated rail and wrapping it around my waist before I brush my teeth and shave, and then pad back into the bedroom, glancing at the wreckage of my bed, the duvet half on the floor, and the pillows scattered, one of them most of the way across the bedside table. If I wasn't so worried about Nicki and what I'm going to say to her, I'd be tempted to smile. My dream was clearly every bit as good as the parts of it I can remember.

I wander down the side of the bed, picking up my watch from the floor. God knows how it got there, but given the state of the bed and bedside table, anything is possible. I turn it over and gasp. How the hell can it be a quarter past ten? I know I struggled to get off to sleep, beating myself up over what happened last night, but I never sleep in this late… except it seems I do.

I startle at the sound of knocking on the front door of the pub. That'll be Leanne, and I'm not even dressed yet.

I drop my watch on the bed and go out onto the landing, running down the stairs and into the pub, letting out a groan when I remember the decision I made after closing last night, that I'd leave the clearing up until today... which seems like the stupidest idea in the world now. I grab the keys, just as Leanne knocks on the door again, and rush over, opening it.

"Keep your hair on."

She looks up at me. She's wrapped up in a thick coat and scarf, although I can still see her face, her short dark hair, immaculately styled as ever, her eyes wandering over my bare chest and down to the towel that's still wrapped around me.

"Did I disturb something?" she asks, with a twinkle in her eye.

"No. And get in here, will you? It's freezing."

She comes inside and I close the door, locking it again, but leaving the keys in the lock this time. When I turn, she's standing with her hands on her hips, not looking at me, but at the bomb site that should be a pub, almost ready and waiting to be opened for a day's trade.

"I offered to stay and help clear up," she says, turning to me and narrowing her eyes.

"I know."

"And you sent me home, telling me you'd manage."

"I know that too."

She waves her arm around at the mess of glasses, crisp packets and general detritus. "Is this your idea of managing?"

"No. It's my idea of leaving it until the morning, and then oversleeping. Okay?"

She glares at me and then lets out a huff. "I suppose I'd better get on with it. And you'd better put some clothes on... unless you're otherwise occupied upstairs?"

"No, I'm not. And before you do anything else, can you put the coffee on?"

"Yes, boss."

"And don't even think about turning on those damn lights until I've had at least two cups, or I'll fire you."

She chuckles, wandering over to the bar and depositing her handbag on top of it while unwrapping her scarf from around her neck. "You can't afford to fire me."

She has a point, although it's not one I'm going to acknowledge… certainly not while I'm standing here in just a towel.

"I'll be down in ten minutes," I say, heading for the back of the pub.

Leanne doesn't reply, but I hear the clink of glasses and know she's making a start on clearing up without me. That doesn't mean I can rest on my laurels, though. There's a lot to do, and not much time in which to do it. I run back up the stairs, depositing the towel on the floor, and grab some underwear from the drawer, pulling it on, before I add my jeans and a white shirt. As I'm doing it up, I glance back down at the bed again. I haven't got time to make it now, but the memory of my dream is still there… as is the thought that I won't be able to make it to the hotel this morning.

"Damn," I mutter under my breath, putting on my watch before I sit on the edge of the bed and lace up my shoes.

I had such plans…

It's only a few days until Christmas and I would have thought people had better things to do than go out for lunch… except it seems not, because even though Reece came in at eleven-thirty, not long after we opened, we've been rushed off our feet since noon.

Every time the doors have opened, I've looked up, hoping to see Nicki, although why she'd come here, given the way I treated her last night, God only knows. I suppose I've been hoping she might, just because I can't get to her, but as the day has worn on, my hopes have turned to fear... fear that I offended her so much last night, she might have left the village.

It's three o'clock now and things are finally quietening down. Reece took his lunch at just after one, and I let Leanne have a break about an hour ago, although I've worked straight through myself.

"You can go upstairs for a while, if you like," she says, coming over to me with a couple of glasses in her hands. "I'm sure Reece and I can manage."

"Okay, but if it gets busy again, give me a shout."

She nods her head, and I duck out through the back corridor and up the stairs. I wasn't about to say 'no' to her offer, because although I can't leave the premises and go to the hotel, I can at least phone...

I've barely made it up the stairs before I pull my mobile from my back pocket, looking up the hotel's number and connecting a call.

"Seaview Hotel, Kieran speaking... how may I help?"

Kieran? I smile, leaning back against the wall between the kitchen and the living room, remembering the conversation between Rory and Laura last night, and his momentary fit of jealousy.

"I believe you have someone called Nicole Woodward staying there?"

"Yes, we do."

"So she hasn't checked out then?"

"No. Would you like me to put you through to her room?"

"No." My reply is fast... too fast, and I cough, trying to give myself time to calm down. "No, thank you."

"Can I tell her you called?" he says.

"No, that's okay. I just wanted to make sure she hadn't left, that's all."

I hang up, feeling like an idiot. Why did I say that? I could have just said 'no', and left it at that. Come to that, I could have said 'yes', and let him put the call through. Except I'm not sure I want to have my next conversation with Nicki over the phone. And in any case, I can't be sure she'd have spoken to me. The thought of that rejection is like a burning hot nail driving through my heart. The pain sears, catching my breath, and I slide down the wall to the floor, my knees bent and my arms resting on them.

This isn't the same as the pain of losing Suzannah. That was something else, something I wouldn't wish on my worst enemy. But I've felt this before…

I felt it when I saw disappointment in Suzannah's eyes, and knew I'd put it there… like when I talked her into moving here, using emotional blackmail to get my own way, even though I knew this wasn't the life she wanted. It was there when I persuaded her we should spend our savings on fixing up this place, because it was better for the business. And it almost broke me, when she sat me down, years later, and told me the real reason she'd never wanted to come here… and what I'd denied her.

The thing is, that's all in the past, and no matter how much pain I caused then, to both Suzannah and myself, there's nothing I can do about it now.

I can do something about this pain, though. I can make this better… or I can at least try.

Because I can't make the same mistakes again.

"Boss?"

Leanne's voice echoes up the stairs.

"Yes?"

"Sorry, but it's getting kind of crazy down here again."

I suck in a breath and stagger to my feet.

"Okay. Give me five minutes."

She doesn't reply, but I know she'll have gone back to the bar, and I head into the kitchen, grabbing a glass of water and swallowing it down. I haven't eaten yet today, and I don't care. I can do that later. For now, I need to focus on how I'm going to make this up to Nicki. It doesn't look like I'm going to get to the hotel today, but at least I know she's still here… and there's always tomorrow. I'll set my alarm and wake up early, so I can go down there and get back before opening time. If I'm lucky, she'll let me explain. God knows how I'm going to do that… but whatever I do, or say, I've got to do it in person. I need to see her face, to read her eyes… and to let her read mine. Hopefully then, she'll see that this is real… and that I love her.

Chapter Eleven

Nicki

There's no way I can spend another day in my room.

I did that yesterday, ordering room service, staying shut away, and reading. At least, I tried reading, but I spent a lot of time crying, trying not to think, and veering between anger and humiliation.

The trying not to think part wasn't overly successful. I was so confused about why Ed had asked me to the pub, just to embarrass me, to make me feel unwanted. I kept trying to tell myself it was my own fault… that I'd read too much into a casual invitation. Except it didn't feel very casual. I'd just told him my marriage had failed, and been doomed to failure from the beginning, because Terry wasn't him. He told me – he expressly told me – he wanted to see me again. So, was he lying? Or did he change his mind? Or was it something deeper than that? Was it something to do with Suzannah?

I couldn't work it out, and ended up exhausting myself going round in circles, and giving myself a headache.

That's one of the reasons I need to get out today. Not only am I sick of trying to work out the reasons behind Ed's behaviour, but I need some fresh air.

I wrap up warm, putting on my black boots over my jeans, and shrugging on my jacket, before tying my scarf around my neck. It's overcast outside, and I can tell from the way the boats are bobbing on the water that there's a wind blowing up.

At the bottom of the stairs, I quickly glance around, struggling not to heave out a sigh of relief, when I realise there's no sign of Laura. She's the other reason I stayed shut up in my room. Don't get me wrong, I like Laura, but I couldn't face her yesterday. I even ordered my breakfast upstairs this morning, just to avoid seeing her.

I start for the door, pulling on my gloves and check the clock on the wall. It's not nine o'clock yet, so hopefully the harbour won't be too busy and I can take my time and clear the cobwebs.

"Nicki?"

I stop dead at the sound of my name and turn to see Laura coming out from behind the reception desk. She wasn't there a moment ago, but I can't ignore her now… she's walking straight towards me. I plaster a smile on my face and I step back from the doorway.

"Hi," I say, trying to sound cheerful.

"Are you okay?" she asks. "I didn't see you yesterday."

"Yes, I'm fine." I don't feel like explaining my absence. "I was just going out for a walk."

She nods her head. "It looks like it might rain."

"Well, I won't be out for long."

I move towards the door again. "Nicki?" I turn around. Her face is full of concern, and she steps closer, lowering her voice. "I know it's none of my business, but try not to think too badly of Ed."

I look over her shoulder at the Christmas tree, the lights blurring, haloed by my tears. "I'm trying. But it's very hard when he keeps humiliating me."

She puts her hand on my arm, and although I'm wearing a thick coat, I appreciate the friendly gesture. "I don't think he means to. He's just struggling with how he feels."

"I know. I get how hard it is for him, and how much he loves Suzannah still, but…" My voice catches and I struggle to swallow down the lump in my throat, holding up my hand.

"I'm sorry," Laura says. "I didn't mean to upset you."

I shake my head, still unable to utter a word, and I turn away, going straight out through the door this time, wishing I'd been able to articulate myself better. Laura seems really nice, and easy to talk to, if the other night is anything to go by, but how can I explain it when I don't understand what's happening myself?

I make my way down Bell Road, stopping on the corner, the wind pulling at my hair, and catching my breath. It's stronger than I thought, and I wonder if this was such a good idea, after all. I can see the waves beyond the harbour, crashing into the defensive wall, and dark clouds gathering on the horizon. They're not necessarily coming this way; they could skirt along the coast, but either way, this wind is freezing.

I decide to brave it, at least for a while, and turn onto the harbour. Not surprisingly, there aren't very many people out this morning, but my heart lurches in my chest when I notice Ed striding towards me. He's by the florist's, wearing dark jeans and that same overcoat he had on the other morning, but with the collar turned up today, against the wind. He's looking at the pavement in front of him and hasn't seen me yet. I could run back to the hotel. It's not like he'd follow me there… he doesn't want to see me.

I'm about to turn when he looks up and breaks his stride, surprise etched on his face. I'm not sure which of us is more embarrassed, but my moment for running is lost, and he waves, picking up his pace.

As he gets closer, I fight my feelings for him… and lose. I've loved him all my life, and there's no way I'm ever going to stop, no matter how much time and space I try to put between us.

"Hello," he says, coming to a stop right in front of me.

"Hello."

He smiles and I feel that familiar warmth in the pit of my stomach. Why does he have to be so damn gorgeous? And why can't he want me, just a little?

"I was just coming to see you." My mouth drops open, his words surprising me even more than his appearance on what I'd hoped would be a solitary walk.

"You were?"

"Yes."

The wind catches at my hair again, blowing it across my face and Ed reaches forward, pushing it back, his fingers touching my cheek. The contact makes me gasp and I look up into his eyes. *Don't hurt me. Please don't hurt me again.*

"It's too cold out here," he says, looking around, his eyes settling on the café behind him. "Come on, I'll buy you a coffee."

He doesn't give me a choice, but takes my arm and steers me towards the café, opening the door and letting me pass through ahead of him.

Inside, it's warm and quiet, most people having presumably stayed indoors on such a morning. There's an older couple sitting near the back, and a young family who are at a table by the counter, but after a moment's hesitation, Ed guides me towards a small table near the window. The glass is slightly steamed up, but it's not as though we're unfamiliar with the view.

I unwrap my scarf and undo my coat, although I don't take either of them off, and Ed unbuttons his coat and puts the collar down, before we both sit opposite each other.

We stare for a moment, neither knowing what to say, I don't think. I'm not sure I'm the one who should start the conversation.

He said he was coming to see me, and I'm presuming he had a reason for that. He opens his mouth, just as a man appears at our side.

"What can I get you?"

I look up, taking in his dark blond hair and tan, wishing he'd leave us alone, although I suppose that is unreasonable, given we're in his café and it's his job to serve us.

Ed glances at me. "Coffee?"

I nod my head. "Coffee's fine."

He looks back at the man beside us. "Two coffees, thanks Carter."

Carter nods and moves away again, and Ed returns his gaze to me, letting out a sigh. I sit back, waiting for him to say something, but he doesn't and, being as I don't really know why we're here, I glance around the room.

"This is different. I remember it being a lot more impersonal than this."

He follows my gaze, and while it's still quite small in here, there's no denying, it's a lot more cosy and welcoming than the café of my memories, which had blank white walls and no personality whatsoever.

"It was," Ed says. "Carter put in the wood panelling when he moved here, and he added the bookshelves."

"I like the newspaper racks too. At least it gives people something to do over brunch."

"Exactly. That's why he did it."

"The paintings are a nice touch, too."

He nods his head, just as Carter comes back, bringing two large mugs and a cafetière of hot black coffee, which he places on the table, along with a jug of warm milk.

"Thanks, Carter," Ed says, and turns to me. "Shall I pour?"

I nod my head, watching while he pours our coffee, leaving me to add my own milk. He takes his black, pulling the mug closer to him and putting his hands around it, as though to warm them. "It's cold, isn't it?" I say and he looks up, frowning.

"Yes." He pauses. "Sorry, I don't really want to talk about the weather."

"What do you want to talk about, Ed? Why were you coming to see me?"

He leans forward. "To apologise."

"What for?"

A blush creeps up his cheeks. "For inviting Rory and Laura to the pub the other night. I was going to come and see you yesterday, to try and explain, but I overslept, and work got in the way… and I—I'm sorry about that too." The words pour out of him, but eventually he stops talking and gazes at me, doubt written in his eyes.

I reach across the table and he stares at my hand for long enough to make me wonder if I should pull it back again. But then he lets go of his cup and mirrors my action, just letting our fingertips touch for a while, before he clamps his hand over mine. The contact sends shivers down my spine and I suck in a sharp breath.

"It's okay," I whisper. "You don't have to apologise for being busy."

He tilts his head. "But I do have to apologise for inviting Rory and Laura to the pub?"

"I don't understand why you did that. Why did you want to humiliate me?"

"I didn't." He pushes his cup aside and pulls my hand closer, holding it tighter. "I never want to humiliate you, or hurt you. I'm just not very good at this."

"Neither am I. But what I don't understand is why you couldn't just talk to me. If you were worried about being alone with me, why couldn't you say? Not that we'd have been alone in a pub full of people, but if you needed Rory there for moral support or something, I wouldn't have minded... I'd just rather you'd been honest about it, instead of making me feel like you didn't want to see me."

"Is that how I made you feel?"

"Yes." I can't see the point in lying, or dressing it up.

He frowns, shaking his head. "I'm sorry, Nicki. That was the last thing I wanted." He takes a sip of coffee. "To be clear, though, I didn't need Rory there for moral support."

"Then why did you invite him?"

"Because I was scared."

"Scared of what? Me?" I shake my head. "I'm really not that scary, Ed."

"I know. And I'm not saying I was scared of you. I—I was scared of how I feel about you."

My heart skips a beat and I can't help the smile that twitches at the corners of my lips. "W—What does that mean?"

He gazes at me for a second. "I—It means I'd like to try again."

That might not be the answer I was hoping to hear, but it holds a promise of things to come.

"Try again at what?"

"At spending the evening together. I'll have to work, obviously, but if you want to come to the pub again tonight, I promise I won't invite anyone else this time."

"So it'll just be us?"

"Well... us and however many customers are brave enough to come out in this weather." I chuckle and he smiles. "Does that mean you'll come?"

I stare into his eyes for a moment, seeing something that looks like hope reflected back at me and I nod my head, unable to resist. "Yes... I'll come."

We both take a sip of coffee, still holding hands, and although I'm trying very hard not to read too much into his words, or his actions, it's hard not to wish, and to hope… even though I've had my wishes and hopes dashed before.

"So, apart from this place, what else has changed?" I ask him.

"Pretty much everything, I should think. It's been a long time."

"I know." I gaze into his eyes and for a moment, neither of us blinks, until someone out of sight drops something, which crashes to the floor and we both jump.

"Are you okay?" he asks.

"Yes, I'm fine." I sip my coffee again. "Did I notice the toy shop had gone?"

"It hasn't 'gone' as such, but Michael and Melissa took it over from their father and turned it into a gift shop."

"What happened to Mr Cole? I remember he was always so jolly."

He smiles. "He was. But that was part of the problem. He was so busy enjoying himself, he forgot about the fact that he was in business, and that he needed to make a profit. The business was failing, and then he was diagnosed with dementia."

"So Michael and Melissa took over?"

"Yes. They still sell toys, but they realised they needed to branch out if they were going to survive."

I nod my head. "I see the flower shop is still there."

"Yes, but it's changed hands. It's owned by Imelda Duffy now." He smiles. "She's a character."

"Really?"

"Yes… not one I can easily describe. Gemma works there as well."

"Rory's daughter?"

"Yes."

"It's funny, thinking about the two of you having grown-up children."

He leans a little closer. "Did you never want to have any yourself?"

It wasn't that I didn't want to have children, but I'm not sure I can explain the reality… not sitting in a café.

"I never had the opportunity."

That sounds reasonable, and he nods his head, glancing up at the clock on the wall. "I'm going to have to go," he says. "I need to get back to let Leanne in and open up."

I turn, looking at the clock myself, surprised to find it's already coming up for ten o'clock.

"I'm sorry. I shouldn't have kept you so long." We both get to our feet and he looks down at me as I fasten my coat before doing up his own.

"Don't apologise. It's been lovely, just sitting here talking." He's not wrong… it has. "I'll just go and pay."

"Let me…"

"I wouldn't dream of it." He smiles and wanders over to the counter, taking just a few moments to pay the bill before he returns to me. "Okay?" he asks and I nod my head, letting him lead me to the door, which he opens, allowing me to pass through ahead of him.

Outside, the wind is still blowing hard. "Gosh, it's not letting up, is it?" I look up as he raises his collar again.

"Shall I walk you back to the hotel?"

I shake my head. "No, I'll be fine. You've got work to do."

He hesitates for a moment or two. "Are you sure?"

"I'm positive. I'll see you tonight."

He smiles. "I'm looking forward to it."

"So am I."

We both stare at each other for a second or two, like neither of us can decide what to do next, and then he says, "Goodbye then," and I repeat his words back at him, wishing I'd had the courage to lean up and kiss him… and wondering how he'd have reacted if I had.

I've spent the afternoon watching a film and replaying my conversation with Ed over and over in my head. He said he was scared of how he feels about me, and while a part of me wants to take heart from that… and from the fact that he invited me to the pub again tonight, I'm not sure I should get my hopes up. After all, being scared of your own feelings isn't a great place to start, is it? Ed's desire to see me again might have felt promising, but he could have just been being polite… wanting to make amends for his earlier mistakes. It doesn't mean he wants the same things I do. It doesn't mean he wants anything at all. The reality is, it's just confusing. I don't know what to make of Ed, or his actions, or what he's said… but hopefully, things will become clearer tonight.

It's rained for most of the afternoon, although it's stopped now, and I turn off the television, the film having just finished, and check the time. It's six-thirty, and while Ed didn't give me a time to go to the pub, I don't want to waste my time here, when I could be there with him. Even so, just like the other night, I don't feel as though I want to go there for dinner. It feels too presumptuous… so I grab my bag and head downstairs to the dining room, taking a seat at my usual table.

I pick up the menu, noting that today's special is Coq au Vin, which sounds perfect, considering how cold it is, and I don't bother checking out anything else, but put down the menu again, just as Kieran approaches, a smile on his face.

"It's good to see you again," he says. "I missed you last night."

"Oh… sorry. I had a headache." I don't know why I'm apologising. That's not entirely dishonest. My head was splitting, although that wasn't the reason for my absence from the dining room.

He frowns. "Are you feeling better today?"

"Yes, thank you."

He nods at the menu. "Have you decided what you want already?"

"Yes… the Coq au Vin, please."

"Good choice. Can I recommend a glass of Pinot Noir?"

"You can… thank you."

He smiles, picking up my menu, before he departs.

It's busier in here tonight, and I glance around the room, observing the couples and families, all smiling and laughing, enjoying these last few days before Christmas. There are two women sitting on the far side of the room, clinking their wine glasses together before taking a sip, and smiling, their heads bent together as they resume their conversation. The younger woman laughs, throwing back her head, and the older one stares at her with such a loving expression on her face, it's impossible not to be touched by it. They look very similar, and are clearly mother and daughter, and I'm suddenly overwhelmed with regret… and with tears welling in my eyes.

"There you—" Kieran puts down my wine, his words cut short as I look up at him and his face falls. "Are you okay?"

"I'm fine. Sorry."

"You're not fine. And why are you apologising?"

"Because… well, I don't know, really. It's just…" I glance over at the two women again. "I was thinking about my mum."

"Your mum?"

"Yes. She… she died a few weeks ago."

"Oh… I'm so sorry."

"It's the main reason I came here… to avoid spending Christmas on my own."

Why did I tell him that? He's a stranger.

"What was the other reason?" he asks, presumably because he feels awkward, although he doesn't look it, and I wonder if he said that so I wouldn't have to dwell on my mum.

"I grew up here."

"Really?"

"Yes. I moved away over twenty years ago."

"Not by yourself, surely?"

"Why not?"

"You can't have been old enough."

I giggle, unable to help myself. "I'm older than you think."

He pauses for a second, studying me, although his scrutiny doesn't make me feel uncomfortable. Then he shrugs his shoulders. "Age is relative, though, isn't it?"

"Relative to what?"

"How old you feel." I'm not sure how to answer that, but right at that moment, someone attracts his attention. "Excuse me for a moment, will you?" he says and, with a smile, he walks away.

A few minutes later, a young woman, dressed in a black skirt and white blouse, brings out my dinner, placing it before me with a smile.

"Can I get you anything else?" she asks.

"No, thank you."

She turns away, and I notice her glance over at Kieran, who's just moving back to the centre of the room. She catches his eye and smiles, her eyes sparkling, and although he smiles back, there's no emotion to his expression. He darts towards the back of the room, clearly having seen someone else requiring his attention, and I notice her shoulders drop. She's obviously interested in him, but it doesn't look as though he returns her affections. I know how that feels... poor girl.

The Coq au Vin is delicious, the chicken so tender I barely need a knife to cut it. The wine compliments it perfectly, too, and I make short work of finishing my meal.

"Can I get you anything else?" Kieran's beside me in an instant.

"No, thank you."

"You're not a dessert person?"

"Oh, I am... but I'm going out tonight."

"Meeting up with old friends?"

"Something like that."

He stands behind me, holding my chair, while I get up. "Enjoy your evening," he says, and I look up into his handsome face, his eyes sparkling down into mine.

"Thank you. And thank you for recommending the wine. It went very well."

"It's a pleasure."

We stand for a moment, but I can't think of anything else to say, so I simply smile and pick up my bag, heading for the door.

The wind has dropped considerably, and I'm glad it's not raining anymore, as I walk along the harbour, making for the pub. I haven't bothered to change tonight, not because I don't care, but because I'll run out of clothes if I'm not careful. And besides, Ed said he wanted to see me again, in which case he won't care what I'm wearing, will he? I know that sounds like I'm letting myself hope again, and maybe I am... but I can't help it. I can't help smiling either.

I'm going to see Ed... so smiling comes naturally.

Inside, the pub is just as busy as it was the other night, and I catch Ed's eye almost as soon as I walk through the door. He smiles, his eyes twinkling in the fairy lights, and I smile back, making my way to the bar.

"Hello," he says as I undo my coat and perch up on a stool. I've chosen one at the end of the bar, where it's quieter, in the hope we'll be able to talk here.

"Hi."

"What can I get you to drink?"

"A red wine, please."

He tilts his head to one side. "Will you let me buy it for you?"

"Okay."

He smiles and moves away, pouring me a glass of red wine, which he brings back, pushing it across the bar.

"Are you not having one?" I ask.

"I won't, if that's okay. I'm practically on my own tonight, so…"

"Practically on your own? What does that mean?"

"It means Leanne had to go home early, because she wasn't feeling well, and…" He leans closer, lowering his voice. "And while Reece means well, he's not fully trained yet. So, I might as well be on my own back here."

"I see. Would it be better if I wasn't here?"

"Why?"

I want to suggest I might be a distraction, but I realise how big-headed that sounds. "I don't know. If you're busy…" I can't think what else to say.

"I might be busy, but I still want you here." He ends his sentence abruptly, and I wonder if he meant to say that. It was lovely to hear, but I don't think it was intentional.

"I'll stay then," I murmur and he smiles, before he turns his head, and then looks back at me.

"Sorry… I'll be back in a second."

There's a man at the end of the bar, holding up a pint glass and Ed heads straight for him, chatting while he pours him a refill. He's just taken the man's money when a young lad comes out from the corridor at the back of the bar and goes to Ed, whispering something to him. Ed rolls his eyes and shakes his head, and then follows the young lad back down the corridor, leaving the bar unattended. He's only gone for a minute or two, but during that time, three more people appear at the bar, wanting drinks. They wait patiently, but when Ed reappears, without the young man, he's kept busy, sorting out their orders.

'A second' becomes an hour, which soon becomes two, during which we've barely snatched more than half a dozen words together. It's clear Ed is rushed off his feet, and I'm not sure whether this is better or worse than the other evening. I don't feel so humiliated as I did then, but I don't particularly like sitting here by myself, either, just watching him. At least the other night I had Rory and Laura for company. Now, I feel even more lonely than I did sitting in the hotel restaurant, watching that mother and daughter, and remembering better times.

Ed might have invited me. He might have hinted at having feelings for me and said he wanted me here, but watching him work isn't getting us anywhere, is it? All it's doing is reminding me that I don't matter… not enough, anyway.

I glance at the clock behind the bar. It's nearly ten to ten, and I've had enough.

I jump down from my stool, fastening my coat, and Ed clearly notices the movement, and even though he's in the middle of serving someone, about to pour white wine into a glass, he puts down the bottle and comes straight over.

"Are you leaving?"

"Yes."

"But it's not long until closing time."

"I know. But then you'll have clearing up to do."

He frowns. "Nicki… I'm sorry I haven't had more time. Please…"

I hold up my hand, and he stops talking. "It's okay. I've had a nice evening, anyway."

He narrows his eyes. "Why don't I believe you?" I can't think how to answer him, so I don't say a word. "It wasn't meant to be like this. I didn't realise Leanne would have to go."

"It doesn't matter… really." It does, but what can I say? I can't say anything. My voice won't work, so I just smile as best as I can, and turn away, getting to the door before he tries to stop me. Not that I think he will, but it seems best to get out of here before I actually cry in front of him.

Outside, the wind has dropped completely, although it's still chilly… not that I care anymore. My tears freeze as they hit my cheeks and I reach into my handbag for a tissue, wiping them away.

I knew it was a mistake to get my hopes up, to let myself dream…

He might not have invited anyone else to share our evening, and it might not have been his fault that we had so little time together, but that doesn't make this feel any better.

I hurry back to the hotel. Ed can't leave the pub, so I know he won't follow me tonight, but that doesn't mean I want to be out here, facing the reality of another wasted evening.

Once inside the hotel, I make my way straight over to the stairs, without looking up, undoing my coat as I go. It's warm in here compared to outside, and I'm already feeling it.

"Miss Woodward?" I turn at the sound of my name, to see Kieran come out from behind the reception desk, his head tilted slightly, and a frown etched on his face, as he walks towards me. "Are you all right?"

"Yes, thanks."

He narrows his eyes just fractionally, and I can tell he doesn't believe me. "Did you have a nice evening?"

"It was okay."

He tips his head the other way, like he's thinking about something, and I take another step towards the stairs. "Nicole?" he says, using my first name.

"Yes?"

"I—I'm about to finish work for the evening. I know it's late, but would you like to have a drink with me? The bar here is open until eleven-thirty. We... We could just talk... if you like."

I shake my head. "Sorry, Kieran. I really can't."

He takes a deep breath, and it's impossible not to see the disappointment in his eyes. "Whoever he is, I hope he appreciates you."

"How do you know there's a he?" I'm intrigued. I haven't said anything about Ed, or anyone else for that matter, and I'm not sure how I've given myself away to someone who barely knows me.

"I'm not so arrogant as to think you should fall at my feet just because I've asked you to have a drink with me... and that because you've said 'no', there must be another man involved."

"I'm pleased to hear it. But what gave me away?"

He smiles. "Nothing... until you said that. Before that, it was just a hunch... and a bit of guesswork."

"Guesswork?"

"Yes. You had a phone call yesterday, from a man."

"I did?"

"Yes. He wanted to know if you were still staying here."

"He didn't leave a name, or ask to speak to me?"

"No. He said he'd only called to make sure you were still here."

"That's odd."

"Is it? He seemed relieved that you hadn't left. I—I got the feeling it mattered... that you mattered. And that being the case, it doesn't seem odd at all... not to me." He gazes into my eyes for a moment, and then lets out a long sigh before he turns away, going back to the reception desk.

I stare after him, hoping I haven't embarrassed him, although I'm not sure what I can do about it if I have. I don't think I led him on, and if I did, I didn't mean to... and in any case, my head is too full of that phone call, and what it might mean. It can only have come from Ed, but what I don't understand is, why he didn't just talk to me... and why he hasn't mentioned calling. We might not have spoken much this evening, but we talked for ages this morning... so why didn't he say something?

Chapter Twelve

Ed

I watch Nicki leave, my heart sinking. This feels like a repeat performance of the other night, except I don't have Rory and Laura here to talk things over with. If I did, at least they might be able to stop me feeling like a complete idiot… although I doubt it.

I'm sure Nicki can't think very highly of me for inviting her to join me again, making such a big deal of it, and then ignoring her for most of the time she's been here. It might not have been my fault, but I can't imagine it made her feel very good. And I wanted to make her feel good… to make amends for the other night, and to try and work things out between us.

Except I failed, dismally… again.

Meeting Nicki on the harbour today felt like fate… like it was meant to be. I won't deny that she looked a little wary, but I can't blame her for that. I'd let her down, and we both knew it. Still, she agreed to have coffee with me, and although I appreciate she might have only done so to be polite and get out of the cold, I'd like to think there was more to it than that. The reason for my optimism? I got tongue-tied and nervous, sitting opposite her in the café. I couldn't think of a single thing to say to her. Even though I'd planned on telling her everything, there was a disconnection between my brain and my mouth. Nicki filled that, talking about the café and how much it had changed since she left. She didn't have to do that. She could have left me hanging. I deserved it, after all. But she made conversation until I finally found my courage and made my apology. I might have fallen over my words a bit, in my desperation to get them out, but she understood. I know she did… because she held out her hand to me… in the most perfect gesture of acceptance. Maybe there was something else behind that offer, too. Friendship? Pity? I don't know. I just know it felt good to hold her hand.

It felt good enough that I admitted to her that I hadn't invited Rory to the pub for moral support, but because I was scared of my feelings for her.

I couldn't explain exactly what I meant, but that was mainly because I wasn't scared anymore. Looking into her eyes, which was something I did a lot while we were sitting together, I couldn't feel anything but love. There was no fear, no doubt… not even any guilt. Just love. I know I should have told her that, but I couldn't. It didn't feel right to open up like that in the café. I thought, maybe here, on familiar ground, I might find it easier to explain, which is why I wanted her to come back here tonight. The mixed messages I've been sending out have got to be confusing her. They're confusing me, so heaven knows how she feels. But I know I want us to be together, more than anything, and it seems only fair to tell her that, so she's not in any doubt.

The thing is, it's complicated. I might love her, and want her, but I'm not sure I'm ready to do anything about it yet. This all feels like it's happening really quickly, and I guess I might need to ask her to wait… to give me some time to work things out in my head. I want to do that, though, because I don't want her to think I'm not serious about this.

The problem is… how am I supposed to go about doing any of that when we're never alone? None of this is going to be easy for me to say, but if we're always going to be surrounded by other people, I can't see how it's ever going to happen.

"Boss?"

"Yes, Reece?" I try to keep the impatience out of my voice. It's not his fault my evening has been ruined, any more than it's his fault Leanne had to go home early. He was just as disappointed when she left as I was… although not for the same reasons.

"Should I re-stock the tonic water?"

I glance down at the shelf. "No. We've got enough for tonight. I'll do it in the morning."

He nods his head. I know he was looking for a reason to look busy, to avoid having to serve any customers, but he's got to learn sometime, otherwise there's not much point in him being here.

Ben Atkins catches my eye and I give him a nod to let him know I'll be with him in a minute.

"Come on, Reece. This is an easy one for you." He looks at me, frowning. "This is Ben Atkins," I murmur, keeping my voice low. "He always orders a vodka and tonic, ice, no lemon." Reece nods his head.

"So, I put a measure of vodka into the glass and give him the opened bottle of tonic?"

"Yes. But don't forget to put the ice into the glass first."

"Oh… yes… right."

I accompany him to the end of the bar, where Ben smiles at us both. He's a little taller than me, but not by much, and his hair is greying at the temples, which it probably should be, considering he's a lot nearer to fifty than I am.

"I'm just training Reece," I explain, and Ben nods his head.

"We've all got to learn our trade somehow," he says and then turns to Reece. "I'll have a vodka and tonic, please. Ice, but no lemon."

Reece nods and turns away, reaching for completely the wrong glass. I don't make a big deal out of it, but just hand him a hi-ball, and tilt my head towards the ice, so he doesn't forget.

"Was that Nicole Woodward I saw earlier?" Ben says, getting his wallet out ready to pay.

"Yes, it was."

"I thought so. I haven't seen her for years."

I can't help but notice the sparkle in his eyes. It doesn't surprise me. Nicki's a very beautiful woman.

"She's come back for a visit," I say, feeling slightly alarmed by how possessive I feel of her… by the fact that I want to tell him to back off and leave her alone, even though he hasn't done anything. "Her mum's just died, and she felt like getting away."

"Oh, that's sad… about her mum, I mean. They used to live in Garden Close, didn't they?"

"Yes."

He nods his head. "I thought so. I did the conveyancing when Mr and Mrs Woodward moved out." He looks up, like he's trying to work something out. "That must be over twenty years ago now."

"Something like that."

Reece returns with Ben's glass and the opened bottle of tonic water, and even quotes him the correct price, handing him the chip and pin machine, when Ben makes it clear he wants to pay by card.

"Well, say 'hello' to Nicole for me, won't you?" he says, putting his debit card away, although I'm surprised he's not suggesting that he'll say 'hello' to her himself. He picks up his drink, and gives me a smile, and just a very slight nod of his head, before turning away.

"Did I do okay?" Reece says.

"You did very well." I don't mention his mistake with the glass. He'll probably get it right next time.

"So, who's Nicole?" he asks, having clearly picked up on the end of my conversation with Ben.

"She's someone who used to live here."

He gives me an odd look, like he expects me to elaborate, but I'm not going to, and after a second or two, he turns, glancing around the pub. "Shall I collect some of the empties?"

"Yes, please." It'll be one less job for me later on.

He smiles and heads off to make himself useful, while I wipe down the bar and contemplate that momentary surge of jealousy. I haven't felt like that for years... not since before I got together with Suzannah, when the thought of Nicki liking Rory used to drive me insane. Knowing it was me she liked all along makes all those adolescent resentments seem like such a waste of time and energy now. Still, it's easy to be wise after the event...

I jump, startling from my thoughts, as Adrian Roskelly puts his glass down on the bar in front of me. He's six or seven years younger than me, a little taller, with dark hair and broad shoulders, born of labouring on the farm he owns, which is two or three miles outside of the village.

"You off for the night?" I pick up his glass.

"I should have gone about an hour ago," he says, glancing at the clock behind me and shaking his head. "The cows will still want milking in the morning, even if I don't feel like getting up."

"I don't envy you those early starts... especially at this time of year."

He rolls his eyes. "It was murder this morning. I could hear the wind and rain pelting against my bedroom window, and I'd have given fairly important parts of my anatomy to pull the duvet over my head and stay in bed for another hour or two."

I smile at him. "Did you have something – or someone – worth staying in bed for then?"

"I should be so lucky. It's been years since I've had someone worth staying in bed for."

"It can't have been that long."

He looks up, like he's thinking it through. "Three years… no, three and a half."

"Oh… since Teagan Penrose left for university, I suppose."

"Teagan?" He raises his voice, just slightly. "What on earth made you say her name? She and I were never together."

"Really? Everyone thought you were."

He shakes his head, letting out a sigh. "Well, we weren't. Aside from the fact that she was far too young for me, and that she was trouble with a capital 'T', the only interest I ever had in Teagan was that she's Ember's sister."

"Ember? Were the two of you…?" He shakes his head, but I sense he regrets that, which means I'm not about to question him. I know how painful regrets can be. "And there's been no-one special in all these years?"

He smiles. "There's been no-one at all… special or otherwise." He leans a little closer, his elbows on the bar. "Although unless I'm much mistaken, you don't have any such problems yourself."

"Sorry?" I feel my brow furrow.

"The lady who was sitting at the end of the bar for most of the evening," he says, nodding over my shoulder, to the space Nicki vacated not so long ago. "She couldn't take her eyes off of you."

"Oh… you mean Nicki Woodward."

He frowns now. "Nicki Woodward? That's a familiar name."

"It probably is. She used to live here. Her parents had a house in Garden Close." His frown clears and he nods his head.

"I remember. She left, didn't she… quite suddenly?"

"Yes." *Because of me.*

"And she's come back to see you?"

"No… she's come back because her mum's just died."

"But her mum didn't live here anymore. Her parents moved away, didn't they?"

"Yes. Not long after Nicki left."

He tilts his head to one side. "Well, you can keep telling yourself she didn't come back here to see you, but any fool can see she did. Hell... I've had nothing but cows for company for the last three and half years, and even I could see she's in love with you."

"I—In love...?" He can't mean that... can he?

He smiles, with a pitying look on his face. "The whole time she was here, all she did was gaze at you, like nothing else existed... like she'd have sold her soul for a crumb of attention."

"I was busy."

He shakes his head. "If I were you, I'd make myself a lot less busy... before she gets tired of waiting and finds someone who's willing to give her the time of day." He stands up straight, tapping his hand on the top of the bar. "Goodnight, Ed."

"'Night, Adrian."

I feel like I'm in a daze. Can Nicki really be in love with me? She's never said so in as many words, and she made a point of telling me her feelings for me were in the past, but thinking about this logically, if that's the case, why is she still spending time with me... especially given the way I've treated her? Why did she tell me she ended her marriage because of me? It has to mean something, doesn't it? And even if it's not love... there's the chance it could be. Unless she gets tired of waiting... or of being ignored.

I check the clock. It's ten-twenty-five, which is close enough for me and I ring the bell behind the bar, calling 'time', and waiting impatiently for the customers to finish their drinks and leave. I can't throw them out, but I wish I could, and I can feel myself becoming more and more restless as their numbers dwindle.

Eventually, the last of them leaves and I turn to find Reece standing behind me.

"You can go," I say to him, walking down the corridor behind the bar to pick up my coat, shrugging it on as I come back towards him.

"Don't you want me to help clear up?"

"No... it's fine. I'll do it in the morning." This is becoming a bad habit with me, but tonight it's also a necessary one.

I grab my keys and usher him through the front door, locking it behind us. His car is one of only three in the car park, and he wanders towards it with a wave of his hand. I'm already starting along the harbour, pulling up the collar of my coat against the cold. It might not be as windy as it was earlier, but there's a definite chill in the air.

It only takes a few minutes to get to the hotel and I step back as a man comes out of the door. He looks up, acknowledging me with a slight nod and a smile, although I can't help noticing the sadness in his eyes. He's young and very handsome and I wonder for a moment what can have caused so much unhappiness. Still... I don't have time to dwell, and I enter the foyer, going over to the reception desk. Anthony Harvey is sitting there, staring at a computer screen. He's maybe fifteen years older than me, and lives with his wife Brenda in a house in Chapel Mews, off of Church Lane. They can't see much of each other, considering he's on duty here all night, and she has a job at the out-of-town supermarket during the day, but they've been married for as long as I can remember, and have two grown-up children, so I guess the arrangement works for them. He looks up as I approach, a smile forming on his lips.

"Hello, Ed. We don't usually see you in here."

"No. I've come to visit Nicole Woodward. She's staying here... although I don't know her room number."

He glances at his watch. "Is she expecting you?"

"No."

He nods his head, uncertainty crossing his eyes. "I can call up to her room…"

I lean over the reception desk and lower my voice. "If you do that, there's every chance she'll refuse to speak to me."

"In which case…" He looks even more doubtful than he did before.

"Anthony… I've screwed up in so many ways with Nicki, I—"

"You mean, you and she are…?"

"I don't know yet, but if you don't give me her room number so I can go and apologise to her, I might never find out."

He bites his lip, looking a little pained, and then suddenly taps on the keyboard in front of him, before he looks up at me again. "She's in the Harbour View Suite," he says. "Go up the stairs, through the door on the left, and along the corridor. It's at the end, on the right."

"Thanks, Anthony. I owe you."

"I'll let you buy me a pint," he says and I smile, nodding my head, as I turn away and head for the stairs, taking them two at a time. Now I'm here, I don't want to waste another moment, and once I reach the top, I pull open the door on the left, entering a long corridor. Making my way down it, I ignore every other door, until I reach the last one on the right, which has a wooden plaque on it, engraved with the words 'Harbour View Suite'.

I'm suddenly nervous, my heart beating loud in my chest, but I raise my right hand and knock on the door, taking a breath as I stand back slightly and wait.

After just a few moments, the door cracks open, and Nicki's face appears. Her eyes widen and she opens the door a little further, revealing that she hasn't changed out of her sexy, tight jeans and sweater, although she has taken off her black boots, making her even shorter than usual, and I have to look down into her upturned face.

"Ed?"

"I'm sorry." It's the best place to start. It needs to be said before anything else.

She frowns. "You're sorry? What for?"

"Everything. Anything. Whatever you need me to be sorry for." I step a little closer. "I wasn't ignoring you on purpose tonight, you know that, don't you?"

"Is that supposed to make it any easier?"

"No. But this isn't easy for me either."

"Because of Suzannah?"

"Yes."

She nods her head. "If you still have feelings for her..."

"I'll always have feelings for her, Nicki. There's nothing I can do about that. But I meant it when I said I wanted to try again with you. I know I keep screwing up, but if my feelings for Suzannah are something you can live with, do you think we could spend some more time together to see if I could stop getting it wrong all the time?"

"You're not getting it wrong all the time."

"Okay... just most of the time, then."

"You're not even getting it wrong most of the time... but you didn't let me finish."

"Finish what?"

"I was going to say, if you still have feelings for Suzannah, I'm okay with that. I understand, Ed. You loved her... you still do."

"Yes, I do."

She looks up into my eyes and hesitates for a moment before she says, "Do you want to come in?"

If that isn't acceptance of the situation, I don't know what is... and I won't say I'm not tempted, because I am. Very.

"I think it's best if I don't." She takes a half step back, the hurt in her eyes cutting through me like a knife, and I know I have to tell her the truth. "It's not that I don't want to."

"Then why don't you?"

"Because we need to talk… and if I come in there, I don't think that's what we'll be doing."

She understands what I'm saying. I know she does. Her eyes widen, she swallows hard, and she whispers, "Oh," a flush creeping up her cheeks.

"Besides, it's late, and I've got an early start."

"You have?"

"Yes. It's Christmas Eve tomorrow. The pub is always busy, and I haven't cleared up from tonight yet."

"So, when are we going to see each other?"

"You could come to the pub again, if you like?"

"So you can ignore me?"

"I won't. I promise. If you come down around nine-thirty tomorrow night, you'll only have to put up with me being busy for an hour before closing time, and then we can be alone for once. We can go upstairs…"

"And talk?" she says, blinking and licking her bottom lip.

"Yes. There are things that need saying." We may have cleared the air a little, but there's still a lot more to be talked through. Hopefully, given some time and the privacy of my flat, I might be able to rectify that.

"Okay. I'll come down at half-past nine."

"And you'll stay afterwards?"

"Yes." She nods her head and then tilts it slightly. "Can I ask you a question?"

"Of course."

"Did you call here yesterday afternoon? Not in person, but on the phone?"

I can feel myself blush, but I know I have to be honest. "Yes, I did."

"Why?"

"Because I was worried I might have hurt you by inviting Rory and Laura to the pub. I was scared you might have gone home, and I wanted to make sure you hadn't."

"Why didn't you talk to me? They'd have put the call through to my room."

"I know. The man I spoke to offered. But I didn't want to talk to you over the phone. I wanted to see you face-to-face. That's why I came to see you this morning… or tried to."

"I see."

She tilts her head the other way, studying me, and I do the same… just staring at her beautiful face. I want to kiss her so much, but she's inside the room and I'm in the hall. She feels too far away. I'd have to step in there and risk the consequences. And I think there would be consequences… ones I'm not sure I'm ready for yet.

Chapter Thirteen

Nicki

He said he wanted to see me face-to-face.

He said he wanted to talk to me... upstairs in his flat.

I can't have misunderstood the meaning behind any of those words.... any more than I can have misunderstood what he meant when he said that if he came into my room, we wouldn't be doing much talking. That had to mean we'd be doing something else. A tingle spreads through my body at the thought of 'something else'.

Even now, as dusk gathers on a chilly Christmas Eve, with yet more festive films on the television, I can't stop thinking about it.

I can't wait to see him again, either, knowing we'll be spending the whole evening together, and that once we've said the things that he thinks need saying, we might be able to move onto 'something else'... after all this time.

I decide to eat early in the hope the restaurant will be quieter, and then I can take my time getting ready, and because it's Christmas Eve and I feel I should make the effort, I change out of my jeans and top, putting on a skirt and blouse. I've already laid out the trousers and sweater I'm planning on wearing to the pub, but the skirt and blouse are more than smart enough for the hotel restaurant.

Downstairs, the dining room is a little busier than usual at this time, but it's not too bad, and I take my seat, picking up the menu to see there's a more festive offering available tonight. There's no roast turkey, because I presume they're saving that for tomorrow, but they are offering roast beef with all the trimmings. I'm not in the mood for something that heavy, though, and instead I opt for the salmon fillet with a dill crust.

"Hello." I startle at the sound of Kieran's voice and look up to see him smiling down at me. "How are you?"

"I—I'm fine thanks."

He nods towards the menu. "Have you decided what to have?"

"Yes. The salmon, please."

He smiles. "Good choice. A glass of Chablis to go with it?"

"That would be lovely."

There isn't even a trace of awkwardness as he reaches for the menu. "I'll be back in a minute," he says and leaves. You'd never know he asked me out last night... or that I turned him down.

I glance around the room at some of the other guests who've chosen to eat early. They consist mainly of families with young children, eager-eyed and desperate for tomorrow, and I can't help smiling. I'm past feeling sorry for myself over the fact that I'll never get to experience any of that first-hand. It's not something I even think about anymore.

"Your wine..." Kieran puts the glass down in front of me and I turn to face him.

"Thank you."

"So, have you got any plans for tonight?"

I wonder if this is his way of asking me out again, or whether he's just making conversation, and decide it's best to be honest. "Yes. I'm meeting the man who called for me the other day."

146

He nods his head. "So, I was right… you do matter to him."

"I hope so."

"Is it serious then?"

"I'd like it to be… very serious."

He sighs and leans down a little. "I hope he knows how lucky he is," he whispers and then stands up straight again, smiling down at me before he moves away. I can't help feeling a little sorry for him, and in other circumstances, I wonder if things might have been very different…

The noise in the pub is deafening. I honestly would have thought people would have had better things to do with their Christmas Eve than drinking it away in the pub… but what do I know?

I've been here for nearly an hour already, and I'm relieved I didn't come earlier. Ed might have greeted me warmly and told me how beautiful I look tonight, but he's barely had five minutes to spare, and I've been watching the clock ever since. It slowly creeps around to ten-thirty, and Ed rings the bell behind the bar, calling 'time' in a voice loud enough to be heard.

Slowly but surely, people wend their way home, some in a better state of sobriety than others. Ed lets his staff go, too, wishing them a Happy Christmas, and as he ushers the final customers out of the door, he locks it behind them, leaving the keys in the door and turning back to face me.

Our eyes meet and he walks over, holding out his hand, which I take in mine, jumping down from the stool I've been sitting on for the last hour, putting my bag over my shoulder and folding my jacket over my arm.

"I'll tidy up later," he says, gazing down at me, and pulls me towards the back of the pub, down the corridor and up the stairs.

At the top, he hesitates for a moment.

"Would you like a coffee?"

"Not particularly."

He nods his head and leads the way into his living room, flicking on the lights to reveal a large, cream-coloured corner sofa with a blue and cream striped rug set in front of it, two low tables at either end, and a couple of bookcases against the far wall.

"This is nice," I whisper, as we walk further into the room, coming to a stop in front of the sofa. He looks down at me, and for a second or two, the air around us stills and crackles. I put my jacket and bag down on the end of the sofa and lean up on my tiptoes at the same time as he bends his head and our lips meet in a hesitant kiss. I've both longed for and dreaded this moment… fearing it might be disappointing and shatter all of my dreams, but my fears are proved unfounded as Ed steps closer, letting go of my hand and pulling me into his arms, tilting his head and deepening the kiss. His tongue clashes with mine and a low groan from deep in his throat echoes through my body. I moan my reply, my hands wandering up and down his muscular back.

Eventually he breaks the kiss and leans back, staring down at me, and I feel as though the time for talking has passed… or it hasn't arrived yet. Either way, it isn't now.

Now is the time for actions, not words, and without taking my eyes from his, I slowly drop to my knees before him. I've never been so bold before, but his eyes widen, and he sucks in a stuttered breath as I reach up and unfasten his belt, undoing the button and zip of his jeans and lowering them slightly. He's wearing trunks and I pull them down, his erection popping up and into my waiting hand.

"Oh, God…" I whisper, my fingers barely fitting around him, and he groans, gazing at me as I stroke him, and then lick the tip of his arousal, before taking him in my mouth.

"Oh, Nicki… yes. Please, yes." His words come out on a whispered breath, and he reaches down, gathering my hair and holding it behind my head as he flexes his hips. That feels so good and, my body on fire, desperate for more, I keep still, letting him dictate the pace, until his breathing changes, becoming more ragged, and he pulls out of my mouth, dragging air into his lungs.

I'm not ready to stop, and I get to my feet, leaning up and claiming another kiss as I unbutton his shirt, pulling it from his shoulders. He fumbles between us, finding the fastening of my trousers and undoing it. They fall, pooling at my ankles, and his hands come around behind me, feeling me through the thin silken material of my underwear. His breathing alters again, and I push down his jeans and trunks, and we both move back for a second, stepping out of our clothes, before I yank my sweater over my head. He stops, staring down at me, and then reaches behind me, unfastening my bra, which joins the rest of my clothes in a pile on the floor.

He's breathing hard, but so am I and I take a moment to calm myself, to take in his hard, toned chest and muscular arms, before I push him back onto the sofa. He rights himself, sitting up slightly, and I lower my knickers, trying to kick them off. I'm still wearing my black boots, and my knickers get caught on the heel, so I stand on one leg, yanking them off. I wonder if I should take off my boots too, but I can't be bothered, and I kneel up, straddling him. He puts his hands on my backside, raising me up over his erection, and then lowers me. He keeps still, letting me decide how much of him I can take, which is just as well, because the stretch is almost too much for me. I manage it though, inch by perfect inch, until I'm settled on him. I clench my internal muscles and he sucks in a breath, sitting us both up slightly as I start to move. Clamping my hands on his shoulders, I rise and fall, over and over, harder and harder. He keeps one hand on my behind, while the other grips the back of my neck, our eyes locked, our lips barely an inch apart, my breasts grazing against his chest.

I don't know whether it's because this is Ed, and I've dreamt of this moment for so long, or whether he's just exceptionally good at this, but it doesn't take long before I feel a long-forgotten quivering deep in my core. I wonder if Ed can feel it too, because he raises his hips, higher and higher, matching my rhythm.

"Please…" I whisper, grinding out the word, and he moves his hand from behind me, bringing it between us, his thumb finding that perfect sweet spot and rubbing against it. That's all it takes… and I throw my head back, screaming his name, as my body succumbs to wave upon wave of pleasure. Spasms rock through me and I struggle for control, even as he closes his eyes, his grip tightening on the back of my neck, and I feel him swell deep inside me.

"Nic… Nic…" He can't seem to speak, but then he roars, the sound coming from deep inside him, filling the room, as he fills me.

I flop forward onto his chest, breathing hard, listening to the sound of his heartbeat as it slowly returns to normal… not that anything will ever be 'normal' again. Not after that.

The hand that was behind my neck flops to the sofa, and he moves his other hand from between us. But otherwise, he remains completely still. He doesn't put his arms around me, or utter a sound, and I'm scared… scared he'll regret what we've just done… what I've just done.

I don't want him to have any regrets. I don't want him to think about Suzannah, either. Not now, and I lean back, raising my hand, and brushing my fingers down his cheek. He seems to startle to life, focusing on me, like he's suddenly remembered I'm right here with him… joined to him, although the pain in his eyes cuts right through me.

"I—I need the bathroom," I murmur, kneeling right up and disconnecting us in the most awkward of moves as I stumble to my feet. He's still aroused, and although I'm not sure that's normal either, I focus on finding my knickers, feeling the need to cover myself. I pull them on, wishing now that I'd taken off my boots, as the heels catch yet again. Ed sits forward, reaching out to steady me, but I ignore him, and grab my sweater, pulling it over my head, before I rush to the door, yanking it open. I stop on the threshold. "Which way?" I say, not daring to look back at him.

"To your right, last door on the left."

I dart out into the hall, taking two steps before I stop and cover my face with my hands. Could that have been any more humiliating? Well… I suppose he could have said out loud that he wished we hadn't done that… but he didn't need to. His eyes did the talking for him.

"Hello?"

I let my hands drop, spinning around at the sound of an unfamiliar voice coming from the top of the stairs. Facing me is a young man, probably only twenty years old, with shoulder-length blond hair and a deep tan. He's very good looking, but I've got no idea what he's doing here. I open my mouth to ask, just as his eyes rake up and down my body, and I remember I'm standing here in just a sweater, my knickers and my knee-length boots.

"Oh, God…" I grab the hem of my sweater, pulling it down and run along the hall to the bathroom, slamming the door behind me, locking it, and leaning back against it.

"What on earth are you doing here?" I can hear Ed's voice and I stand away from the door again, holding my breath.

"I thought I'd come home and spend Christmas with my dad." Oh… this must be Dan. I suppose, now I think about it, there was a resemblance between him and Ed.

"Some warning might have been nice." Ed sounds disgruntled.

"Clearly." Dan sounds like he's smiling. "Sorry to interrupt. I didn't realise you had a girlfriend."

"I—I haven't. It's not like that."

There's a kind of ringing in my ears, and their voices become muffled as I struggle between anger and tears. How could he say that, after what we've just done? Because it meant nothing to him, I suppose… because he wishes we'd never done it in the first place.

I unlock the door again, pulling it open, and step out into the hall. Dan is still at the top of the stairs and his father is facing him. He's wearing his jeans, which are now refastened, and has pulled his shirt back on, although he hasn't done it up, and they both turn to face me. I can feel myself blush, so I focus on the carpet and dash along the hall, ducking between them and back into the living room, closing the door behind me. My trousers are still on the floor, so I sit, pulling them on, even though they snag on my heels. "Come on…" I whisper, tugging them harder, and then I stand to do them up. My bra is lying at my feet, but I just shove it into my bag, shrugging my jacket on before I go back to the door. Father and son are in exactly the same places as when I last saw them, and when I step out into the hall, Dan looks away, but Ed turns, staring right at me.

"Nicki? Where are you going?"

I don't answer him. Instead, I move to the top of the stairs and tilt my head at Dan, who's still standing on the second step down. He hesitates but then moves aside, making space for me to pass.

"Thank you," I mutter.

"Nicki?" Ed's voice rings out as I run down the stairs, but I ignore him, turning at the bottom and going down the corridor, into the deserted pub. I move around to the other side of the bar, making for the door, grateful that Ed left the keys in the lock and as I turn them, I hear him shout, "Nicki, come back!"

There's no chance of that. Not this time.

This time, I've had enough.

It's drizzling, but that's not the reason I'm running. Ed might follow me. I'm not sure he will… but he might, although he'll need to finish getting dressed first, which gives me a slight head start, and that's a good thing, because I've got no intention of being at the hotel when he gets there.

I'm out of breath and a little bedraggled by the time I fall through the door, but I rush over to the reception desk, relieved that Kieran is off duty now. At least I don't have to face him, and admit I don't matter to Ed at all… that I got it all wrong. The man who is on duty – the night porter – looks up, a startled expression on his face.

"Is everything all right, Miss?" he asks.

"Yes. Everything's fine." That's a lie, but I'm beyond caring. "Do you think you could prepare my bill for me?"

"You mean, you're leaving? Now?"

"Yes. I'll be back down in five minutes."

He looks a little flustered but nods his head and I dart to the stairs, running up them and straight to my room. I let myself in, and go to the wardrobe, grabbing my suitcase and throwing my clothes into it, along with my toiletries, my Kindle, and everything else I can find that I brought with me. To be honest, I don't really care if I leave anything behind… as long as I've got the essentials, and once I'm sure I have, I close my case and lug it off of the bed, carrying it back downstairs again.

The man at the reception looks up as I approach, reaching into my handbag for my purse.

"You're booked to stay until New Year's Day," he says, biting his bottom lip.

"I know. I understand I'll have to pay until then."

He nods, looking relieved, as though he was expecting me to argue, and he pushes a piece of paper across the desk at me. I don't even bother to check the figures, I just pass over my credit card and he puts it into the machine for me, my hand shaking as I tap in my pin number. We wait for what feels like forever, and eventually, the machine spews forth a slip of paper, which the man tears off, handing it to me, together with my credit card.

"Please come and stay again," he says and I nod my head, even though I know I'll never set foot in Porthgarrion for as long as I live.

"Thank you."

I turn, rushing from the building, replacing my purse in my bag as I retrieve my car keys. Out in the car park, my Mini is where I left it on the day of my arrival, and I dash over, putting my case in the boot before climbing in the front and slinging my handbag into the passenger footwell. I take a moment, just to catch my breath, and then I start the engine, turning on the windscreen wipers and reversing out of the space. I struggle to engage first gear and feel a lump rising in my throat.

"Stop it… stop being pathetic." I can't afford to cry now. I can do that later… I take my foot off of the clutch and then depress it again, a little harder and move the gear stick over to the left and upwards, feeling it engage properly this time, and I let out a sigh, driving onto Bell Road.

I by-pass Garden Close, remembering my intention of going down there to see my parents' old house, to revisit my childhood memories, but I drive on, wishing I'd never had that stupid idea about laying my past to rest… wishing I'd never come back here at all.

Ever since I first fell for him, all those years ago, loving Ed has always hurt. I just never realised it could hurt this much.

I choke, swallowing down the lump in my throat that refuses to budge, and get to the top of Bell Road. There's nothing coming, so I pull out, turning to the right. It'll only take me an hour or so to get home, and I don't care that the house will be in darkness, with no food, no festivities… and that I'll be spending Christmas by myself. I don't care about any of it.

I turn on the radio for some background noise and then slow, as I approach the left-hand bend, holding up my hand to shield my eyes from the bright headlights coming straight at me. I hit the brakes, feeling the car skid on the wet road, and the last thing I hear is my own scream…

Chapter Fourteen

Ed

"Nicki, come back!" I hear the pub door open and slam shut, my heart lurching in my chest. *God... what have I done?*

"I know my timing sucked," Dan says, getting my attention. "But are you going to just stand there and let her go?"

I turn to face him properly. He's changed. His hair is lighter, and even longer than I remember, his skin darker, and while he looks as carefree as ever, there's something in his eyes that's different. Concern? Disapproval? I can't be sure. But I don't know him very well... not any more.

"It's not that simple."

"Really? It looked pretty damn simple to me. It's fairly obvious that you and the lady who's just run out of here weren't discussing climate change, or the state of the economy... unless you thought getting half naked might help with either of those things, in some way I can't think of." I can't help blushing and he climbs up the last step. He's an inch taller than me and I look up into his clear blue eyes. "Why are you embarrassed, Dad? And why did you say she wasn't your girlfriend?"

"Because..." I can't think what to say. I don't know the answer myself.

"Are you going to say because she isn't? Are you going to tell me you've taken to sleeping around since the last time I was here... because I won't believe a word of it."

"Of course not. I haven't done anything like this since..."

"Since Mum died?" he says, tilting his head.

"Yes."

"So tonight was the first time?" I nod my head and he sighs. "And I suppose you feel guilty, do you?" He pauses, but doesn't give me long enough to answer. "You need to stop this, Dad. It's been years since Mum died, and she wouldn't have wanted you to feel like this."

"You don't understand." I'm not sure I do yet. My head's still swimming, trying to come to terms with it all. "I knew Nicki when we were younger. Your mum knew her too. We all grew up together... went to school together." That's not the main reason I'm so confused, but it's a part of it... the only part I'm going to tell him.

"And?" He shrugs his shoulders.

"And I liked her back then... before I started seeing your mother."

"I'm still not seeing the problem here."

"I would have asked Nicki out when we were teenagers, but I thought she liked Rory Quick, so I backed off."

"Right. And that's an issue now because...?"

"Because it transpires it wasn't Rory she liked... it was me."

His brow furrows, like he's thinking. "I have to question her taste, but I still can't see where you're going with this. You liked her; she liked you, and judging from the look on her face just now, she still does. That doesn't mean you didn't love Mum in between." He rolls his eyes and steps a little closer. "If you didn't learn anything else from Mum's death, surely to God, you learned that life is pretty bloody short... too short to waste over regrets. Especially when there's nothing you can do about them."

I hear every word he's saying. I even agree with a lot of them, although that doesn't help me with the maelstrom of emotions running around in my head… especially now I'm fixating on one particular sentence he just uttered.

"What did you mean about the look on Nicki's face?"

"You hurt her, Dad. Badly. I could see it in her eyes. If you like her in the way I think you do, you need to find her, and you need to apologise."

"Shit…"

I make for the top of the stairs, but he puts his arm out, barring my way. "Shoes would be good, and I'd do up your shirt, if I were you. Pneumonia isn't a good look at your age."

I turn, going back into the living room, and put on my shoes, doing up my shirt at the same time. Dan's standing in the doorway, watching me, but steps to one side when I get back there, to let me pass.

"I'll be back," I murmur and he smiles.

"I'll cope if you don't make it."

I don't answer, and instead I run down the stairs, grabbing my jacket from the peg at the bottom and shrugging it on as I dash through the bar to the front door. It's unlocked, and I grab the keys, going out and locking it behind me, before I make my way out onto the harbour.

I hadn't realised it was raining, but I still pause for just a second, taking in a lungful of air. Then I pick up my pace, images of Nicki filling my head. I hadn't expected things to go so far tonight. I'd thought we'd talk, that I'd tell her how I feel, and she might do the same, and that maybe we'd kiss. When she dropped to her knees, I knew I should have stopped her… but she was about to fulfil one of my greatest fantasies, and the reality was so much better than my wildest dreams. What we did tonight changed everything... broke every boundary, and the thought that I might have hurt her... that I might have lost her...

I start running, rounding the corner into Bell Road and crossing over to enter the hotel, slowing to a walk as I go through the door.

I can still remember the way to her suite, and I make for the stairs.

"Ed?"

Anthony's voice stops me in my tracks, and I turn to face him. "Yes?"

"Are you looking for Miss Woodward?"

"Yes, I am."

"She's just left."

"Left?"

"Yes. She came back here in a bit of a state, asked me to get her bill ready, and then packed her bags, paid in full, and left. You've only missed her by a couple of minutes."

My legs feel like they won't hold me up, but I make my way over to the desk, wishing now that I hadn't bothered to stop and talk to Dan... that I'd come straight here instead. Nicki will be on her way back to Bath, but that's all I know... other than that Bath is a big place, and I've got no idea where she lives.

"Can you give me her home address?" I say to Anthony.

He frowns, shaking his head. "Of course I can't. I'd lose my job if I did that."

"Okay... her phone number, then?"

"The answer's the same, Ed. I'm sorry."

I can tell he means it, and I can't blame him. It's not his fault. It's mine.

The lights are still on in the pub, just as I left them, but I can't face going upstairs and admitting my failings to Dan... Dan, of all people. So I leave my wet coat on one of the chairs and start clearing up. He's probably gone to bed anyway, if he's got any sense, and I need to keep busy… to avoid thinking about what I've done. I've lost Nicki. I've hurt her more than ever, and I can't forgive myself for that.

It takes me a couple of hours, but by just after two in the morning, the pub is as clean as it'll ever be. I'm still not tired, and not yet ready to face the reality of being alone and contemplating what I've done. I gaze over at the optics behind the bar, wondering if I should get myself a drink… except I'm fairly sure that if I started, I wouldn't stop. The pub might not open on Christmas Day, but I need a clear head. My mother's coming over, and somehow, I need to work out what I'm going to do about finding Nicki… and making it right again. I need to explain. I need to tell her what happened tonight… because I'm not giving up. How can I? I love her.

I go behind the bar and reach out to turn off the lights, just as there's a loud knocking on the door.

"We're closed," I call out.

"I know. It's me." That's Rory's voice. "Open the door, will you?"

I do as he says, going over and unlocking the door again, then stepping back to let him in. He's in uniform, which is a surprise at this time of night, and as I push the door closed, a claw of fear creeps up my spine. I've seen that look on his face before… just over seven years ago.

"Oh, God… it's Nicki, isn't it?"

He nods his head, my body numbing, my heart slowing to a stop as all the memories come flooding back. "She's okay." Rory's voice permeates my brain. "She's not even badly hurt… just concussed."

I grip his shoulders. "Promise?"

"I promise. She's at the Royal Cornwall, in Truro."

The numbness doesn't go, but I feel my heartbeat quicken. "I need to go to her."

He nods his head. "I'll take you. It'll be easier."

I grab my coat from the chair where I dumped it earlier and follow him out through the door. There's a police car parked right outside and as I lock up, he climbs inside. I follow, sitting beside him, and he starts the engine.

"Tell me what happened?"

"She was in an accident out on the main road. I received the call just after I'd gone to bed and I got there probably about ten or fifteen minutes after it happened. Her car was lying in the ditch at the side of the road."

"You… you mean she'd just driven it off the road?" Please don't let that be it… I couldn't bear it.

"No. There was another car involved. It was crashed into the wall opposite."

"Was Nicki conscious?"

"Not when I got there. But she came round just before they put her into the ambulance. She said your name a couple of times, and then drifted off again." He glances at me every so often while concentrating on the road. "I don't suppose you know what she was doing on the main road at that time of night, with a suitcase in the back of her car?"

"I might do."

"And would you care to enlighten me?"

"If I must." He waits, although he's staring straight ahead now, giving me time, not scrutiny. "Nicki was at my place tonight, after closing time. We… we went upstairs, and although my intention had been that we'd have a coffee and talk, we…"

"Got carried away?" Rory says.

"Something like that."

"Okay, but I still don't understand why she'd leave the village."

"Probably because things didn't go according to plan."

"I know it's been a while, but…"

"That's not what I mean. I hadn't intended for anything to happen… not tonight. But it did, and afterwards… immediately afterwards… well, I wasn't perhaps as demonstrative as I might have been."

"Why on earth not?"

"I was confused."

"You mean, you regretted it?"

"No. Well, yes."

"Which is it? Yes, or no?"

"Neither… and both. It's complicated, but I think Nicki picked up on something."

"Why? What did she say?"

"Nothing. Not about what we'd done, anyway. She just said she needed the bathroom."

"That's not unusual."

"I know. I can remember that much. She'd only been gone a few seconds, when I heard voices."

"Whose voices?"

"Hers… and Dan's."

"Dan's back?"

"Yes. Only I wasn't expecting him."

"Obviously not. Was Nicki wearing anything?"

"Yes… thank God. She'd put her jumper and knickers back on… and she was wearing her black boots."

I hear him suck in a breath. "I imagine that gave Dan something to think about."

"Hmm…" I recall how sexy she looked, especially in those black boots, and I wish she'd put her trousers back on now. Still, it's too late to worry about things like that, and in the grand scheme of things… "They only exchanged a couple of words and then Nicki bolted to the bathroom. I just about had time to pull on my jeans and grab my shirt, but it was obvious what we'd been doing."

"So what? You're both consenting adults, and Dan's twenty-one, not twelve."

"I know, I know. It's just… he said something about Nicki being my girlfriend."

"And?"

"And I denied she was. I told him it wasn't like that."

"Why, for God's sake? Why would you say that?"

"I don't know." I do. It was because I was awash with guilt at the time. But I can't explain that. Not to him… and not yet. "Anyway, Nicki overheard."

"Of course she did. She was only in your bathroom."

"Exactly… and she came straight out again, got dressed and left without saying a word."

"You're surprised by that?"

"No. Dan gave me a quick lecture about life being too short, and then I went after Nicki… to find she'd already checked out of the hotel."

"And had an accident," he says, sounding grim.

"Yes… and it's all my fault."

"I think you'll find the driver of the other vehicle had a lot to do with it. I haven't been able to breathalyse him yet, because of his injuries, but he reeked of booze and, judging from the position of the vehicles, and what I've been able to make out of the skid marks in the dark, I'd say he was on the wrong side of the road."

"You're missing the point, Rory. If I hadn't behaved the way I did, she'd never have run out on me. She'd have stayed, we'd have talked. Hell… we'd probably still be talking now, and she'd never have been on that road in the first place."

"I know. But that's just a set of circumstances. It's called life, Ed."

Rory parks in front of the hospital, in one of the spaces reserved for emergency vehicles, and we both get out, walking through the main entrance and up to the reception desk.

"We're looking for Miss Nicole Woodward," he says. "She was brought in by ambulance earlier this evening."

The lady smiles up at him. "Yes, Sergeant." She taps on her keyboard a few times and reads from the screen. "She's in bed M… through the double doors and on your left."

Rory nods his head and thanks her. I understand now why he said this would be easier if I came with him. I doubt they'd have let me in if I'd come by myself, being as I'm not related to Nicki. I'm nothing to her, really. Especially not now.

"Come on." He leads me through the double doors, as instructed, and I follow him into the main Accident and Emergency department. There are curtained bays on either side of us, and we by-pass all of them until he stops by one with the letter 'M' above it. He clears his throat, just as a doctor in blue scrubs comes around the corner.

"Are you looking for Miss Woodward?" he says, smiling.

"Yes." Rory gets in a reply before I can and the doctor looks at me, expectantly. "This is her boyfriend." I'm not sure how accurate that is, but I don't argue, in case they throw me out.

He nods his head and pulls back the purple curtain, and my breath catches in my throat, my chest hurting intensely as I gaze down at Nicki, lying in the bed before us. She looks even smaller than usual, and so vulnerable, dressed in nothing more than a hospital gown, with a pale blue blanket pulled up over her legs. There's a dressing on her head, just above her right eye, and tears fill her eyes as she glances from the doctor, to Rory, and then to me. I don't hesitate, and walk around the bed, taking her hand in mine, and although she visibly stiffens at my touch, she doesn't pull back.

The doctor coughs and we both look over at him. "You'll be pleased to hear the cut on Miss Woodward's head is superficial." He addresses me with a smile and then looks down at her. "And we've just had the results of your scan. Everything's fine. We'll keep you in overnight, just to be on the safe side, but you can go home tomorrow… providing someone can be with you for the next day or two." He looks up at me and raises his eyebrows.

Before I can speak, Nicki gets there first. "I live alone. I'm not —"

"You can stay with me." I interrupt her and she turns, raising her head with the greatest of care, her eyes settling on mine.

The doctor doesn't give her a chance to argue, thank goodness. "That's good." He steps towards the curtain again. "You'll be moved to a ward soon, and then you'll be able to get some sleep. I imagine you'll be discharged sometime tomorrow morning… and you'll get home just in time for lunch, which is a good thing. Even on Christmas Day, the food in here doesn't get any better." He smiles and looks at me again, before his gaze returns to Nicki. "Get some rest over the next couple of days. Your head will probably hurt a bit, so let your boyfriend look after you."

"I will," I say, before Nicki can contradict him about my role in her life.

He nods his head, ducking through the curtain and disappearing.

"You're looking a lot better than you did earlier," Rory says, and Nicki looks up at him. "I'll need to take a statement from you, but it can wait. Right now, I have to find the idiot who caused the accident." He looks over at me. "I'll be back later."

"Okay." He goes too, leaving us alone, and I lower my gaze to Nicki, still gripping her hand as I suck in a deep breath. "I'm sorry."

Chapter Fifteen

Nicki

I look up into his eyes, seeing the pain and worry he's doing a poor job of disguising, and although I want to hold him and tell him it's okay, I can't. I'm still too angry… too hurt.

"I thought I'd lost you… twice," he says, his voice cracking slightly. "I came to the hotel, and you weren't there… and then Rory turned up at the pub, and…"

"I'm not yours to lose, Ed."

He sucks in a breath, like my words have hurt him. But I know how that feels. I can remember the pain of his words, too.

"Yes, you are."

"No, I'm not. You can call yourself my boyfriend, but we both know it's not true."

"Yes, it is. At least, I want it to be."

"In that case, why did you tell your son I'm not your girlfriend?"

He sighs, gripping my hand a little tighter. "Because I wasn't expecting to answer questions about you… about us. Not yet. I hadn't told you how I feel about you, so I certainly wasn't ready to tell Dan."

"And how do you feel about me?"

"I'm in love with you."

He says the words so simply, but with such certainty, I almost believe them. "You don't play fair, Ed."

He frowns. "I'm not playing. I'm serious."

"You might be now, when I'm lying in a hospital bed with a bandage on my head, but what about earlier? I could see the regret in your eyes, so don't try to pretend you were happy about what we did. And what's it going to be like in the cold light of day, when I'm not in a hospital bed? What's it going to be like tomorrow, and the next day, when those regrets creep back in? When the guilt about Suzannah gets the better of you?"

He leans in a little. "The honest answer to that is, I don't know what it's going to be like. What I do know is, this has nothing to do with Suzannah, or regrets, or with you lying in a hospital bed. It doesn't even have anything to do with what we did earlier." He perches on the edge of my bed, keeping hold of my hand, and looks into my eyes. "I won't insult you by saying my head isn't still in a mess. I think we both know it is, but I know without a doubt that I love you."

"Because you nearly lost me?"

"No. I knew I loved you before tonight. I've known for ages, and I wanted to tell you before we…"

"Before I rushed us into making love?"

He shakes his head. "You didn't rush us."

"Oh, I think I did. You weren't ready, were you?"

He reaches out with his free hand, caressing my cheek with the backs of his fingers. "I wanted you, Nicki. I still do. To be honest, I thought I'd made that fairly obvious, even before tonight."

"That might be true, but it doesn't alter the fact that you weren't ready. You're still not ready… for us."

A sharp pain stabs at my head, slightly above my eye and to the right of where the cut is, and I wince in agony.

"Hey... are you okay?"

"No. It hurts. They promised me some painkillers over an hour ago."

He nods his head and gets to his feet. "I'll go and chase them up." He lets go of my hand and leans over me, kissing my forehead. "I'll be back in a minute."

He's gone before I can say a word, and I nestle into the pillow behind me. The pain isn't subsiding, and I close my eyes against the lights, hoping that might help. It seems to, just a little, and rather than pain rattling round my head, I hear his words... "I'm in love with you."

I've waited all my life to hear him say that, so why don't I feel elated? Aside from the pain in my head and the concussion, why am I not jumping for joy? I suppose it's because I'm right. Whatever he says, he's not ready.

I hear the curtain being pushed aside and crack my eyes open. Ed's back and he comes around the bed again, taking my hand in his once more.

"The nurse says she'll be here in just a minute with your painkillers. And they're going to move you, too. I'll have to leave then, evidently." He perches up on the bed. "I'll call the hospital in the morning to check what time they're discharging you, and I'll drive over and collect you."

"You don't have to do that."

"Yes, I do." He sighs, shaking his head, and moves closer. "I know I didn't handle things very well earlier, and I'm sorry about that... more sorry than I can begin to explain. I also get that you don't trust me not to hurt you again, not after what I've done... but I'm not giving up."

"On what?"

"Us."

"Is there an us?"

"Yes. I don't blame you for doubting me. I've hurt you too many times. But please don't doubt my love for you."

Tears well in my eyes, and I struggle to fight them. "Y—You didn't want me."

"Of course I wanted you. Did I seem like an unwilling participant?"

"Not before, or during... but afterwards, yes."

"That was... that was the guilt."

"You're not supposed to feel guilty. Not at a time like that." I look up at him as the first tear falls. He moves closer, cupping my face with his hand, wiping the tear away with his thumb.

"Please don't cry, Nicki. I'm trying to be honest here... to tell you how it felt. I told you, my head's a mess."

"And I told you... you're not ready."

He opens his mouth, but at that moment, the nurse comes in, carrying a small beaker, which I know will contain my painkillers. I'm desperate for the relief now, and I feel like Ed and I are going round in ever decreasing circles... leading nowhere.

She hands over the beaker and pours some water from the jug beside the bed into a plastic cup.

"Take these and you'll soon feel better." I'm just swallowing them down, when Rory appears at the gap in the curtain and the nurse turns to him, smiling. "Did you get what you needed?" she asks.

"Yes. They've taken some bloods, so we can see what his alcohol levels were."

She nods her head. "I don't think there's any doubt about the answer to that question. He smelt like he'd bathed in whisky."

"Even so, I'll need evidence if I'm going to take it further." He turns to me, smiling. "How are you feeling?"

"Tired."

"Her head's hurting too," Ed says.

The nurse checks my chart, writing something down and looks pointedly at Ed. "The painkillers will help with that, but she needs to get some rest now."

"I think that's our cue to leave," Rory says.

"Before you go, what will happen about my car?" I haven't even thought about it until now, but I need to know. Ed might have offered me somewhere to stay, but I need to go home… and soon. I don't belong here anymore.

"The damage is quite bad." Rory pulls a face that suggests it could be a lot worse than 'quite bad'. "As you're going to be staying with Ed for a while, I'll have it taken to the garage in the village. Tim can take a look at it, and if necessary, your insurance assessors can view it there."

That wasn't what I wanted to hear. "My suitcase… my handbag…" It was bad enough that I wasn't wearing a bra when I got here and they helped me undress. The last thing I need is for someone to find it in my handbag.

"They're in the boot of my car," he says with a smile. "I'll leave them with Ed, shall I?"

I look up at Ed, and he nods his head. Neither of us says a word, but I'm not sure we know what to say anymore.

"I'm sorry to wake you… I just need to take your blood pressure."

The nurse smiles down at me, her blonde hair tied back in a tight ponytail, a pair of glasses perched on the end of her nose, and I smile back. They've woken me every ninety minutes since I came onto the ward, so even though I have a room to myself, any hope the doctor had of me getting some rest was ill-founded.

She wraps the cuff around my arm and presses a button on the monitor she wheeled in with her, waiting a few moments while it hums and the cuff inflates.

"Happy Christmas," she says.

"Oh, yes… Happy Christmas." I'd forgotten today was Christmas Day, and I glance towards the window.

"It's raining." She answers my unasked question. "But I think it's due to brighten up later."

The cuff deflates, and she pulls a notepad from her pocket, writing down the result, presumably to transfer to my chart, which isn't here with me anymore, for some reason. Then she removes the cuff again, wrapping it around itself and putting it back into the basket beneath the monitor.

"Can I get you any more painkillers?" she asks.

"No, thanks."

I've still got a slight headache, but it's nothing I can't tolerate.

She smiles and leaves again, taking the monitor with her… presumably to go and disturb someone else, and I turn over in bed, facing the window. I don't know what time it is. There's no clock in here and my phone is in my handbag, which is now at Ed's place. It feels early, though… too early to be awake, and I close my eyes, thinking about Ed, and about our conversation last night… well, this morning really. He told me he loves me, but is that enough when he's so wracked with guilt all the time? Is there any hope for a relationship that's founded on regret? In the cold light of Christmas morning, I want to hope it is. I want to hope he meant every word he said… but I just don't know…

"Breakfast!"

I startle awake and turn to see a man coming into the room, carrying a tray. He's smiling, his sandy-coloured hair combed neatly back from his rounded face.

"Oh… what time is it?"

"Just after seven-thirty. We're running a bit late today."

Late? It still feels horribly early to me.

He puts the tray down on the over-bed table and wheels it into place, pausing while I sit up. I look down to see a plate, with a silver-coloured cover. There's some cutlery and paper pouches with salt and pepper in them, along with two plastic containers, one for ketchup, and the other for brown sauce. There's also a cup of tea, which is the most welcome sight in the world.

"Now, don't get excited," the man says, his smile widening. "I don't want to get your hopes up, just because it's Christmas." He removes the silver cover with a flourish, and my tummy grumbles at the sight of a cooked breakfast.

"Well… I didn't expect that."

He chuckles. "Like I said, don't get excited. The bacon isn't exactly what you'd call crispy, and the eggs will still be tasteless and rubbery, but if you add some pepper and a dollop of ketchup, they'll be passable… and it's better than porridge."

"It certainly is."

I pick up the pouch of ketchup, struggling to open it. "Here, let me." The man takes it from me, opening it with ease, and hands it back. "I'll leave you to get on," he says and goes over to the door.

"Thank you."

He smiles, nodding his head, and disappears, leaving me to my breakfast.

He wasn't wrong, the bacon is far from crispy, but the eggs are okay, especially with the addition of a little black pepper, and when mixed with the baked beans. The mushrooms are heavenly, as are the grilled tomatoes, and by the time I've finished gulping down the last of my tea, I'm feeling almost human again.

I'm also in desperate need of the bathroom, and I push back the table, swinging my legs off of the bed and sitting up, surprised by the swirling sensation in my head.

"Oh… Oh dear."

I take a moment, and eventually the room stills and I get to my feet, hanging on to the side table, just in case. I feel remarkably wobbly, but I know I have to get across the corridor to the bathroom. Taking a deep breath, I place my hand on the wall for support and gingerly put one foot in front of the other, making it to the door, and pulling it open. The corridor is deserted and I tiptoe across it and into the bathroom. It's dark in here, so I turn on the light, wincing at the brightness. I still cling to the wall for support and make it to the toilet, grateful for the opportunity to sit down.

When I come out, I'm greeted by the nurse who saw me earlier.

"Ahh… I was just looking for you."

"Oh?"

She walks with me back to my room. "Yes. Your boyfriend just called to see how you are, and we've told him you'll be ready to leave by eleven."

"Will I?"

"Yes. The doctor's already checked your notes, and he's happy for you to be discharged. We've asked your boyfriend to bring you some clean clothes because yours are soaked and muddy."

She opens the door to my room and I pass through, stopping to take a breath. "Where are my clothes?"

"They're in a bag in the locker." She nods towards it.

"Okay." I put my hand out for the wall again. "Is it… is it normal to feel this weak and dizzy?"

"Yes. That's why the doctor wanted to be sure someone would be with you for the first day or so. It will pass… probably quite quickly, if you get plenty of rest."

I've lost track of time again, but I turn as the door opens a crack, half expecting to see another nurse, and stifle a gasp when I see Ed poking his head through the crack.

Oh, God… I love him so much. Despite everything that's going against us, regardless of all my doubts and fears, I'm his. I always will be.

"Can I come in?" He enters, and I notice that, rather than wearing his coat, he's got on a thick, navy blue sweater. He's carrying a jute shopping bag, which he puts on the end of the bed, and then he leans over, kissing my cheek. I look up through my tears and he steps closer, cupping my face with his hand. "Are you okay?"

"I'm feeling a lot weaker than I expected, but the headache is better, thank you."

He nods his head. "I've got so many things I need to talk to you about, but before we get into any of that, I—I never got to finish what I was trying to say to you last night."

"No… you didn't."

"I was going to send you a text message when I got home, but then I realised I didn't have your number."

"It wouldn't have made any difference. I don't have my phone… it's in my handbag."

"Oh. I see." He perches on the bed.

"What were you going to say?"

"I was going to ask you – no, to beg you – not to give up on us. I get that it's a big ask, after everything I've put you through, and I know you're still angry with me, but…"

I reach out, touching his arm, and he stops talking. "You're not wrong. I was angry with you. In fact, I was furious… so furious I was trying to work out how I could get home today without a car." His brow furrows and he shakes his head. "You hurt me, Ed, and I thought I never wanted to see you again. But this morning, I've realised that's not true."

"Which part?"

"The part about not wanting to see you again. You still hurt me… but I don't want this to be the end. I can't give up. I wouldn't know how to." He smiles, leaning closer and rests his forehead against mine.

"Thank you. The confusion – the mess in my head – I will work it out. I promise." He sits back again, looking down at me. "Do you want to get dressed?"

I wonder for a moment about all the other things he said he wanted to talk through, but I guess he's decided they can wait, and I'm quite relieved about that. My head is spinning.

"I'm not sure I can. I had trouble standing up earlier."

"Then let me help you."

I pull back slightly. "You can't. I mean, I can't. It wouldn't be..."

He smiles again, shaking his head. "Were you going to say it wouldn't be right?"

"Yes."

His smile widens, and he stands up, reaching for the bag at the bottom of my bed. "I don't see why not. We need to be practical about this, and besides, I've already seen you naked..."

"No, you haven't. I kept my boots on." Why did I say that? Neither of us needs reminding about last night.

Ed nods his head very slowly. "Hmm... I remember. And if you're that particular about it, I promise not to look at your feet, or your lower legs. Okay?"

I stare up at him, and we both start laughing at the same time.

"Sorry. I made that unnecessarily awkward."

"No, you didn't," he says as he unpacks my clothes, although I have to smile when I see he's brought my jeans and a grey sweater that really needs a t-shirt, or blouse underneath it, because it's so itchy. Still, he wasn't to know...

"Shall I undo this?" he says, tugging at the sleeve of my hospital nightgown.

"Okay."

175

I look up into his eyes, but he focuses on the job in hand, taking off the nightgown and dropping it onto the mattress. I'm naked before him, but he doesn't bat an eyelid and helps me into my underwear, holding me steady while I have to stand for him to pull my knickers up. My jeans follow, and then the sweater, and although I'm hot now, and there's no getting away from the itchiness of this jumper, I'm grateful to be dressed. Ed's been very business-like in putting my clothes on, and a small, perverse part of me can't help feeling disgruntled about that. He's brought my flat shoes and slips them on, before standing back and gazing down at me.

"Shall I check if it's okay for you to go home?" he asks. I nod my head and he turns, leaving the room, while I get to my feet again, and bend to retrieve my bag of clothes from the locker. My boots are there too, and although they're a little damp, they seem perfectly okay. I pick them up, along with the bag, and put them on the bed, just as Ed comes back in. "Are you okay?"

"Yes. I was just getting my things ready. Am I allowed to go?"

"You are. They've said I can give you paracetamol every four hours, if you need it. You evidently haven't had any since the ones you had in A&E, is that right?"

"It is."

He nods, coming over and putting all my things into the jute bag, before he holds out his hand. I stare down at it for a moment and then take it. Aside from the fact that I want to hold it, I feel the need for something steadying.

Outside, there's still a light drizzle, and although I don't have a coat, because it's screwed up in the bag, Ed reassures me his car is parked close by.

"Which one is it?"

"The Range Rover." He nods towards a dark blue tank, and I have to chuckle.

"Does it come with a set of steps?"

He laughs. "No, but we'll be fine."

He takes out his keys, opening the car as we approach, and puts the bag on the back seat before opening the front passenger door. I raise my foot, but before I can put it anywhere, he leans down, lifting me into his arms, and deposits me straight onto the seat.

"There," he says. "No steps required."

I gaze at him, but he just passes me the seat belt, and closes the door, walking around to the driver's side and getting in beside me. He starts the engine and I strap myself in before he pulls out of the parking space.

We're on the main road, heading towards the roundabout, when he turns to look at me. "Do you remember me saying earlier that there were things I needed to talk to you about?"

"Yes."

"Hmm… I would have brought this up when I was helping you dress, but I got distracted."

"You did? What by?"

"You, of course." He makes it sound like I should have been able to work that out for myself, and I feel myself blush, realising that he wasn't perhaps as unaffected by helping to dress me as I'd thought.

"Oh… sorry."

"Don't be sorry. I like being distracted by you."

I'm not sure how to reply to that. It feels like we're still on slightly rocky ground, and besides, he mentioned needing to talk… which has me a little nervous. "What was it you needed to say?"

He hesitates for a moment, negotiating the roundabout and then speeds up, sucking in a breath. "I've got something I need to apologise for… well, something else I need to apologise for."

"What's that?"

"Last night… I should have… I mean, when we…"

God… could this be any more embarrassing? "Please… please don't apologise for what we did. None of it was your fault. We've already established I'm the one to blame for what happened."

"No, we haven't."

"Okay, but we've agreed you weren't ready."

"I don't remember agreeing with you on that either. As far as I recall, the nurse interrupted us before we got to finish that conversation. And before you start telling me you rushed things again, you didn't… okay? My apology has nothing to do with that."

"Then why are you saying sorry?"

"Because I forgot to use a condom."

I try not to smile, feeling relieved. "You don't have to apologise for that. Believe it or not, I had noticed."

He turns, staring at me, before he looks back at the road. "Can I take it from your calmness that you're on the pill?"

"No." His body tenses, his muscles tightening, his fingers gripping the steering wheel, and I reach over, placing my hand on his arm. "It's okay, Ed."

"No, it's not. I should have…" He shakes his head. "I'm sorry, Nicki. My only excuse is that it's been a very long time since I've had to think about things like that, and…"

"Can you stop panicking?" I interrupt him and he glances over again, frowning. "It really is okay, Ed. I—I can't have children."

He takes his foot off of the accelerator, looking at me for a little longer this time. I see confusion in his eyes, but he turns away before I can say anything, focusing on the road again. Up ahead, there's a sign for a parking lay-by, and he indicates, pulling into it and skidding to a halt before he pulls on the handbrake and slams the car into 'park'.

"You can't?" he says, twisting in his seat, so he's facing me, his voice soft and considered, like it matters… like I matter, although I'm not sure I want to think about that.

"No."

"Do you mind me asking why not?"

"Of course not. I'm used to it all now." Being used to it doesn't make it any easier to say, and I take a breath, knowing this conversation could change everything between us. "I have something called POI, which stands for premature ovarian insufficiency… but you'd probably know it better as premature menopause."

He doesn't say a word to start with, but I can see the shock written all over his face, and I swallow down the lump in my throat.

Eventually, he coughs and takes a breath. "Menopause?"

"Yes."

"But you're only forty-one."

"I know. That's what the premature part means."

"Sorry. I'm being stupid."

I reach over, putting my hand on his arm. "No, you're not. When it happened, even I didn't notice anything was wrong."

He frowns. "If it's not a silly question, how could you not notice?"

"Because of the timing, I suppose… and the fact that my periods had never been very regular. So, when I missed one, I didn't worry. I knew I wasn't pregnant. I hadn't slept with Terry for nearly three months by then."

"You hadn't?"

"No. That was what I meant when I said the timing was important. This all happened around the time we split up. I'd moved out of the house and was living in a rented flat. I'd changed jobs, too, because we couldn't work together anymore, and we were going through the process of getting divorced and selling our home. It was... difficult."

"I can imagine." He shakes his head for a moment. "Sorry. That was an insensitive thing to say. I can't imagine how it felt at all."

"It's okay."

"Is it?"

I smile. "Not really. But there's nothing I can do about it now."

He sucks in a breath, letting it out slowly. "How did you find out there was something more serious wrong?"

"That took a while. After I'd missed three periods, and started having hot flushes, even I realised it wasn't normal, and I went to see my GP. He told me it was probably stress, and with everything that was going on, I believed him. Terry and I had sold the house by then, but after paying back the mortgage, there wasn't enough left to buy anywhere else."

"So you stayed in the rented flat?"

"Yes. I didn't like it very much, which probably wasn't helping with the stress, so I went along with that diagnosis for a while longer, until it all got too much. I was crying all the time, and I had trouble sleeping. It was horrendous... so I went back to the GP again. Fortunately, my own doctor was on holiday, and I saw a locum. She arranged a blood test, which showed my hormone levels were within the menopausal range."

"What did you do?"

"Once I'd recovered from the shock, I had some more tests done, initially to try and find a cause."

"And?"

"They couldn't find one. Evidently, that's not at all unusual. Then I had a few other tests done, and once the diagnosis was confirmed, I was put on HRT."

"And that helped?"

"Oh, God... yes."

He smiles at my reply, and I have to smile back. "I felt like a human being again... although obviously I had to face the fact that I'd never have a child of my own. I was given leaflets, and pointed to websites about egg donation and adoption, in case I needed them in the future, but to be honest, having just got divorced, it was the last thing on my mind."

"You and Terry never wanted to have children?"

"We talked about it before the wedding, and both agreed we didn't. I'm not sure of Terry's reasons, although I imagine they had something to do with the fact that he never really wanted to settle down in the first place."

"And your reasons?"

"There was only one man I ever wanted to have children with... and he was married to my best friend. That ship had sailed as far as I was concerned."

I gaze up into his eyes, seeing something that looks like regret reflected back at me... although I'm not going to read too much into it. It's probably pity, anyway... not regret.

"And how do you feel about it now... not being able to have children, I mean?"

"Like I said, I'm used to it."

"So you don't feel like it's something you've missed out on? It never came up with your other boyfriends, before Terry... or since?"

"I haven't had any other boyfriends."

He leans back slightly. "W—What? None at all?"

"No. Terry was my first, and until last night, he was my only."

He closes his eyes, like he's in pain, which is hard to see, but not as hard as the torment in his eyes when he opens them again. I hate the thought that what we did is so difficult for him to bear, and I wish now that I'd done things differently... that I'd waited.

"You're seriously saying you've never been with anyone else in all these years?" he says.

"Yes, I am. But you haven't either, have you? It was always about Suzannah for you." He bites his lip, shaking his head, and goes to open his mouth to speak. I reach up, covering his lips with my fingers. "Don't… please, Ed. I don't want to hear it. This is hard for you, I get that. I know how conflicted you are."

He pulls my hand away. "I don't think you do," he says, kissing my fingers, just gently. "I'm sorry, Nicki… for all of it."

"You need to stop apologising. You don't regret marrying Suzannah, so why apologise for it?"

"That wasn't what I was saying sorry for. You're right, I don't regret marrying Suzannah. But the reason I keep apologising is because I hate the idea of hurting you… or of you hurting at all, for that matter." He selects 'drive', releasing the handbrake. "I might be conflicted," he says, staring at me. "But don't for one second think that means I don't love you." He checks his mirror and pulls out onto the road, speeding up. "Because I do, Nicki… more than I'm capable of explaining at the moment."

Chapter Sixteen

Ed

I thought dressing Nicki at the hospital was hard. It was a struggle to control my reactions and not take her in my arms and kiss her. But that was easy compared to the conversation we just had at the side of the road. That was so much more than I ever thought it would be… just like everything with Nicki, it seems.

She thinks she understands my conflicts? Hell, I don't even understand them myself yet… so there's no way I'm ready to explain them.

As for the rest? I don't know what to say, which is probably why we've said nothing since I pulled out of that parking bay… and we're nearly back at Porthgarrion now.

I can't imagine what she went through… what it meant to discover she couldn't have children. It's a life-altering thing to hear and she would have been by herself when that happened, too, with no-one to turn to for support. I hate that thought, and I wish it could have been different for her, that someone could have been there for her. That *I* could have been there for her. Except I wasn't. No-one was… because it seems she's only ever been with one man… until last night. Of course, she was right when she said the same applied to me. I'd only ever been with Suzannah, too.

I'm not going to think about that now, though. It's too confusing, and I've got other things to think about… like Nicki.

I still feel guilty for not using a condom, even though there are no consequences. I wasn't to know that, and I should have been more careful. Not that I was aware of being careful at the time. I wasn't aware of anything… other than Nicki, and what she was doing to me, and how it felt.

It didn't even register with me that I'd forgotten to take more care of her until after Rory dropped me back at the pub in the early hours of the morning. He left to go home to Laura, and I carried Nicki's bags upstairs, sitting in the kitchen and staring at my phone for ages, while I tried to work out how to phrase a text message that I hoped would explain what I wanted to put into words. It was only when I got into my message app that I realised I didn't have Nicki's number, and that the whole thing had been a waste of time.

After that, I made up the spare bed, putting her things in there, and had a shower.

It was then, while I was leaning back against the tiled wall, thinking about Nicki, picturing her kneeling before me and re-living everything that followed, that I realised what I'd done. I panicked… not surprisingly. Then I beat myself up for a while, and then I got out of the shower and dried off, resolving to speak to Nicki, to apologise and then reassure her… not that she needed reassurance. Not in the way I expected.

Once I was dressed, I went and sat in the living room, but I ended up staring at the sofa… at the place where we'd made love, or rather, where Nicki had made love to me. My mind was racing… thoughts of what we'd done mingling with memories of Suzannah, the guilt building and rising with every second. I tried so hard not to make comparisons, but it was impossible, and I recalled a gratified, loving, pleasing satisfaction and contrasted it with a breathless, heady, consuming, insatiable desire. No matter how much I wanted to block those memories… to obliterate the obvious differences, I couldn't. They were staring me in the face.

In the end, I moved to the kitchen, just for a different view, and made myself a coffee, and that's where Dan found me a short while later. He was shocked when I told him what had happened, and he joined me at the table, helping me make plans…

"Oh… God…" Nicki's whispered voice startles me back to reality.

"What's…?" I turn. She's staring out of the window, her face pale and I suddenly realise where we are. We're coming up to the spot where her accident happened. I reach over and take her hand in mine. "Hey… it's okay. I drove this way earlier. The cars have been moved. There's nothing to see." She's shaking and I slow down, gripping her hand even tighter. "You're safe, Nicki, I promise."

"Get me home… please?" Her voice is a frightened murmur, and although I keep hold of her hand, I put my foot down again, whisking us past the accident site and taking the turning into the village.

I park at the back of the pub and switch off the engine, twisting around to face her.

"Are you okay?" She nods her head, even though I know she's not, and while a part of me wants to tell her she doesn't have to pretend with me, I can hardly criticise her when I know I'm not telling her everything myself… albeit that our reasons are probably very different. "Do you want to go in?" She nods again and I get out of the car, going around to her side and lifting her into my arms once more. "Shall I carry you?"

"No... I'm fine. Honestly."

I feel a little disappointed, but I set her down on the ground before opening the rear door and retrieving the bag. She's standing, staring out onto the harbour, taking deep breaths, and I give her a minute before I hold out my hand to her. She takes it and without a word, I lead her inside through the back door.

"I forgot to tell you earlier, but my mother's here."

She looks up at me, startled.

"She is?"

"Yes. It's Christmas Day. She always comes over... or she has since Suzannah died. We used to go to her before that."

Nicki pulls back. "I shouldn't be here. I—I can go back to the hotel."

"Over my dead body. It'll be fine. Dan's explained to Mum about your accident."

"He has?"

"Yes. We discussed it earlier."

"So she knows about us?"

I hesitate for a moment. "She knows you're staying here because you've just had an accident..."

"But you didn't want her to know about us?"

I can see the doubt and hurt in her eyes and as she tries to pull away, I hold on tighter.

"You didn't let me finish. I was going to say that Dan and I agreed I should be the one to tell her about us."

"Oh."

"The problem is, I had to leave before she arrived."

"So she still doesn't know?"

"No."

She nods her head gingerly and glances up the stairs. "I could do with a shower, if that helps?"

I smile and lean down, kissing her forehead. "It might make things easier."

We climb the stairs and I show her to the guest room, which is next to my bedroom. Her suitcase is open on the bed, along with her handbag.

"I hope you didn't mind me going through your things. The nurse at the hospital told me to bring clean clothes, so..." I let my voice fade and she smiles up at me.

"It's okay, Ed."

I put down the bag containing her dirty clothing, and go out into the hall, where I open the airing cupboard and retrieve a towel, which I bring back to her.

"I—I know where the bathroom is," she says in a quiet whisper and I nod my head, unwilling to think about the how and why of that.

"If you need me, shout. I'll be in the kitchen."

"Good luck," she whispers.

"I won't need it."

She nods her head and I leave her to it, going along the hall to the kitchen, where Dan looks up from his seat at the table. Mum is sitting beside him. She's wearing a smart woollen dress, her blonde hair cut shorter than the last time I saw her, roughly two weeks ago. It appears they've been chopping vegetables. They both put down their knives and sit back, looking up at me. "We heard you come back, but didn't want to get in the way," Dan says. "How's Nicki?"

"She seems to be okay. She's tired, and she says she feels weak."

"That's to be expected."

"She's just having a shower."

He nods his head and I turn to Mum. "And how are you, Ed?"

"I'm okay."

"Really? From what Dan's been saying, you haven't had any sleep."

"I'll catch up, don't worry." I pull out a chair and sit down opposite them, just as Dan gets up, going over to the coffee machine, and pouring some out into a large mug. He brings it back, putting it in front of me. "Thanks." I take a sip, putting the cup back down again, before I focus on him. "Are you sure about helping downstairs?"

"Of course. I just wish you'd woken me when Rory Quick came round last night."

"It wasn't really last night, Dan… it was two o'clock this morning, and to be honest, the only thing going through my head was getting to Nicki."

"You could still have woken me," he says, sitting back down. "Either then, or when you got back from the hospital."

"I know, but I wanted to make up Nicki's bed, and have a shower."

I take a breath, wondering how to broach the subject of my relationship with Nicki. My mother thought the world of Suzannah, so it won't be easy, and I stare out of the window at the grey sky, the rain dripping down the glass pane.

"Nicki was always such a lovely girl," Mum says and I glance back at her, noting the twinkle in her eyes.

"I know. We're… um…"

She chuckles. "I know you are."

I look at Dan. "Don't blame me," he says, holding up his hands. "Nan guessed there was something going on between you, and I wasn't about to lie to her."

"I'm surprised you haven't mentioned it before," she says.

"It wasn't going on before. Nicki's only been back for a very short time."

"Oh… so it's early days, is it?"

"Yes, I suppose so."

"What does that mean?"

"It means I'm in love with her, and even though it's complicated, I'm going to work it out… as long as she can forgive me, that is." I guess that's about as plain a way of putting it as there is.

"For the whole girlfriend-not girlfriend thing, you mean?" Dan says, and I glance at my mother.

"Dan explained that to me, too." She shakes her head in a disapproving way.

"Thanks, Dan."

"Anytime."

"Is that what you're worried about?" Mum asks.

"Oh, it's way more complicated than that."

They both nod their heads, although neither of them asks for an explanation, which is good, because I don't have one.

"She's here, isn't she?" Dan says.

"Yes. I just told you, she's in the shower."

He rolls his eyes. "That's not what I mean. She's here, Dad… when she could be somewhere else. She chose to come back with you."

"Only because she doesn't have anywhere else to go."

"I don't believe that for a minute. And that's not entirely what I meant, either."

"Why? What did you mean?"

"That she's here." I frown at him. "And she's going to be here, under your roof for the next couple of days, while she recovers… so use the time wisely."

He has a point, I suppose, and while I've got no intention of taking advantage of Nicki's enforced stay, it wouldn't hurt for us to spend some time together.

"Are you both okay with this? Whatever this is?" I say, looking from my mother to Dan. "Nicki isn't trying to replace your mum, you know?"

He nods his head. "I get that, Dad. And as for being okay with it, I think the answer to that should be obvious. You've been bloody miserable since Mum died. If you've got the chance to be happy again with Nicki, I think you should take it."

"I couldn't have put it better myself," Mum says with a sympathetic smile, which I return.

"How's the lunch going?" I ask, keen to change the subject. Before I left for the hospital, Dan offered to take charge of cooking Christmas lunch with Mum's help, and I wasn't about to refuse.

"The turkey crown is in the oven already," he says, "and we're just finishing the vegetables. I had to raid the kitchen downstairs for some more carrots and potatoes. We're just doing a tray of roasted veggies… keeping it simple."

"Simple works for me."

He nods his head. "I also found some individual portions of Christmas pudding, and some brandy butter," he says.

"Did you go through the entire pub larder?"

"Pretty much." He grins. "But who's going to complain? You own the place."

"True."

We all turn at the sound of a slight feminine cough coming from the door, and I shoot to my feet. Nicki's standing on the threshold to the kitchen, her hair damp around her shoulders. She's wearing the same jeans she had on earlier, but with a different top. This one is cream and much thinner than the jumper I took over to the hospital for her. She's also wearing a navy blue cardigan over the top, and she looks worn out and so frail, I want to wrap her up in my arms, and keep her here… forever. I go to her, putting my hands on her waist. She doesn't object, so I step closer, looking down into her upturned face.

"Are you okay?"

"Hmm… just exhausted."

"Come and sit down." I turn, putting my arm around her, and steer her towards the table. Dan gets up, holding out a chair, and Nicki sits in it, looking up at him.

"Thank you," she says, and he smiles.

"Happy Christmas, Nicki," Mum says from her seat opposite.

"Happy Christmas to you too, Mrs Moyle."

"I think you should probably call me Ellen, don't you… in the circumstances?" Mum glances up at me and then smiles back at Nicki again, who nods her head and then tips it back, looking up at me.

"Happy Christmas, Ed. Sorry. I forgot to say that earlier."

"So did I, so don't worry."

"You've both had other things on your mind… what with the accident and everything," Dan says, saving us from our own apologies, before he looks back at Nicki. "Can I get you a coffee?"

"It's okay. I'll do it," I say, but Dan holds up his hands.

"Sit down, Dad. I can manage. You haven't slept, remember?"

Nicki looks up at me, frowning. "You haven't slept? Not at all?"

"No." I sit next to her, taking her hand in mine. "It was nearly five when I got back here, and it didn't seem worth going to bed."

Dan brings over a mug of coffee, offering Nicki the milk and sugar. She accepts milk, but declines sugar, and once Dan's stirred her coffee, she lifts the cup, taking a sip.

We both stare at each other, feeling a little awkward, although she doesn't pull her hand from mine, and I don't release her.

"I think we need to get these vegetables into the oven, don't we, Nan?" Dan says, breaking the silence. "Do you think we've done enough?"

"I don't know. I'm used to cooking for one," Mum says.

He tips the roasting tray in our direction and Nicki laughs. "How many people are you feeding?"

"Just the four of us."

"That's enough," I tell him and he nods his head, taking the tray to the oven and putting it inside. I watch him, and when he turns around, I can't help smiling. "It's lovely to see you and everything, Dan… but weren't you supposed to be taking part in a special surfing competition, or something?"

He grins. "You remembered that?"

"Yes. Believe it or not, I pay attention to your text messages, when you can be bothered to send them."

He rolls his eyes, coming over to the table and clearing away all the vegetable peelings, while Mum sits back in her seat, taking events in her stride. "The competition was cancelled," he says. "The waves weren't high enough, so I'm going out there again on New Year's Eve."

"Can you afford to keep flying backwards and forwards like this?"

He frowns at me. "Just about."

"And was there a reason you didn't make it home in the summer?" I turn to Nicki. "Dan usually comes home during the summer to teach at the local surf school. It enables him to finance his lifestyle for the rest of the year."

Dan shakes his head. "That's not the only money I earn, you know? I do occasionally win the competitions I enter."

He tilts his head at me, but I just shrug my shoulders. "How would I know about that? You never tell me."

He shrugs too, wiping down the table where he and Mum have been working. "Well… either way, the reason I didn't make it back last summer was because I met someone."

This is news to me, and judging from the look on Mum's face, it's news to her, too, although not entirely unexpected news as far as I'm concerned. "A girl, I take it?"

"Yes, Dad… a girl. A French girl, called Simone. We spent the summer together at her parents' place near Nice."

"You could afford to take the entire summer off, could you?"

"I earned some money while I was out there, doing bar work… and it felt important at the time."

"Oh? Was it serious then?" Mum asks before I can.

"Evidently not." He shakes his head, like he's remembering something. "I thought it might be, but when I asked her to come back out with me on the circuit, she said 'no'."

"And you didn't think about settling down with her?"

He frowns. "Settling down? No. Of course not."

Mum chuckles and I nod my head. "That probably told you everything you needed to know then, didn't it?"

"Yes, it did. I liked her, but I wouldn't have given up anything for her… and she felt the same, I guess."

"You guess? You mean, you didn't ask?"

He shrugs again. "It was one of those things."

"Have you spoken to Sam?" I ask, and then turn to Nicki again. "Sorry… I should probably explain. Sam is Dan's boss at the surf school."

She nods. "I know. Rory explained… remember?" She doesn't go into any more detail, but I guess that's because Rory's explanation came on the night I invited him and Laura to the pub… and she'd probably rather forget that, as would I. She turns to Dan, who doesn't seem to have noticed her embarrassment, or mine.

"He called me in the spring to see how I got on at one of the competitions I'd been in, and I told him then I didn't think I'd be back. I'd just met Simone, and… well, she'd already mentioned spending the summer together, so…" His voice fades, and I can't help feeling a bit hurt that he's clearly spoken to his boss more than he speaks to me.

"Has he kept your job open? Will you be able to work there next summer? Assuming you come back, of course."

He laughs. "To be honest, I wasn't sure he would, but he called me a week or so ago, just to catch up, and he was telling me that the guy he hired last summer to cover for me was absolutely useless. They had lots of complaints, evidently, so I think he's quite keen for me to come back. I thought I'd try and go over there in the next few days, if I can find the time."

Nicki sits forward a little. "Why wouldn't you be able to?"

"Because I'm going to be helping downstairs, covering for Dad," he says.

"You are?" Nicki turns to me, tilting her head.

"Dan and I talked it through this morning, and we've planned it all out. I've spoken to Leanne, too, and she said she'd liaise with Reece, so between the three of them, they can cover everything downstairs, and I can look after you."

She blinks two or three times in quick succession, and sucks in a stuttering breath, like she might cry. "You don't have to do that, Ed."

I grip her hand a little tighter and move my chair closer to hers. "Yes, I do."

"That was a fabulous lunch." I lean back in my seat and look over at Dan, who's smiling, rather pleased with himself, even though he had help from Mum, especially with the gravy.

"It was." Nicky nods her head in agreement. "I didn't realise how hungry I was."

Not only did Dan and Mum cook us an excellent lunch, but he even made the table look festive, having brought up some candles from downstairs.

"Do you two want to go and put your feet up?" he says, stretching his arms above his head, before getting to his feet. "Nan and I can clear away."

"I'm not leaving you to do all this." I stand too, but Dan shakes his head, nodding towards Nicki.

"We'll be fine, Dad. There's not much to do… honestly."

He's got all the subtlety of a rhinoceros, but I'm too tired to argue, and I look down at Nicki. "Do you want to join me in the living room?"

"Only if your mum's sure she and Dan don't need any help."

"We're positive," Mum says, and I know at least part of her motive for staying out here is to grill Dan about Simone, and probably me and Nicki, too… not that he knows very much about us.

Dan stacks up the dishes, moving them to the draining board and opening the dishwasher. "This won't take five minutes, will it, Nan?"

"If you say so, Daniel."

Nicki nods her head and I hold her chair, pulling it back as she stands, and then I take her hand, leading her from the kitchen.

"Thanks, Dan," I call over my shoulder.

"Any time."

The living room has smaller windows and is quite dark by comparison with the kitchen, so I turn on the side lamps as Nicki takes a seat, sitting at the opposite end of the sofa to where I sat the other night… when she made love to me. I take a seat beside her, not too close, but close enough that I can hold her hand, and when I do, she gives me a gentle squeeze. I raise my head, my eyes locking with hers, and I'm about to ask if I can kiss her, when she winces.

"Are you in pain? Is it your head?"

"It's okay. It's just…"

"Do you want some painkillers?"

"I'll give it a little while and see if it wears off, now we're sitting quietly."

"Okay. But if it gets worse, or you change your mind, just tell me."

She nods and then twists in her seat, so she's facing me. "It hurts, doesn't it?"

"What?"

"Dan, not communicating with you."

I move a little closer to her, and she raises our hands, putting them onto my leg. "How did you know?"

"It was written all over your face."

I suck in a breath, letting it out slowly as I shake my head. "I know things were hard between us when Suzannah died. It was my fault. I shut down for a while and left him to cope by himself. Mum helped, but he was still so young. He needed me, and I should have done a better job, especially considering he found her body. I should have tried harder… been there for him. I think he found it hard to forgive me for that. But I don't think it would kill him to tell me where he is once in a while… or let me know what he's doing and when he's coming home." I stop talking, remembering the scene in the hall last night, when he came back so unexpectedly… and what it led to.

Nicki leans in to me. "Do you ever contact him?"

"How do you mean?"

"Do you ever just call him, or text him, for a chat?"

"We've never been that chatty." As I'm saying that, I think about the last twenty-four hours, and how good it's been to talk to Dan… and how understanding he's been.

"Are you sure about that?" she says, looking right into my eyes.

"Not really." I sigh. "In case you haven't noticed, I'm not sure about anything at the moment… other than loving you."

She smiles, looking a little shy, which is very cute. In fact, it's adorable. "You should try it," she says.

"Try what?"

"Calling him. I think he'd like it. I think you would too."

I put my arm around her and, after just a second's hesitation, she nestles against me. "Thank you," I whisper.

"What for?"

"Everything."

Chapter Seventeen

Nicki

We've spent the afternoon sitting in the living room with Dan and Ed's mum, watching films. We chose quiet ones, that my poor head could cope with, and Ed's made several cups of tea. At about six o'clock, Ellen and Dan went and prepared some sandwiches from the leftover turkey, and after we'd eaten them, she said she needed to go home. Ed didn't seem surprised, and I gathered she has a cat that needed feeding… so at least I wasn't the cause of her departure. As she left, she kissed me briefly on the cheek, and although she didn't say a word, there was something welcoming in that gesture.

Once Ellen had departed, Dan left us to ourselves, claiming that he had friends to catch up with online, although I'm sure he's been able to do that from wherever he's been in the world.

Ed and I have started another film, but I can't get into it, and to be honest, even though it's only the middle of the evening, I'm struggling to keep my eyes open.

"I know I'm pathetic, but would you mind if I went to bed?" I gaze up at him. He looks as tired as I do.

"I don't think you're pathetic at all. I was just about to suggest the same thing... and I didn't have an accident in the early hours of this morning."

"You didn't get any sleep, though," I say as he gets up, switching off the television and then turns to help me stand.

"No. I'm starting to feel a bit like I've got a hangover."

"Without the advantages of having got drunk first?"

"Exactly. I don't remember feeling like this when I was younger and went without sleep."

"That's because we're not young anymore."

He moves a little closer. "We're not old either, Nicki."

"No, but we're both exhausted."

"And you need to rest."

He steps away again, switching off the lamps and plunging us into semi-darkness, the only light coming from the hall. He comes back, taking my hand and guides me around the furniture and out into the hallway, where I blink against the bright light and let him lead me along to the guest bedroom. Stopping outside, he turns to face me.

"I'm just next door, if you need anything." He tilts his head backwards to the door behind him.

"Okay."

He looks down at me, his eyes boring into mine, and I wonder if he's going to kiss me. I thought he might earlier, when we first went into the living room after lunch, but he didn't... and he doesn't now. Instead, he steps away and releases my hand.

"Goodnight, Nicki."

"Goodnight."

I open the door to the bedroom and pass through it, closing it behind me. I'm not going to deny I'm disappointed, but I'm also beyond tired, and rather than dwelling on Ed and all the issues that seem to surround our relationship, I walk over to the window and close the curtains, undressing quickly and climbing into bed…

The headlights come straight towards me, faster and faster and try as I might, I can't slow the car. The brakes won't respond, even though I hit them again and again. Nothing happens. I turn the wheel, but the car doesn't deviate, and the lights get bigger and bigger, stronger and stronger, blinding me. I scream… and scream… and scream…

"Nicki… wake up."

I open my eyes to see Ed, perched on the edge of my bed, and I burst into tears.

He reaches for me, pulling me into his arms and holding me there, against his bare chest, the fine hairs tickling my cheek as I sob.

"I couldn't stop the car… the brakes…"

"It was a nightmare. It's not real." He strokes my hair. "I've got you. You're safe now."

I suck in a breath, tilt my head back and look up at him. He's turned on the side light and I can see his face is full of concern, his eyes locked onto mine, and as he brings his hand around from behind my head, cupping my cheek, I let out a sigh, leaning in to him.

"Are you okay now?" His voice is slightly hoarse.

"Yes, thank you."

"Are you sure?"

I nod my head, and he moves his hand away, releasing me and getting to his feet. I hadn't expected that and I lean back, realising now – somewhat belatedly – that because I never wear anything in bed, I'm naked. Grabbing the duvet, I pull it up, although it seems a little pointless now. He's just been holding me, crushed against him… skin to skin.

He steps towards the door, but I reach for his hand, pulling him back.

"I'm sorry, Ed."

"What for?" He frowns down at me.

"For waking you."

His frown deepens, and he tilts his head to one side. "Is that really why you're sorry?"

I hate that he can see through me so easily. "No. If you want me to be honest, I'm sorry that you don't feel you can stay with me."

His frown clears, and he sits back on the edge of the bed. "Do you want me to stay?"

I nod my head. "More than anything." His eyes widen, just slightly. "I want you, Ed. I want us… but you're still so messed up, aren't you?"

He sighs and I sit forward, letting the duvet fall again. I don't care though, and I grab his other hand… his left one… my fingers finding his wedding ring, not that he seems to notice.

"This is my fault," I whisper, staring at his chest.

"No, it's not." I raise my head, looking into his tortured eyes and wishing things could be different.

"Yes, it is. I shouldn't have rushed you."

He shakes his head. "Your memory seems to have been affected by the accident. We had this conversation already. Twice. I told you… you didn't rush me."

"Yes, I did. You said we needed to talk, and I knew that, deep down, myself. Only, I didn't want to wait." A very slight smile twitches at the corners of his lips. "I should have done, though. I should have let you take things at your pace… not mine."

"I know you think I do, but I don't regret it."

"I do."

His face falls. "Why? Did I do something wrong?"

I release his right hand, holding onto the left one still, and place my free hand on his chest, flat against his warm, toned skin.

201

"No, Ed. You did everything right. It was perfect… right until the end, when I realised it was too soon for you. Even now, it's still too soon, isn't it? I know you've said you'll work things out, and I believe you. But think about it… I'm staying here with you for the next few days, and you've put me in the guest room."

"Of course I have. Did you think I'd assume that you'd want to sleep with me after everything that happened? You walked out, Nicki. Actually, you ran out. I don't blame you for that… I hurt you. We might have talked at the hospital, but I don't think we'd resolved anything. We still haven't… not really, so there's no way I was going to presume anything."

He's right, and I know he is. "Okay… but look at us now. I've had a nightmare and you don't even want to stay with me…"

"You think? You think I don't want to get into bed with you and hold you… and comfort you?"

"Then why don't you?"

"Because I wouldn't just be holding you."

"And you think I'd have a problem with that? I already told you I want you, Ed."

He releases his hand from mine and grabs me, pulling me close to him. "I know," he whispers in my ear. "But you've just been in an accident. You're concussed… and besides, you're right… I'm a mess." He leans back, capturing my face with his hands and gazing deep into my eyes.

"You still feel guilty about Suzannah, don't you?"

"Yes. But not for the reasons you think."

He lets me go and stands up again, lifting me up the bed a little and lying me down, my head on the pillows. Then he pulls the duvet back up, covering me, and turns off the lamp again, plunging us into darkness. He doesn't leave, though. Instead, he leans over, his hands either side of me, pinning me to the mattress. I can make out the shadow of him, and feel his breath against my cheek.

"I'm trying to do the right thing here, Nicki, but please don't think this is easy."

"What? Being so messed up? Feeling so guilty?"

"No… walking away from you, going back to my room, alone." He bends his head a little further, his lips brushing against mine, although he doesn't prolong the kiss. He stands up straight. "Get some sleep. I'll see you in the morning. If you need me in the meantime… if you need painkillers, or you have another nightmare, or…" He stops talking and sighs, like he wants to add to that list, but can't. "If you need me, just call."

He leaves, closing the door softly behind him, and although I feel like calling out, 'I need you,' I don't. It wouldn't be fair… to either of us.

I wake, cracking my eyes open, and stretch my arms above my head.

"Ouch!" God, my back hurts and I turn over, hoping to ease the pain. It doesn't work, although I notice the sunlight around the edges of the curtains and wonder what time it is. There's no clock in here, and my phone is still charging in the kitchen.

I sit up, arching my back, which hurts even more, and I twist around, putting my legs over the side of the bed. My feet won't touch the floor, but I shimmy forward until they do, curling my toes into the thick carpet. I need the bathroom, but I can hardly wander around naked, and I didn't bring a bathrobe, either. I correctly anticipated that the hotel would provide one, and I made use of it while I was staying there. A glance at the back of the door tells me there's nothing hanging there, so I get up and wander to the wardrobe in the corner, pulling it open. Peering inside, I discover it's full of shirts, mostly white ones, presumably belonging to Ed, and I reach in and grab one, shrugging it on and letting out a half-laugh when I realise how big it is on me. I'm swamped by it, but that's not a bad thing. At least everything's covered.

I quickly fasten all the necessary buttons and crack open the door. The hall is empty, although I can hear noises coming from the kitchen and I hesitate for a moment or two, wondering if Dan might be in there.

"Ed?" I call out and after just a couple of seconds, he appears at the kitchen door, looking down the hallway at me. He's holding a tea towel, although he lets his hands drop to his sides and gazes at me.

"Y—Yes?" he stutters.

"Is Dan around?"

He smiles. "No, he's downstairs. You're safe to come out."

I step into the hallway, feeling his eyes rake up and down my body as I walk towards him.

"What's the time?"

"Nearly eleven."

"Eleven?" I can't believe it. "Are you serious?"

"Yes. I was going to wake you in about ten minutes. Rory's coming over at twelve to take your statement."

"Oh, good God… I need to shower."

"Don't panic. You've got plenty of time. I'll make some coffee while you're in the bathroom."

"Okay. Thanks."

I head towards the bathroom. "Hey," he says, calling me back.

"Yes?" I turn to face him.

"My shirts never looked that good on me."

I reach for the hem, holding onto it. "I didn't have anything else to put on… sorry."

"Don't apologise. I like it."

I nod my head and duck into the bathroom, leaning back against the door and letting out a long sigh. He might think this isn't easy for him, but it's just as hard for me… especially when he says things like that.

We haven't had time for breakfast, and it was too late for it, anyway. After my shower, Ed changed the dressing on my head, telling me the wound looked better than he'd expected, and Rory arrives a few minutes later, not long after I've finished getting dressed. I'm still sitting in the kitchen drinking the last of my coffee as he gets to the top of the stairs.

"Dan said it was okay to come up," he says with a smile. It might be Boxing Day, but he's in full uniform, and is carrying a small briefcase.

"Of course it is." Ed's over by the sink, but he turns when Rory comes into the room.

"I see you've got him working down there."

"He volunteered, so I can look after Nicki."

Rory turns to me. "How are you feeling?"

"Better than I was, although my back is killing me. Do you think that's normal?"

Ed comes over and stands opposite me, his hands resting on the back of the chair. "You didn't tell me you had backache."

"I didn't get the chance."

"How bad is it?"

"Tolerable. It feels bruised, I suppose."

Rory nods his head, stepping further into the room and sitting down at the head of the table, placing the briefcase on the floor beside him. "I imagine you're going to feel bruised for a few days."

Ed sits too, staring across at me. "Next time something hurts, could you tell me?"

"If you insist."

Rory chuckles, shaking his head slightly. "Can I get you a coffee?" Ed offers, ignoring him.

"Yes, please."

Ed turns to me. "Would you like another?"

I nod my head and he gets up again, making a fresh pot, while I turn to Rory.

"What happens now?" I ask him.

"Well… normally, I'd just make a few notes, and then you'd come over to the station at some point and sign a full statement, but I thought I'd save you the bother." He reaches down for the briefcase, lifting it onto the table and opening it. He pulls out a large notepad before disposing of the briefcase again and pulls a pen from one of his many pockets. "It might take a little longer, but I'll write out the statement now, and you can sign it before I leave."

"Okay. Then it's all done, is it?"

"It should be. The man driving the other vehicle was over the limit… not by as much as I'd expected, but it's enough to charge him. We're also waiting for the results of a toxicology report, which has been delayed because of Christmas."

Ed comes back over, standing beside me, his hand on my shoulder. "Toxicology?" he says.

"Yes." Rory looks up at him.

"You mean he'd been taking drugs?"

"We can't be certain yet, not until we get the results, but when we went through his car first thing this morning, we found what appears to be a small quantity of cocaine in the glove compartment. That's got to be tested too, although Tom's fairly sure he's right about it being cocaine, and he's more experienced with drugs than I am."

"Who's Tom?" I ask and Rory smiles.

"PC Tom Hughes," he says. "He works with me, although he's soon to be my son-in-law."

I nod my head and return his smile.

"I can't believe this," Ed says, and I feel him tense beside me. I place my hand over his, looking up into his livid face.

"Hey… it's okay."

"No, it damn well isn't."

I twist around slightly, so I can see him better. "I'm here, aren't I?"

"Yes, but only because you had the sense to bury your car in a ditch, rather than letting that idiot hit you."

"Is that what I did, then?"

Ed frowns and glances at Rory. "Don't you remember?"

"No."

I turn to Rory, who sucks in a breath, flipping over the first page of his notepad and taking the lid from his pen. "What do you remember?" he says.

"Starting when?"

"Do you remember getting into the car?"

"Yes. It was raining."

He writes everything down as I say it, and Ed gives my shoulder a squeeze, moving away to continue making the coffee. "Had you been drinking?" Rory asks, looking up at me again.

"I had a glass of wine with dinner, much earlier in the evening, but I'd only been drinking tonic water at the pub."

"Okay." Rory makes a few more notes and then sighs, leaning back in his seat, his expression much more serious. "Were you… feeling all right?"

"How do you mean?"

He glances at Ed. "Were you upset?" I wonder how much he knows… whether Ed's told him what happened on Christmas Eve.

"I was, but if you're asking whether I was in control of the car, the answer is yes. I wouldn't have driven if I wasn't."

He nods his head. "I'm sorry. I had to ask."

"It's okay. You're just doing your job." I smile at him. "It's the first time I've really seen you being a policeman."

"Hmm... it's just a shame you're getting to see it as the victim of a crime." Ed comes over and puts our coffees down in front of us, sitting beside me now, rather than on the other side of the table, and Rory takes a deep breath. "What can you remember after getting into the car?"

"Driving away from the hotel. There was no traffic, and I got to the junction and turned right onto the main road. I put the radio on and then slowed down to take the bend... and then..." My voice cracks. "And then the headlights were coming straight at me." My hands are shaking. "I—I couldn't see properly. I was blinded by the lights, and I started to scream."

Ed puts his arm around me, pulling me closer to him. "Can you remember anything else at all?" Rory asks.

"Not really. I just remember screaming and then it all went black. I don't recall actively thinking about driving into the ditch, or even doing anything to avoid the other car. He was going to hit me... I was convinced of it." I shudder, and Ed holds me a little tighter. "There was rain on my face, though... I remember that." I turn to Rory, feeling confused. "And you were looking down at me. I wanted Ed, too... but he wasn't there."

Rory smiles. "That was later, when the paramedics were putting you into the ambulance. You were asking for Ed, and I told you I'd get him."

"Did you? I don't remember that. I don't remember anything at all after that... not until I woke up in the hospital."

Rory nods his head. "Okay. Talk amongst yourselves for a few minutes while I just write this up, then you can sign it and I can get out of your hair." He takes a sip of coffee and puts pen to paper, while Ed turns me in my seat so I'm facing him.

"You wanted me?" he says, with a slight smile.

"Didn't we already establish that… last night?" I whisper.

"Yes, but Christmas Eve was different. I'd hurt you. Badly. And yet you still wanted me?"

"Hmm… it's an instinct, I think. I was angry with you. I'm not going to say I wasn't. What you'd said to Dan had hurt me a lot, but I've wanted you all my life, Ed. You're like a magnet, and I don't think I can stop being drawn to you… not now."

He gazes right into my eyes. "That's good to know."

"Why? Are you planning on hurting me again?"

"No. But I know I'm asking a lot of you. I guess it's just nice to know you're not going to give up on us."

"Honestly… I thought I was the one with concussion, not you. I told you yesterday morning at the hospital, I won't give up."

He smiles more fully. "I know, but after last night, I thought you might have changed your mind."

"No. You were right about that. I felt rejected when you went back to your room, but…"

"Oh, God… that wasn't what I wanted. I didn't mean for you to feel like that." He sits forward, frowning, and I reach out, placing my hands on his upper arms.

"It's okay."

"No, it's not. Nicki, if I'd stayed…"

"We'd have ended up regretting it. I understand that."

He pulls back. "No. That's not what I was going to say. I wouldn't have regretted it at all. I told you last night, I don't regret what happened between us on Christmas Eve, other than that I hurt you afterwards. What I'm trying to say is, if I'd stayed with you last night, it would just have added to the confusion… up here." He taps the side of his head. "And that's not what we need right now… not when I'm trying to straighten it all out."

Rory coughs and I jump, letting go of Ed, who looks over my shoulder, raising his eyebrows.

"I'm finished," Rory says.

I'd forgotten he was there, and I blush, looking up at Ed, who seems completely unfazed by the fact that we've just been having an intimate conversation in front of our oldest friend.

I turn around, hoping Rory won't notice the flush creeping up my cheeks.

"If you can just read that through," he says, pushing the notepad towards me. "And if you're happy with it, sign at the bottom."

If he has noticed my embarrassment, or overheard any of our conversation, he's polite enough not to comment, and I pick up the notepad, reading his printed words.

"How are Tom and Gemma getting on with planning the wedding?" Ed asks, sipping his coffee.

"All I'll say is, thank God I've got Laura to keep me sane." Rory's reply makes me chuckle under my breath, but I don't say anything and keep reading.

"Why?" Ed asks. "From what Gemma told me when she and Tom came to talk to me about the reception, I thought everything was under control."

"It is."

"Then I don't understand what the problem is."

"The problem is Tom."

"Don't tell me you've changed your mind about him?" Ed says. "I thought you liked him."

"I do. I just hadn't realised how much money he got from selling his house up in Wimbledon, or that he'd insist on spending so much of it on the wedding."

"Ahh... and this dents your fatherly pride, does it?" Ed says, and I glance up to see him smiling.

"Yes, if you must know," Rory replies. "The only thing he's let me pay for so far is Gemma's dress."

"You mean, he's paying for the wedding and the reception, and everything?" I ask, interrupting my reading, and Rory looks across at me.

"The wedding's being held at the church, and Tom's paying all the fees for that," he says. "And Ed's refusing to charge a penny for the reception."

I look at Ed, and he smiles, shrugging his shoulders. "It's my wedding present… to Gemma."

"It's a very over-the-top wedding present." Rory sounds resigned, although Ed just huffs, and I go back to my reading, nearing the end. "Oh, I don't know… I'm starting to think I should just give in gracefully, and be thankful for small mercies."

"Such as?" Ed says.

"Such as the fact that I'm fairly sure Tom and Gemma are going to make me a grandfather before too long, and that means they'll need a bigger house. It's good to know he can afford it."

I put down the notepad, my reading complete, and as I sign my name at the bottom, I can't help chuckling. "Who'd have thought…? Rory Quick, a grandfather."

"Not just a grandfather. Keep it to yourselves, but with any luck, I'll be a father again before too long."

I drop the pen and Ed reaches out, putting his arm around me.

"Sorry," Rory says. "Did I say the wrong thing?"

"No, it's fine." I look up at him. "It's just that…" I can't say the words and I turn to Ed.

"Nicki can't have children," he says.

"Oh, God… I'm sorry." Rory looks so troubled, I put my hand out to him across the table, and he takes it.

"It's okay… really. I've had years to get used to it. It never normally bothers me. I expect it's just the accident making me more emotional, or something."

Neither of them says a word, and I pull my hand back and push the notepad over to Rory.

"I didn't realise Laura was pregnant," Ed says, frowning. "She was drinking white wine the other night, and…"

"She's not pregnant yet," Rory says, smiling again. "She wanted to have all the work done on the house first, and she's been really busy at the hotel lately, but we're…"

"Getting there?" Ed says, grinning.

"Something like that." Rory looks down at the notepad, checks everything, and then picks up the briefcase from beside him, putting the notepad away again. "I'll leave you two in peace," he says, getting to his feet and looking down at me. "Your car's at the garage and Tim's said he'll call you in the next few days."

"You've spoken to him already? Even though it's Boxing Day?"

"Yes. He didn't mind. And I hope it's okay, but I got Laura to give me your mobile number, which I've put on the file and passed on to Tim. I didn't want to disturb you, and I knew she'd have it at work."

"Of course I don't mind."

He nods his head. "You should probably contact your insurance company too… not that they'll be open today."

"No. I'll do it tomorrow."

"I'll help you, if you like," Ed says, and I turn and give him a smile.

He stands and shows Rory to the top of the stairs, although he insists he can find his own way out from there, and Ed comes back into the kitchen.

"I don't know about you, but I feel like some fresh air."

"Shall we go to the café for lunch?"

"Could we?"

He smiles. "Of course. Go and get some shoes on."

I do as he says, but I'm just slipping them on when I realise I've got a problem, and I go back out into the hall again, to find Ed waiting for me with his coat on, and a fleece hoodie in his hand.

"This is going to be enormous on you," he says, holding it up for me to put on, and I turn and let him slip it over my shoulders. "But it'll be better than nothing."

"I was just coming to tell you I don't have a wearable coat… but it seems you worked it out for yourself."

"Yes. Yours is going to need dry cleaning."

"If it's even salvageable."

"Well, you can worry about that another day," he says, turning me around to zip up the hoodie. "The main thing is, you're in one piece." He smiles, "And you look utterly adorable."

"This is very warm." I hug all the excess material around myself.

"That's just as well, because it's freezing outside." He offers his hand and I take it. "Ready?" he says and I nod my head.

He's not wrong. It's freezing cold. But at least it's not raining, and the sun is trying its best to shine. Ed holds my hand and together we wander along the harbour, stopping when we reach the café. He opens the door, and we're greeted by a waft of warm air and the smell of coffee and bacon. I go in ahead of him, instantly reminded of the last time we came here, when he apologised for inviting Rory and Laura to the pub.

"Shall we sit over there?" he says, nodding to a table nearer the back of the café, well away from the one we sat at before.

"Okay." I lead the way, stopping by the vacant table, and he holds my chair while I sit down, before removing his coat and taking a seat opposite me.

The man who served us last time comes over, looking down at me. "Are you feeling better?" he asks, and I smile up at him.

"Yes, thank you."

"Good," he says. "I'll give you a minute or two to decide what you want."

"Thanks, Carter," Ed replies, and the man goes away again.

"How did he know?" I whisper, leaning across the table.

"This is Porthgarrion. Everyone knows."

I smile, and he hands me a menu. I decide on the goat's cheese and pepper toasted sandwich and after some deliberation, Ed says he'll have the same and when Carter comes back, Ed gives him our order, adding two coffees.

He reaches for my hand and I take it, waiting while he shifts his chair a little closer to the table and leans forward. "Can I ask you something?" he says in a low voice.

"Of course."

"Why did you really get upset when you told Rory you can't have children? It wasn't anything to do with the accident, was it? And you didn't get upset when you told me, so…" His voice fades, like he doesn't know what to say next.

"I suppose it was thinking about the two of them having a baby… about Rory having a second chance at fatherhood, and realising you'll never know how that feels, if we're together."

"That's not an if," he says, raising his voice slightly above its earlier whisper.

"So, you're okay with it? I mean, it's easier for me. I'm resigned to it now, but this is all new to you. If you need some time to think it over…"

"I don't."

"But Ed… we never really talked about how you feel, did we? We didn't discuss how this impacts on you."

"No. Because we don't need to. I love you for you, Nicki."

"Thank you." I smile at him.

"You don't have to thank me for loving you."

"I wasn't."

"Then what were you thanking me for?"

"Being you."

He shakes his head and opens his mouth to reply, just as Carter arrives with our coffee, and I'm pleased for the interruption. I'm sure Ed had been about to tell me that being him isn't such a great thing right now, or words to that effect, and I'd just like to enjoy the moment, knowing that us being together isn't an 'if', and that he loves me.

Lunch is delicious and when Ed's paid – which he insisted on – we leave the café and make our way slowly back along the harbour. It's been nice to get out, but I'm tired again now, and the sofa is beckoning…

"Nicole? I mean… Miss Woodward?" I turn at the sound of my name and almost groan out loud when I see Kieran crossing the road towards us. We stop walking as he steps up onto the kerb and he glances at the dressing on my head. "How are you? I heard about your accident."

"It seems everyone did," I say with a smile. "And I'm fine, thank you."

"Really? That looks painful."

"It's not that bad. Honestly, Kieran."

"You checked out of the hotel. Are you…?"

"I'm staying with Ed," I say, leaning in to him just a little. Ed squeezes my hand, and Kieran glances at him before returning his gaze to me.

"Oh… I see. Well, I hope you get better soon." He seems embarrassed now and before I can say anything else, he nods his head and turns, walking away, towards the hotel.

Ed looks down at me, but doesn't say a thing, and we turn in the opposite direction, making our way back to the pub.

Once inside, we go upstairs and he takes off his jacket, leaving it over the banisters before he leads me into the living room, turning to me before we've sat down.

"So, that was Kieran?"

"Yes."

He nods his head. "Strange, isn't it… to think Rory was worried about him, when it should have been me all along?"

"You think you should have been worrying about Kieran?"

"Yes."

I step closer, looking up into his eyes. "You've got nothing to worry about, Ed."

"Really? He's very good looking."

"I know. He's also very young. Can you believe, he asked me out?"

"Yes, I can. I think I even know when he did it."

"You do?"

"Yes. It was the other night, when you came to the pub and I was too busy to spend any time with you."

He's right of course, but… "How did you know?"

"Because when I got to the hotel, coming to see you, he was just leaving. He looked miserable."

"He did?"

"Yeah. I didn't understand it at the time, and to be honest, it was none of my business, and I was more concerned with seeing you and apologising. But now, it makes sense. If he'd asked you out, and you'd turned him down, his reaction is perfectly understandable."

"How do you know I turned him down?" He frowns, like he's unsure of himself, and I lean in a little closer. "It's okay. You don't have to look so worried. I might have been upset that night, but that didn't mean I was going to jump at the next man who came along."

He grabs me, pulling me into his arms.

"That's a relief."

He blinks twice and then, with a low growl, he closes the gap between us, crushing his lips to mine. He deepens the kiss, our bodies fused, and as he flexes his hips, I feel his arousal, pressing into me. His breathing changes and his hands come between us, undoing the zip of the hoodie. He doesn't take it off, just pushes it open, his hands wandering… one of them roaming around my back, resting there and pulling me closer, while the other caresses my breast through the flimsy material of my blouse.

He pinches my nipple, squeezing it between his finger and thumb, and I squeal, then sigh into him, pleasure pooling at my core. I want him so much, and it feels like he wants me too. I bring my hands up onto his shoulders and he stills, then stops, and finally pulls back, my hands falling to my sides again as he steps away, pushing his fingers back through his hair.

"I'm sorry, Nicki," he says, breathing hard. "That really wasn't playing fair. I shouldn't have done that."

So much for enjoying moments.

"Didn't you want me, then?"

"You know I did. You know I do." He turns, looking up at the ceiling. "It's just…"

"It's too hard, isn't it?" He doesn't answer, but he doesn't need to. We both know I'm right. I reach out, letting my fingers caress his arm, just to get his attention, and he looks back at me, a pained expression on his face. "Can you take me home, Ed?"

The pain becomes shock. "Are you kidding?"

"No. I think you need some time alone to work out all the conflicts in your head. You said earlier that staying with me last night would only have added to all your confusion, and now, look at you… you're beating yourself up over a kiss. I think it would be easier for you if I remove myself from the scene to give you some space to think… by yourself."

"Well, I don't agree." He shakes his head. "And I also don't believe you."

"What about?"

"About the reasons you want to go home. You told me I was a magnet for you, and now you want to leave? That doesn't make sense... unless there's something you're not telling me."

"Well, if you think it's got something to do with Kieran..."

"I don't care about Kieran. I care about you, and why you want to leave me... again."

"Because I need some distance... okay?" I raise my voice, and he reaches out, grabbing me and pulling me into his arms.

"Why, Nicki? Tell me why."

"Because this is really hard for me too, Ed. I love you, and I love hearing you say you love me. I've waited so long to hear those words, and I want that life, all the time. But knowing you're having to fight your demons just to say those things, and just to be with me... it's not a great feeling."

He lets me go, but only for long enough to move his hands up, clasping my face. "I'm sorry."

"Will you please stop apologising? I don't want you to be sorry."

"Then what do you want?"

"You. I've always wanted you, for as long as I can remember. But I can't do this anymore."

His breath stutters and I hear him choke. "N—Nic... wait a second. You said you weren't going to give up. You said you couldn't."

"I know, and I'm not. I'll never give up. But I can't watch you do battle with your memories. I need to be somewhere else while you work things out for yourself."

"And when I've done that?"

"Then come and tell me. Tell me you're free, and you're mine."

"I'm already yours."

"Maybe. But you're not free, are you?"

He sighs, letting his head fall forward and resting it on top of mine. "I'm not taking you home… not today. You only came out of hospital yesterday, and you were just saying this morning about how bruised your back is feeling."

"Okay. If you won't take me today, can we at least compromise on tomorrow? My mum's neighbours will be back by then. They'll keep an eye on me."

He leans back again, looking down at me, an agonised expression on his face. "If you insist, I'll take you back to Bath after breakfast. I should be able to get you there by lunchtime."

I frown up at him. "Bath? I don't live in Bath."

"You don't?"

"No. I live in Mevagissey."

"I thought…"

"Mum and Dad moved to a bungalow in Mevagissey and I moved in with Mum after she had her stroke."

"I see." He lets go of my face and puts his arms around me, hugging me close to him. "This isn't what I want, Nicki."

"It isn't what I want either, but I'll only be forty-five minutes away."

"Forty-five minutes? The moment you walk out of my door, you'll be too far away, but if taking you home means I'll eventually get you back here for good, then I'll do it."

Chapter Eighteen

Ed

I thought about picking Nicki up, carrying her through to my bedroom, throwing her onto the mattress, ripping off her clothes – mine too, obviously – and making love to her. I thought about it for maybe ten or twenty seconds, picturing us writhing in each other's arms, the images searing into my mind… and then I decided against it. As much as I wanted her – and I do want her – making love to her won't help. I can't even kiss her without my memories getting in the way, and I wish now I hadn't done that, even if it felt too good for words.

Maybe she's right. Maybe having her here isn't helping… but watching the process of her leaving is tearing me apart.

She packed her things last night while I made us something to eat. I know this is just about her giving me space, but it feels like so much more, and I didn't want to bear witness to her imminent departure.

It's strange, but I've eaten from the pub menu for ages, rather than cooking just for myself, and when I finally got the chance to cook for someone else, I couldn't enjoy it. I kept wanting to go into Nicki's room and beg her to stay. I pictured her sitting me down on the edge of the bed and explaining to me – yet again – that it makes sense for her to leave. Maybe it does. But that doesn't mean I want her to go.

We ate in the kitchen, in silence, and afterwards, we went to bed. Nicki was tired and I think we both knew there wasn't very much left to say to each other. I lay awake all night, wondering about going in to her. Making love was out of the question… it would have been the ultimate in not playing fair. But I wondered about climbing into bed with her, and just holding her in my arms. She was only a few feet away, and I knew that tomorrow that distance would stretch to twenty-five miles. That thought was killing me, and I got out of bed on more than one occasion, making it to the door and even opening it a couple of times, before common sense got the better of me. I knew if I went to her, it would be impossible for me to ever let her go.

"Ready?"

I spin around at the sound of Nicki's voice, almost spilling my coffee, and I suck in a breath. I wasn't kidding yesterday when I told her she looked adorable wearing my hoodie. It swamps her, but she makes it look so sexy.

I put down my cup and wander over, taking her case, and she looks up into my eyes.

"Are you sure you don't mind me borrowing this?" she says, tugging on the hem of the hoodie.

"Not at all."

"I've got other coats at home, so I can return it to you."

"Keep it. It looks better on you, anyway."

She sighs, glancing around. "I think I've got everything." She heads for the stairs, but then stops and turns. "Say goodbye to Dan for me?"

"You'll see him again, Nicki. This isn't forever."

"I know. But I'd forgotten he was going to see Sam this morning and I feel bad for leaving without saying goodbye."

I nod, unable to say any more. I'd forgotten Dan had arranged to see Sam too, but it's understandable for both of us. We've had a lot on our minds. Nicki smiles, although it doesn't touch her eyes, and then she turns and starts down the stairs. I follow with her case, and when we get to the bottom, she waits while I grab my coat, shrugging it on, and pocket my keys before opening the back door. She takes a half step forward, but as she does, I slam the door shut again.

"Don't. Don't leave." I drop her case, stepping into her path.

She looks up at me, her eyes filling with tears. "I—I have to, Ed. Please don't make this any harder."

"I'm not." Desperation gets the better of me and I move closer, cupping her cheek with my hand. "I'm not making it hard at all. I'm making it easy. Stay here with me."

"I can't."

"Yes, you can. I love you."

She covers my hand with hers. It feels even smaller than usual. "I know. And I love you too." She sighs, closing her eyes, which releases a single tear onto her cheek. "How many times do we have to have this conversation? How many times do I have to remind you… you're not free."

"What is it you need? Do you need me to say I've stopped loving Suzannah?"

"No. I'll never ask that of you." She frowns. "I don't know how to put this without it sounding like I'm jealous, but I don't want to keep looking over my shoulder, Ed. I know how much you loved Suzannah… I know you always will. She was everything to you, and I can accept all that, but…"

I move my hand, placing my fingers across her lips to stop her from talking. "I need to tell you something. It's something I probably should have told you before now, but I'm not exactly proud of myself, and…"

She pulls my hand away, taking it in hers, and tilts her head, staring up at me. "What is it, Ed?"

"I—I've painted a picture of Suzannah and myself having the perfect marriage."

"That's because you did," she says, her brow furrowing. "You were always so happy together, even when I was living here, before you got married."

"I know. I'm not trying to say we weren't happy, but if I'm being honest, I think I was happier than she was."

"What do you mean?"

"I mean, I was selfish. I didn't realise at the time how selfish, but when we took over the pub, I just assumed she'd want to go along with it."

"I know. You told me about this."

"I didn't tell you everything. I didn't tell you I guilt-tripped her into letting me spend our savings on fixing up the kitchens here, and that she went along with it… because she loved me."

"So? People do things like that all the time. It's called making compromises."

"In this instance, it should be called making sacrifices. I was so busy thinking about what I wanted, I never really considered her feelings, or what she was giving up for me."

"Why? What was she giving up?"

I take a breath. "I've never told anyone this… not even Rory, but Suzannah wanted us to have more children."

Nicki frowns. "Why couldn't you?"

I shrug my shoulders. "I suppose there was nothing stopping us. Except I didn't know it was what she wanted… at least not until she laid it all out before me."

"When was that?"

"Oddly enough, it was her last Christmas."

"She waited that long to tell you?"

"Yes. And even then, it only came up by accident, really. We were being a bit nostalgic, sitting upstairs and talking about the past, and I asked her if she had any regrets. We'd made a genuine success of things here, and I suppose I half expected her to say she regretted moving here still, and that I'd be able to counter that argument with how well we were doing… except she didn't say that at all. She told me she'd wanted us to have more children."

"But surely you still could have done. She wasn't that old."

"No, she wasn't. I told her it wasn't too late, but she said 'no'. We'd made our lives here, thanks to me. Dan was a teenager, and the thought of that kind of age gap was too much for her… so that meant no more kids."

"Why didn't she mention it sooner, then?" Nicki asks, shaking her head. "If she had, there wouldn't have needed to be such an age gap."

"I don't know. I didn't ask her. To be honest, I was in too much shock to think straight. I just felt that I'd let her down… again."

"But you weren't to know… not if she hadn't told you."

"I think she thought I should have worked it out without her having to tell me… and I should have done, shouldn't I? We were supposed to know everything about each other."

"No… you were supposed to tell each other everything. You're not psychic."

I smile, unable to help myself. "That's why I hate it when people say there's nothing wrong, even when there is. Suzannah used to do that all the time… and look where it got us. I couldn't give her the thing she wanted most, because I didn't even know she wanted it."

"Why are you telling me this?" she asks, tipping her head to one side. "Are you trying to warn me off?"

"No. I know I was selfish back then, but I changed a lot when Suzannah died."

She shakes her head, bringing up her free hand and resting it on my chest. "You weren't selfish, Ed. I loved her dearly, but in this instance, I think Suzannah was the selfish one."

"How do you work that out?"

"Because she made the decision about you having more children all by herself. She didn't give you any say in the matter."

"No… it was the other way around. I was the one who moved us here, to a place where she didn't want to live, let alone raise our child… or children."

"That's not what I'm hearing. She could have said 'no' to moving here, and to spending all your savings, but she didn't. She said 'yes'…"

"Reluctantly."

"Even if it was with some reluctance, she still said 'yes'. And then she took the unilateral decision that, as a result, you wouldn't have any more children… without even discussing it with you. If she'd explained at the time that she'd wanted to have another baby, but that moving here would make it impossible for her, what would you have done?"

"I don't know. It would have complicated everything, but I'd probably have found a way around it. We could have moved in here for a while, maybe done the work and got this place up and running and then found a house somewhere and installed a manager to run the pub, I guess. Something like that, anyway."

"Exactly. You'd have compromised."

"Yes, but I didn't, did I? Because I wasn't listening."

"No, Ed. Suzannah wasn't talking. She wasn't telling you how she felt, or what she wanted. If she had been, you'd have moved heaven and earth to make it happen… because you loved her. Only she didn't give you the chance. Even later on, once you'd made a success of things, she still could have told you how she felt, so you could have worked things out… but she didn't, and you can't keep blaming yourself for that. It was her decision, Ed. She chose to live the life you'd both made for yourselves…"

I gaze down into her eyes. "God… I love you."

She smiles. "I love you too. But you still haven't explained why you're telling me this story."

"I suppose it's because I want you to understand that things aren't always what they seem. Everyone thought Suzannah and I had the perfect marriage, but scratch the surface and…"

"It was still pretty damn perfect, Ed. Don't kid yourself."

"I'm not. Suzannah and I were very happy together, and I still love her very much… I always will. But I suppose what I'm trying to say is, don't be fooled by appearances. The muddle in my head… the guilt over being with you… it's not what you think it is."

She gazes up at me. "Whether it is, or it isn't, I can't stay. That muddle in your head is still there, and until you work it out, we can't be happy together."

She may be right, but I wish it didn't have to be this way.

I park my car outside a neat-looking bungalow. It's rendered and painted white, with a ramp leading up to the front door. The bungalows on either side have steps, so I guess the ramp might have been installed after Nicki's mum had her stroke. There's a garage to one side, with a narrow driveway – too narrow for my car – and the small garden is paved, with a few pots scattered around. They're barren at the moment, but that's to be expected at this time of year.

Nicki looks over at me and I open my mouth to beg her to let me drive her back to Porthgarrion. I stop myself from actually saying the words, but that doesn't mean I want to leave her here, any more than I did when I finally closed the door on the pub, having told her about Suzannah. I felt I had to tell her that, to let her know that my marriage hadn't always been perfect… and that I'm certainly not. Her response was so typical of Nicki, though. She's always been so fair… so reasonable, and while I know she probably just wanted to make me feel better, I have to admit, she was right. Suzannah could have told me sooner. It was one of the things I struggled with the most after she died… the time we'd wasted, that could have been spent making her even happier, giving her what she wanted, if only she'd been honest. I used to be overwhelmed with guilt that I'd denied her all of that, but in reality, Nicki's right. Suzannah denied it to herself.

And to me.

"Okay?" I say, instead of, 'Please come back with me,' and she nods her head. I manage a slight smile and get out of the car, going around to Nicki's side to help her. I don't lift her out, just like I didn't lift her in, but I hold her hand while she jumps down, and then I release her, opening the back door to retrieve her case.

Inside, the house feels reasonably warm and as she puts her keys away, she turns to me. "I left the heating on low while I was away, just so it didn't get too cold in here."

"Good idea." I'm still holding her case. "Where would you like me to put this?"

"Oh… my bedroom," she says, and I glance around at the four closed doors I can see from here, not allowing for the fact that the hall goes around a corner, and that there are presumably yet more rooms.

"Which way?"

She smiles and turns to her left, ignoring all the doors, and walks around the corner, opening the one at the very end.

"This used to be Mum's room," she says as I follow her in, observing the double bed and fitted wardrobes, and the view over the back garden. There's a door in the corner which is open and seems to lead to an ensuite bathroom.

"Used to be?"

"Yes. Dad liked to be able to look out over the garden, so they chose it as their bedroom and had the ensuite installed. Don't worry, I haven't moved myself in here since Mum died. But after her stroke, we quickly established that the ensuite wasn't practical for her anymore. It's not very big, and she was using a walking frame, and couldn't turn around, so we moved her into the bedroom that's right beside the main bathroom, and had them both adapted." I put her case down on the end of the bed and turn to see her looking around the room. "It worked out well," she says, like she's thinking it through. "At least I got to feel like this was my private space… like I hadn't given up everything."

"Even though you had." I wander over, putting my hands on her waist and looking down into her eyes. "I'm sure she appreciated it, Nicki."

Her eyes fill with tears. "I know she did." She blinks a few times and smiles up at me. "Shall I make some coffee?"

I nod my head, even though I'm not sure it's a wise decision. Staying and having coffee feels like we're just prolonging the inevitable pain of leaving, but I don't want to go yet, and I follow her back the way we came, by-passing three more closed doors, until we come to one that Nicki opens, revealing a kitchen, with cream coloured units and a granite work surface. It's spotless and functional, but I suppose it probably had to be. Nicki goes to the corner, picking up the kettle, and then puts it down again, turning to me, her hand covering her mouth for a second, before she lowers it.

"I've just realised. I don't have any milk. In fact, I don't have anything at all. The fridge is bare and the cupboards are fairly empty, too… and I don't even have a car to get to the supermarket, do I?"

I go over, taking her hands in mine and holding them between us. "No." I want to say that this is another good reason for her to come back home with me, but I don't. "We'll worry about food in a minute, but speaking of your car, I said I'd help you with the insurance claim today, didn't I?"

"I know, but it's fine. Gerald won't mind going through it with me."

I take a half step back, staring down into her eyes. "Um… who's Gerald?"

She smiles and pulls one of her hands from mine, resting it on my chest. "No-one for you to worry about. He's the next-door neighbour. He and his wife, Shirley, have known my mum for years, and since I've been living here, they've been really kind to me. They're coming back from their daughter's sometime today."

I nod my head. "I see… these are the people you said would keep an eye on you?"

"Yes."

"And you're sure Gerald won't mind helping?"

"I'm positive. I'm more concerned about the fact that I've got no food."

"I'll go to the supermarket for you, if you like, while you unpack."

"I think I'd rather come with you. I can unpack later. It'll give me something to do… to take my mind off…"

"Off what?"

"Missing you."

"I'm so glad you said that." She stares into my eyes. "I'm going to miss you, too." I don't know what I'm going to do to take my mind off of how empty my flat is going to feel without her. Avoid it, I suppose, and work.

She smiles. "I'm glad you said that, too. But I think I should come shopping with you, anyway. I don't know when I'll have a car, so I'll need to stock up."

"Okay… although I don't think you'll need to panic. Your insurance company will probably sort you out a courtesy car quite quickly."

She nods her head and steps closer, her hand still burning a hole in my chest. "Maybe they will… but I'd rather spend a little more time with you."

I smile, resisting the temptation to kiss her and then lead her back out of the house and into my car.

The supermarket is fairly quiet and although Nicki hasn't made a list, we make quick work of filling a trolley with everything she thinks she'll need for the next few days. She still doesn't seem convinced about the courtesy car, but reassures me that either Shirley or Gerald will pick up anything she runs out of… or even give her a lift to the supermarket, should it be necessary.

When we get back, I help her unpack everything and then she makes us a coffee, while we both set out the cold meats and cheeses we've just bought for lunch, along with the bread, and put it all onto a tray, which I carry through to the living room, setting it down on the low coffee table in front of the sofa. This is another functional room, with what appears to be a recliner chair set well away from the far wall, and a large television in the corner.

"Excuse the lack of festive cheer," Nicki says, sitting on the sofa.

I join her. "Don't worry about it."

She hands me a plate from the tray. "It didn't feel right putting up a Christmas tree before Mum's funeral, and then I decided to go away, so it wasn't worth it."

"You don't have to explain. It may have escaped your notice, but I don't have any Christmas decorations in the flat either."

She frowns. "Is that something to do with Suzannah? Have you not bothered since her death?"

"It's got nothing to do with her. I'll admit I keep it simple. I'm not one of those people who puts up their tree on the first of December, but I usually manage it by the week before Christmas."

"But you didn't this year?"

I shake my head. "No... because there's only so much Christmas a man can take, and thanks to Leanne, the fairy lights in the pub are burning holes in my retina." She laughs, throwing her head back, and my heart lurches in my chest. "God... I love that sound." She stills, looking right at me, and biting on her bottom lip. "Can I call you?"

"Do you want to?"

"Yes. I know I need to think, but there's no way I'll be able to function, let alone think, if I can't at least hear your voice."

"I'll give you my number."

She sits, waiting, and I put down my empty plate, pulling my phone from my pocket and tapping her number into my contacts list as she recites it. Once it's saved, I look up at her.

"I want to call you now, and I haven't even left yet."

"Oh... that's such a lovely thing to say."

"I mean it, Nicki. I'm really going to miss you."

"I'm going to miss you, too."

I want to ask her why it has to be this way, why we have to miss each other at all, but I already know the answer, and deep down, I know she's right.

I'd have happily stayed with Nicki forever. Prolonging the agony didn't matter anymore. I just didn't want to leave. But I kept telling myself I had to, and I set a mental deadline of four o'clock. Any later than that and my stay was likely to stretch into the evening... and maybe beyond.

So, at five to four, I told her it was time for me to be going, and although she hesitated for a moment or two, she agreed, and we headed for the front door, opening it just as Nicki's neighbours came home. I felt a little disappointed by that. I'd hoped for a quiet farewell, and maybe a kiss or two out by my car, so I couldn't be tempted to take it further... but it seemed that wasn't to be. Nicki insisted on introducing me, and I wondered how she'd go about it... what she'd call me. In the end, she just told them I was 'Ed', and nothing more. She didn't call me her boyfriend, and I can't blame her for that... not after everything that's happened. They didn't seem to notice anything odd about her introduction and were far more interested in knowing why she was wearing a dressing on her head, and then hearing all about her accident. Once that had been explained, Shirley asked Nicki to join them for a take-away that evening.

"Oh... I'm not sure." Nicki looked up at me, as though she needed my approval, or maybe just my opinion.

"I think you should." I didn't like the idea of her being on her own, and she turned to Shirley and accepted with a smile.

Shirley and Gerald both reassured me they'd look after Nicki, maybe sensing somehow that I wasn't just 'Ed', but that I meant something more, even if Nicki wasn't prepared to articulate it, and then Nicki walked me to my car. We couldn't have that quiet farewell, and we certainly couldn't kiss – not with her neighbours watching us – so I just told her I'd call, but that if she needed me she had to promise she'd call me. She did, and then I got into the car and drove away.

The journey back to Porthgarrion has been difficult. Every mile feels like it's breaking off another piece of me and by the time I park up behind the pub, it's like there's nothing left... like I'm a shell of the man I used to be. I stare out through the windscreen, unable to focus on anything. I could be anywhere, because without Nicki, I'm nowhere... I'm nothing.

I pull my phone from my pocket, and although I'm desperate to hear her voice, I know she could well be with Shirley and Gerald, and won't be able to talk properly anyway, so I go to my message app, find her contact details and type...

— ***Hi. I just got home, although it doesn't feel like home without you. I'm sitting in the car behind the pub, and I want to drive straight back to you. Would that be so wrong? Would it be wrong of me to drive back there and hold you, and never let you go? I know you're going to say 'yes' to that, because you think I'm not free yet, but I miss you so much, Nicki. xx***

I press 'send' and look up, the lights on the outside of the pub blurring slightly.

"Oh, God..." I mutter and get out of the car. How the hell am I supposed to do this?

My phone beeps in my hand and, although it's cold, I lean back against the closed car door, clicking on the message which Nicki's just sent.

— ***It wouldn't be wrong. It just wouldn't be very wise. We'd only end up back where we started, and I don't think either of us could handle that. I know I asked for this, Ed, but please don't think it's any easier for me than it is for you. I miss you too, and I'd give anything to be in your arms right now. N xx***

I let out a long sigh, staring up at the clear night sky, the stars twinkling and a chill settling around my shoulders, before I look down and type out my reply...

— ***I'm starting to think wisdom is overrated. I promise I will work this out as quickly as I can, but in***

the meantime, will you promise me something in return? xx
— *What's that? xx*
— *Promise you'll wait for me? xx*

My phone rings and I glance down at the screen, pressing on the green button the moment I see Nicki's name appear.

"Of course I'll wait for you," she says before I can even say 'hello'. "I've already waited more than half my life for you, Ed, so what's a little while longer?"

"It's a lifetime. Every second without you is like a lifetime." She doesn't reply, although I can hear her breathing, so I know she's still there. "Nicki, are you okay?"

"Yes... it's just that when you say things like that, I want you to come back and hold me and never let me go. But then I remember how you reacted after we made love, and after you kissed me, and..."

"And you can't forgive me?"

"It's not about forgiving you. There's nothing to forgive."

"Yes, there is. I hurt you."

"I know. But this isn't about that, is it?"

"No." She's right. It's not, and there's no point in me arguing otherwise. We've talked it over too many times now.

"Just promise me that the moment you know you're free... the moment you know you can give yourself to me completely, without looking back, and without regrets, you'll come to me."

"I promise, Nicki. I promise I'll come back to you."

"A free man?"

"A free man. The man you deserve."

She falls silent again and then says, "I'd better go. I was supposed to be at Shirley and Gerald's ten minutes ago."

"I thought you'd already be there. That was why I sent a text message, rather than calling."

"I was on my way out of the door when your message came in."

"Well, you go... and have a lovely evening."

"Without you?" I hear her sigh. "What are you going to do tonight?"

"Work. It's a plan I have to take my mind off missing you. I don't expect it'll succeed, but it's better than sitting upstairs by myself, wishing you could be with me."

"Hmm... I've decided to spend the next few days packing up the house to get it ready to sell. It'll keep me occupied, and stop me from wishing I could be with you, too."

"Why are we punishing ourselves, Nic? Why are we ?"

"Please, Ed... I can't go over it again. We've already said everything that needs to be said, too many times."

"Okay. I'm sorry... I'm sorry, Nicki."

"I'm sorry, too."

"You've got nothing to be sorry for. Go and have dinner with your neighbours. I won't be finished until late tonight, so I'll call you in the morning, okay?"

"Okay... and Ed?"

"Yes?"

"I love you."

"I love you too, Nic."

I hear her sob just before the line cuts out and I drop my phone into my coat pocket as I turn around, resting my elbows against the top of the car, my head in my hands.

I thought I knew everything there was to know about pain... but it seems I was wrong.

Inside, the pub is busier than I'd expected and although I'd intended to pop upstairs for a while, I feel guilty about leaving everyone to cope by themselves, especially when they've been managing without me for the last few days.

So, I take off my coat, transfer my phone to my back pocket, hook up my keys and make my way down the corridor.

The bar is heaving and I look around, spotting Dan at the far end, serving Geoff Carew. He turns to go to the till and sees me, raising his eyebrows in surprise.

"What happened to you today?" he says, ringing up the sale. "I came back from Sam's to find the place deserted... at least upstairs, anyway."

"I took Nicki home."

He freezes, halfway through counting out Geoff's change. "Home?" he says.

"Yes. She asked me to take her."

"Have you broken up?"

"No, but she worked out that I needed to think through a few things... and she decided I'd be better off doing that by myself."

He nods his head. "Are you okay?" he says, his voice filled with concern.

"No." He flinches at my honesty. "Look... give Geoff his change and come back, will you? We need to talk."

He frowns but then continues counting out the coins, closing the till and going back over to Geoff, before he returns, standing right in front of me. Luckily, with Leanne and Reece in tonight, they can cope for a few minutes without us, and Dan and I step into the corridor, where it's quieter.

"I know this could have waited until later, but I wanted to say it now."

"Say what?" he asks, looking confused.

"Sorry."

"Sorry?"

"Yes."

"What for?"

"I let you down... when your mum died. I put myself first and forgot about you and your grief."

His face clears, like he's finally understood. "It's okay, Dad. It was a long time ago."

"It doesn't matter how long ago it was. I haven't been a very good father… and I want to try and make it up to you."

He blushes. "You don't have to. I know it was hard for you."

"It was hard for you, too. You found her body. But even if you hadn't, she was your mother, and yet I was so wrapped up in what I'd lost, I forgot that. I'm going to make more of an effort now, though. I'm going to try harder."

"Has this got anything to do with Nicki?" he says, surprising me.

"Let's just say she's helped me to see the error of my ways."

He smiles. "Well, that's good."

"It is… and I want to try harder. I'm going to call you more often and spend more time with you when you're here."

His smile becomes a grin. "As long as you're not going to try surfing again."

"Surfing? How did you know about that?"

"Sam said something about it earlier, in passing, and when Rory came into the pub just now, I asked him to fill in the blanks. It sounds disastrous, Dad. What were you thinking?"

"I was trying to impress your mother, if you must know. But don't worry, there's no danger of me ever trying to surf again."

"Glad to hear it." I turn to go back into the bar, but he grabs my arm. "It'll be okay, Dad."

"What will?"

"You and Nicki."

"I hope so, Dan." His smile reflects the eternal optimism of youth. "You can take the rest of the night off, if you want. I need to keep busy, and you've more than earned it."

He shakes his head. "No, it's fine. It'll be interesting, working a shift with you."

"Interesting? Why?"

"Seeing how the old-timers do it."

"Old-timers? I might not be able to surf, but I can show you a thing or two about running a pub." He laughs and I follow him back down the corridor, relieved to have cleared the air.

As I come out into the bar, I glance to my left to see Rory and Laura sitting together. He's in uniform, and she's wearing a business suit, which tells me they've both come straight from work, and that although Laura normally finishes much earlier in the day than this, she must have been working late again.

I wander over, leaving Dan to serve another customer, and they both smile when they see me approach.

"Has your boss been keeping you late?" I say to Laura and she rolls her eyes.

"You could say that. It's this wedding venue application."

"Rory told me about that before Christmas."

"Hmm… well, I'd hoped to get the application forms in by the New Year, but Stephen's just thrown a spanner in the works."

"He has?"

"Yes. He's put forward the suggestion that we could offer outdoor weddings in the hotel's garden in the summer months."

"Why is that a problem?" I ask.

"Because we need a licence that covers every part of the hotel in which we want to hold ceremonies. I'd already completed most of the forms, but now I'm going to have to start again, and I'm also going to have to arrange to get some work done on the gardens, too, because according to the regulations, the locations have to be 'seemly and dignified'."

"And the gardens aren't dignified?"

She smiles. "They're okay, but they're a bit overgrown. I think Stephen thought we could get the licence now, and have the work done in the spring, but all the areas have to be approved prior to the granting of the licence." She sighs, taking a sip of her wine, and I turn to Rory.

"I hope you've had a better day."

He shrugs his shoulders. "That depends. We got back the toxicology report on the man who caused Nicki's accident."

"Oh? And?"

"He hadn't taken any drugs, but Tom was right… the packet in the glove compartment contained cocaine. He's being charged with possession now, as well as everything else. I was going to come round in the morning and tell Nicki, but you can pass the message on for me."

"I'll tell her when I call her tomorrow."

He frowns. "When you call her?"

"Yes. She's gone home."

They both sit forward. "As in back to her place?" Rory says.

"Well, it's her mother's place, but yes. She asked me to take her back there this morning."

He frowns, shaking his head. "But I thought…"

"You thought what?"

"I didn't mean to listen in to what you guys were saying yesterday, but I thought I heard Nicki say she wasn't giving up on you."

"She's not. But I'm guessing, if you heard that, you probably also heard me saying how confused I am."

"Yes, I did."

"Well… that's why she's gone home. To give me time to work things out, without the distraction of having her here."

"Is this to do with your late wife?" Laura asks.

"Yes, it is."

"Is Nicki feeling insecure about her, or something?"

"No. It's nothing like that. Nicki knows how I feel about Suzannah. She accepts that I'll always love her."

"Wow… really?" Rory's surprised, and it shows.

"Yes. And before you say anything, I know how big a deal that is. Nicki's a remarkable woman… a lot better than I deserve."

"And there you have it," Rory says, slamming his hand down on the bar like he's frustrated. "The guilt kicks in again. That's what this is all about, isn't it? You feel guilty for being happy."

"Not exactly, no. It's more complicated than that, and it's impossible to explain at the moment… although I suppose it doesn't help that I know I could have tried harder with Suzannah, and I don't want to make the same mistakes again."

"What on earth are you talking about? You did everything with Suzannah."

"I know. But she never wanted us to live here. She wanted the life we started off with."

"You mean the life where you were bored rigid working for the brewery and were living in that dull little house?"

"It wasn't dull… and it wasn't ours. We'd have bought somewhere nicer, if Dad hadn't had his stroke, if I hadn't insisted on moving here…"

"If… if…" Rory rolls his eyes. "Coming back here was the making of you, Ed."

"Maybe it was, but it wasn't what Suzannah wanted. She wanted us to have more children. She wanted a more 'normal' life, whatever the hell that is, but that certainly wasn't what I gave her."

He frowns. "Well, I think you're wrong. She might have wanted more children, and maybe she didn't enjoy living above a pub, but if you'd asked her to swap the life she had for a supposedly 'normal' life with another man, she'd never have done it. Suzannah loved you, Ed. She worshipped you."

"I know. Sometimes I wish she hadn't worshipped me quite so much. Then she might have told me the truth about how she felt before it was too late."

Laura reaches out, her hand resting on my arm. "That's the whole point though, Ed… it is too late. At least, it is to change anything with Suzannah."

"Precisely," Rory says. "This is all in the past, and you need to lay it to rest... along with your memories. You need to stop thinking about Suzannah like she's still here, as though you could still hurt her feelings. She's not, and you can't. But you can hurt Nicki, very easily."

"I know. I know that only too well."

He sighs, staring at me for a moment. "In that case, why don't you start by taking that off?" He nods down at my left hand and I follow the line of his gaze, my eyes settling on my wedding ring. "I get that it's hugely significant, but you can't expect Nicki to believe in your commitment to her, if you're still wearing another woman's wedding ring."

I'd never thought about it like that, but he has a point... and more than that, maybe this is the answer I've been looking for. Maybe this is a way for me to draw a line. Because that's what I need to do. I know that now. I need to draw a line between what happened in the past and where I am now... where I want to be. It's the only hope I have for a future with Nicki.

Chapter Nineteen

Nicki

The last few days have sped past... not that I'm complaining. I've kept myself busy, just like I said I would, and I feel like my feet have barely touched the ground.

I spoke to Tim Burgess from the garage in Porthgarrion the morning after I got home, and although we've never met before, he was very kind and helpful. He explained that he thought my car would probably be a write-off, going into detail about chassis damage or something. I didn't understand a word of it.

"Rory Quick told me you only had a bump on your head," he said once he'd finished his lengthy explanation.

"That's right."

"Well... you were very lucky."

I didn't doubt that for a minute.

He gave me all his details to pass on to the insurance company, and told me if they wanted the car moved to a different garage, he'd arrange that, or they could send an assessor to him... whichever they preferred.

His call reminded me to get the insurance claim done, and I went to see Gerald about it. I'd spoken to him the night before, over our Chinese take-away, and he'd said he'd happily assist me in filling out the forms, which I downloaded from their website. He and Shirley both came back and in the end, the forms didn't take us too long. Afterwards, I made us a cup of coffee while Shirley popped back to their place to fetch the Christmas cake which their daughter had baked and sent home with them. We each had a slice to tide us over until lunch, and I must say, it was lovely, with delicious marzipan, and not too much icing.

We sat in the living room, and Shirley looked at me over the top of her teacup.

"That was a nice young man you were with yesterday," she said, clearly fishing for information.

"Yes." I smiled, wondering how Ed would feel, being referred to as 'young'. She lowered her cup, raising her eyebrows. "We knew each other when we were children, and he married my best friend."

Her shoulders dropped. "Oh," she said, sounding much more disappointed.

"She died a few years ago, and…"

She perked up again, and I almost laughed, wondering if she could be any more obvious. "And what?"

I couldn't think what to say. 'I've loved him all my life, and now he loves me too'? 'He's trying to work out his past, so we can be together'? 'Being without him is killing me, even though I know it's for the best'? They were all true, but I didn't feel like saying any of that.

"And… it's a little complicated, but we're working on it."

"Well… nobody ever said love was easy." She had a definite twinkle in her eyes and I had to smile.

"Is that your way of saying I'm difficult?" Gerald said, and my smile turned into a laugh.

Since then, I've spent a lot of time with both of them. They've been helping me go through the rest of Mum's things and clear up the house to get it ready to sell. We got a lot done on that very first day. Gerald helped with the paperwork, which would otherwise have been tedious, and Shirley and I sorted out Mum's clothes, leaving them for Gerald to take to the charity shop in town. The jewellery was a little harder and I'll admit I shed a few tears… but that was nothing compared to going through her photographs. Some of them were heartbreaking, like the ones of her and Dad when they were young and so clearly in love. They had no idea what the future held… but I suppose that's true of all of us.

That's what I said to Ed when he called that night, just like he has every night since. He'd called me in the morning, too, and told me about the toxicology report on the man who'd caused my accident. I wished he could have been here then, to hold me. Just discussing the accident brought it all back, and I had to sit down to stop my legs from shaking. I think he could hear the fear in my voice, because he kept asking if I was okay, and I guess that's why he avoided talking about it in the evening, when he called again, and instead, I told him I'd spent the afternoon sorting through Mum and Dad's old photographs.

"They were so happy," I said. "You can see it in their eyes, and in the way they look at each other. But Dad died so young, it makes you wonder…"

"Wonder what?" he asked.

"Whether Mum regretted the things they hadn't done. They both worked really hard when I was growing up. It didn't leave a lot of time for anything else."

He fell silent, just for a moment or two, and then he said, "I think, when someone dies, there's always room for regrets. You can't put things right anymore, can you?"

I knew he was thinking about Suzannah, and I had to ask, "Do you have any regrets about things you didn't do with Suzannah?"

"You mean, apart from making her live above a pub when she didn't want to, and not giving her the life I'd promised, or the children she wanted?"

"We've already discussed this, Ed, and it wasn't all your fault."

"I know, but that doesn't mean I don't regret it. Although I suppose if we're talking in more general terms, then I could have worked fewer hours, given her more of my time. I could have talked to her more. Or maybe what I mean is, I could have listened to her more… paid her more attention, so I'd have noticed that she wasn't happy."

"She was happy, Ed. Everyone says so. And I didn't intend for you to beat yourself up again."

"I'm not. I'm answering your question… and while I'm about it, I want to thank you."

"What for?"

"For getting me to see sense with Dan."

"I didn't do anything."

"Yes, you did. You made me realise I needed to apologise for the way I behaved… and start being more of a father to him."

"Have you spoken to him, then?"

"Yes. I talked to him when I got back here last night. I think he was surprised by my apology, but it needed to be said. He and I needed a clean slate. I don't want to keep looking back and regretting things."

"Neither do I."

"Good. Because I've decided, I'm not going to make the same mistakes again. I'm going to make time for you. I'm…"

"Don't be ridiculous, Ed. And don't make promises you can't keep. You can't close the pub at seven o'clock every night, just so we can be together."

"I know. I'm not going to. But I've worked out that, given another week or so, Reece will be competent enough to work unsupervised, and that means he and Leanne can handle the evening shifts by themselves. I'll still work during the day, but I'm going to leave them to it in the evenings."

"And what about during the summer, and when it gets really busy, like it has been over Christmas? You know you'll need three people behind the bar then."

"That's only for a few weeks of the year, and I'll keep my hours down as much as I can."

"How?"

"By taking on part-time staff during the summer. I might still have to work the odd shift, and I imagine I'll have to do a lot more at Easter and Christmas, because it's not so easy getting people in for such a short stint, but that'll only be for a couple of weeks at a time. It always quietens down again afterwards."

"You really have thought this through, haven't you?"

"Yes. You went away so I could think, and even though it's only been a day, that's exactly what I've been doing."

"I see... and have you thought of anything else?"

"Yes. And because of that, I need to ask you a question."

"Oh?"

"I need to ask how you feel about living above the pub. As you know, I never really consulted Suzannah about it, but like I just said, I don't intend making the same mistakes with you... so, how do you feel?"

"Is it optional, then?"

There was a very slight pause before he said, "Well... I, um... I..."

I laughed. "It's okay, Ed. I don't mind living above the pub. I quite like your flat, actually."

"Is there anything about it you want to change? The only thing I've done since Suzannah died is to replace the sofa, but we can get a new one, if you don't like it, or we can..."

"I like your sofa…" I stopped talking, feeling myself blush, and Ed coughed.

"I like my sofa, too," he whispered. "I miss seeing you curled up on it."

That hadn't been what I was thinking about, but I didn't think it wise to mention my memories of his sofa. "Have you really not changed anything else?" I asked instead.

"No. But if you want to, we can. We can rip out the kitchen, change the bathroom… do whatever you like."

"That all sounds like hard work. I was…" I hesitated, unsure whether to voice the thought that had just crossed my mind.

"You were what?"

"I was wondering about your bed."

"My bed?" He sounded confused.

"Yes. If you haven't changed anything other than the sofa, then…"

"Oh, I see what you mean. I'll buy a new one… tomorrow."

"There's no rush."

"Yes, there is."

I wasn't sure what he meant by that, and I was slightly scared to ask.

The next evening, he told me he'd ordered the bed, but that it would take two weeks to be delivered.

"It's because of the New Year." He sounded deflated.

"Two weeks isn't that long." I tried to reassure him.

"I told you, every second without you is like a lifetime."

"I know, and I feel the same. But I don't want you to rush this, Ed. I want us to get it right."

"We will. I'm working really hard at getting everything straight in my head, so I don't mess it up again. But I'm also aware that I don't want us to spend any more time apart than we absolutely have to, because that's just a waste." He stopped talking, but before I could say anything, he said, "When you ran out on me on Christmas Eve, before I came after you, Dan said something to me which showed a wisdom he can only have inherited from his mother, because he certainly didn't get it from me."

"Why? What did he say?"

"He told me that life's too short to waste on regrets… that if I had learned nothing else from Suzannah's death, I ought to have learned that."

"And have you?"

"Yes."

I sighed, letting hope flutter in my chest, even though it had been there before, and been dashed. I didn't think Ed would do that to me again, though… not after last time.

Yesterday, I felt the house was cleared enough to have the estate agents round. When I called, I half expected them to say they'd book me in for sometime in January, but I guess they had nothing better to do, and a young man arrived at three o'clock and looked around the house, commenting on the adaptations that Mum had required, and how they might affect the value. That wasn't news to me, and when he gave me the valuation at the end, I wasn't disappointed.

He came back today, even though it's New Year's Eve, and took the photographs, measuring up the rooms at the same time, and we agreed the house will go up for sale next week.

It was as he was leaving that a van pulled up outside, and a man got out, going around to the back and opening it. He pulled out an enormous bouquet of hand-tied roses, smiling at me as he walked up the driveway.

"Miss Woodward?" he said, checking the card.

"Yes."

"These are for you." He handed them over and I felt myself blush, both men staring at me.

"Thank you."

They stepped away, to their respective vehicles, and I smiled down at the bouquet, admiring the deep red roses, interspersed with yellow ones that had bright red tips on the petals. It was an unusual combination, but it worked, and I carried them into the house, closing the door as I pulled the card from its envelope, and grinning as I read the words written on it.

'I'll never run out of ways to say 'I love you', but being as I can't say it to your face, I thought I'd let the flowers do the talking. E xx'

I hugged the bouquet to my chest, sighing out my happiness as I took it through to the kitchen, putting it down on the work surface, and picking up my phone, which I'd left there.

I knew Ed would be working, so I sent him a text message…

— *Thank you for the flowers. They're beautiful. I'm not sure how they can say 'I love you', but the thought is perfect, and I love you too. N xx*

I was delving in the cupboard under the sink, looking for a big enough vase, when Ed's reply came in.

— *I'll explain the flowers when I see you. It'll be better in person… trust me. xx*
— *That's very mysterious. N xx*
— *I know ;) xx*

I chuckled, and set about arranging the flowers, unable to stop smiling.

I feel like things are finally getting settled. Other than the contents of the kitchen, which I still need to use, and my personal belongings, Mum's house is packed and ready to go up for sale. All I've got left to do is wait for Ed, and work out what I'm going to do with my life… and by life, I mean career. New Year's Eve seems like a good time to be thinking about such things, too. It feels like a time for making plans…

I know that once the sale of Mum's house goes through, I'll have more money than I've ever had in my life, and as such, if I don't feel like working, I won't have to. But I can't imagine doing nothing. I want to work... I enjoy it.

Of course, I could help in the pub, I suppose. Ed wouldn't object, I'm sure, and it would mean we could be together more often... but is that what I really want? I mean, obviously I want to be with Ed, but do I really want to work in the pub and give up teaching? I'm not sure I do. It's something I should talk to him about before making a decision, especially as he took the time to ask me how I felt about living above the pub.

We've already discussed the fact that Ed won't be able to talk tonight, because the pub will be busy, but I can't see the harm in asking.

— Hello. I know you're busy, so don't feel the need to reply straight away, but I've been thinking about what I'm going to do once Mum's house is sold, and I wondered if you've got any ideas. xx

I get up to make myself a cup of coffee, but am halted at the door by my phone beeping and I return, picking it up from the table, to see a message from Ed... already.

— Tell me you're not still thinking about travelling the world? xx

I sit down, quickly typing out my reply.

— Of course I'm not. I meant in terms of my career. There's no way I'm going to travel the world unless you're coming with me. xx

His reply takes a minute or two, but I wait for it, clutching my phone.

— Thank God for that. Your message scared the hell out of me. I'd love to travel the world with you one day, but in the meantime, is there any reason you can't go

back to what you did before? Obviously, you could work here with me, and I certainly wouldn't mind spending all my time with you, but you love teaching. I could see it in your eyes, so if you can, why not go back to it? xxx

I smile.

— *Do you have any idea how much I love you? xxx*

— *Yes. Because I love you more. Sorry, I have to dash. It's crazy here. I'll talk to you tomorrow morning, but don't worry if you don't hear from me first thing. It's going to be a late finish tonight. xxx*

— *Okay. Happy New Year. xxx*

— *It's going to be the happiest New Year ever. Trust me. xxx*

I'm not sure what he means by that, but he's busy and I can't keep texting him. Besides, we're going to talk tomorrow, so I can ask him then.

I go into the kitchen and make that coffee, bringing it back into the living room, and sitting down on the sofa again. My laptop is on the shelf under the coffee table and I pull it out, turning it on and going to a web browser. I know that, even if there are any vacancies at the schools or colleges close to Porthgarrion, I won't be able to do anything about it now. Not at ten to eight on New Year's Eve. But there's no harm in looking.

There's no harm in hoping.

I'm learning that… slowly but surely.

Chapter Twenty

Ed

Working as a publican, I both love and hate New Year's Eve. I do a roaring trade, but because I always get an extended licence to keep the pub open until one o'clock in the morning, I'm exhausted the next day. For most people, New Year's Day is a holiday, but not in this business, and every year in the past, I've woken up on the first morning of the year, feeling jaded, wondering why I do this to myself. Today, though, I'm up, showered and dressed before seven-thirty. Okay, so I'm still exhausted, but I'm very far from jaded. I feel positively wired.

I've got a lot to do, the first part of which is to change the bedding in the spare room. Once that's done and it feels like a more reasonable time of day, I send text messages to Leanne and Rory.

In Leanne's case, I'm asking a favour… namely that she comes in earlier than usual and that she contacts Reece and asks him to come in too. It's a big ask after such a late finish, and she replies straight away with a terse, 'Okay'.

In Rory's case, there's something I need to talk to him about, and I've asked if he'll pop down to see me. Oddly enough, his reply is exactly the same as Leanne's.

I pour myself a bowl of cereal, eating it quickly, along with a cup of coffee, which I gulp down, and then I head downstairs. We didn't finish clearing up last night – well, this morning – and given the favour I'm asking of Leanne, the least I can do is get the pub back into shape before she arrives.

I'm polishing the last of the tables when Rory arrives, knocking on the front door, which I open, letting him in, along with a blast of chilly wind. He's not in uniform today, which I guess means he's lucky enough to have the day off.

"What's happened?" he says, undoing his coat. "Why the urgent text?"

"I needed to tell you something."

"And you couldn't have told me last night? We were here all evening."

"I know. But so were Gemma and Tom."

"And what you need to tell me couldn't be said in front of them?"

"Exactly."

He frowns. "This is very intriguing."

"It's about the wedding."

"What about it? You're not pulling out of doing the reception, are you?"

"Of course not. But you probably noticed that Dan wasn't here last night."

"No… he left earlier in the day, didn't he? To go back to Hawaii. Gemma told me. She was a bit down about it, to be honest, because he told her he wouldn't be able to make it back for the wedding."

"Well, that's the whole point. He will be."

"Then why did he tell her he wouldn't?"

"Because he wants it to be a surprise. There's a competition on over that weekend, but he's going to duck out of it and come back."

"Oh… She'll be thrilled," he says, his face lighting up.

"I know, but don't tell her, will you?"

"Of course not."

"I wanted to tell you because I didn't want you to think badly…" I let my voice fade.

"Of Dan?" he says, finishing my sentence for me.

"Yes. He cares about Gemma, and he wouldn't let her down."

Rory tilts his head slightly. "It's not like you to defend him. Is everything okay?"

"Yes. Everything's fantastic, actually. Thanks to Nicki, I've seen the error of my ways and talked to him a lot more since he's been home. I've also apologised to him for the way I behaved when Suzannah died. It was long overdue."

"And this was thanks to Nicki, was it?"

"Yes."

He nods his head. "How's it going with her?"

"Well… I've worked out what I'm going to do. I've even worked out how I'm going to do it. Now I just need Leanne and Reece to get here."

He frowns, looking confused, but before he can say a word, we're interrupted by a knocking on the door. I open it to be faced with Leanne and Reece.

She glares up at me. "I have two things to say to you," she murmurs through gritted teeth.

"Oh, yes?" I step back to let them enter, and she turns to face me.

"One… you'd better make this worth our while; and two, one of these days, do you think you could give one or other of us a key to this place?"

I smile and nod my head. "The answer is 'yes' to both questions."

"I'll leave you to it," Rory says, coming over and ducking out through the still open door, although he pauses on the threshold, putting his hand on my arm. "Whatever it is you've got planned, good luck."

"Thanks."

He leaves and I close the door, waiting while Leanne and Reece move further into the pub.

"I'm sorry to drag you in early. I hope I didn't interrupt anything important."

Reece doesn't move, but Leanne narrows her eyes at me. "No, nothing at all." It's impossible to miss the sarcasm in her voice.

"Do you have any idea how annoying it is when people do that?"

"Do what?"

"Say that something's unimportant, or there's nothing wrong, or it doesn't matter, when the opposite is so clearly the case."

She puts her hands on her narrow hips and steps closer to me. "Okay. I'll tell you then. When you called me, I was in bed… with Reece… and we weren't sleeping." I look over her shoulder at him, to see a blush creeping up his cheeks.

"I see. So you're…"

"Yes, we are," she says. "He and I have been together since Christmas Eve. In fact, when you called me on Christmas Day and asked me to contact him, he was lying in bed beside me. I've been staying at his place every night… and I think he's absolutely perfect. Is that enough information for you?"

"More than enough, thanks. I think I preferred living in ignorance."

"Don't blame me. You asked."

"And it's not a mistake I'll be making again." She smiles, shaking her head.

Reece steps forward and takes her hand, leaning close to her. "I think you're perfect, too," he whispers and she looks up at him, sighing.

"Before you two get carried away, can we sit for a moment?" I nod towards a table and they sit opposite me, still holding hands. "I didn't get you here early to talk about this, but as we're all together, I might as well tell you, I'm going to be taking more of a back seat in terms of working behind the bar."

"Really?" Leanne frowns at me. "Is there a reason for that?"

"Yes."

"You're not ill, are you?"

I smile. "No, I'm not ill. You'll find out the reason later."

She rolls her eyes. "Now, who's the one being all secretive and mysterious?"

I ignore her and sit back in my seat, looking at Reece. "In light of my decision, I wondered if you'd like to take on some extra shifts. I think you're nearly at a point where you can work unsupervised. I'll still be down here during the day and, to be honest, it's fairly quiet for most of January and February… at least until the half-term holidays, anyway."

"If you think I'm ready," he says, a smile forming on his lips.

I nod my head. "It's not as though I'll be abandoning you altogether. I'll only be upstairs, so if there's anything you can't handle, you'll only have to shout."

"If this is a permanent thing, what are we going to do at Easter, and in the summer?" Leanne says, leaning forward slightly. "If Christmas has been anything to go by, I don't think the two of us could handle the bar by ourselves then."

"I wouldn't expect you to. I'll take on more shifts whenever I have to, and I'll employ part-time staff to help, too. And I'll give you both a pay rise, obviously."

They turn to each other, grinning, and I get to my feet. Leanne looks up at me. "Are you sure you're not ill?"

"I'm positive."

Reece stands too, bringing Leanne with him, their hands still firmly clasped together. "If you didn't get us here to talk about this, then…"

"I got you here to ask if you'd mind managing the pub by yourselves today."

"All day?" Leanne says, wide-eyed.

"Certainly over lunchtime. I'm going out in a minute, and to be honest, I don't know when I'll be back. Hopefully, it'll be before tonight, but I can't guarantee it. We're not usually that busy on New Year's Day, so it shouldn't be too bad."

"I'm sure we'll manage." Reece squares his shoulders before he releases Leanne's hand and puts his arm around her.

She looks up into his face. "If you say so."

"Now… I've got to go," I say, starting towards the bar.

"Already?" I turn, seeing Leanne staring at me wide-eyed.

"Yes. Don't worry. You'll be fine. Fiona and Nancy are both working today. If it should get busy, Fiona can always help behind the bar. She knows what she's doing."

"We'll work it out," Reece says, clearly feeling a confidence that's not shared by Leanne, and I wander back over to her.

"I trust you with this," I say, looking down into her face and she sucks in a breath, nodding her head. I take her hand, dropping the pub keys into it. "You wanted the keys. These are yours until I get back, and I'll get you a set of your own in the next couple of days… okay?"

She nods, relaxing a little and I give her a reassuring smile, before retracing my steps, going around behind the bar and down the corridor, where I put on my coat and grab my keys. When I come back into the bar again, Reece and Leanne are standing face-to-face, staring into each other's eyes.

"I'll be off. Don't wreck my pub."

"No, boss," they say in unison, although they don't even turn to look at me, and I smile as I go back down the corridor again, letting myself out of the back door.

Although it's been overcast all morning, the sky is brightening. It's still chilly, though, and I pull my coat around me.

I don't go straight to my car, but I walk around to the front of the pub, and up Church Lane, passing the police station and Italian restaurant on my right, and Tim's garage on my left. There's no sign of Nicki's car, but the garage is closed up anyway, a heavy padlock on the huge wooden doors.

I keep going until I get to the church, opening the creaking gate that leads into the graveyard, and wandering over to the far corner, by the wall, where Suzannah's buried.

I don't come here as much as I used to. At the beginning, I came every day, blotting out my responsibilities for Dan and the pub, leaving my mother to cope with my son, and my staff to handle my business by themselves, while I sat here, trying to forge a hopeless connection with the woman I loved, and weeping for everything I'd lost. Eventually, of course, life got in the way. My bar staff left, fed up with my perpetual absences, and I was forced to resume my role as a landlord. My mother told me off, too, reminding me of Dan's needs, and that I had a responsibility to him, but I didn't do so well in resuming my role as a father. All of that just added to my already overflowing well of guilt… that I hadn't been here when Suzannah died; that Dan had been the one to discover her body; that I couldn't bear to witness his grief. I resented him and the time my mother was telling me to spend with him. I longed to be with Suzannah, even in death, but my time was being stolen by the living.

I got a lot wrong back then.

When I get to Suzannah's grave, I can't help smiling at the flowers that have been placed in the small vase that's always kept here. I don't bring flowers all the time, like I used to… just on special occasions, like her birthday and our anniversary. But I know these are from Dan. Whenever he's home, he always brings pink and white carnations. I've never asked him why, but the other day, when I went to see Gemma about sending Nicki a bouquet, I asked her if she knew why he chose those particular flowers. She did, and once she'd explained it to me, it made perfect sense. I hadn't realised until then that flowers have meanings, but that's what gave me the idea to send Nicki the roses…

I crouch down beside Suzannah's headstone, running my fingers over the engraved lettering that spells out her name.

"I don't know if Nicki is who you would have chosen," I whisper. "But she's right for me… for who I am now. Loving her the way I do doesn't mean I didn't love you. It doesn't mean marrying you and loving you was the wrong thing to do back then. And that doesn't mean loving Nicki is wrong now. They're two very different things, and you're two very different people. I understand that now, even if it has taken me a while to work it out. I'm sorry, Suze… I'm sorry if I was ever anything less than you wanted… than you deserved."

As I'm talking, the sun comes out from behind a cloud and for the first time in ages, I can see the image of Suzannah's face as clearly as if she were standing before me. Tears cloud my vision and I smile, kissing the palm of my hand and placing it over her engraved name.

"Thank you for that, sweetheart."

I take a deep breath and slowly pull the gold band from my finger, making a small hole in the earth at the foot of Suzannah's gravestone and dropping my ring into it, before covering it over again.

"I love you," I whisper, and then I get to my feet, turning away.

This won't be the last time I come here. I'll come back, often. And I'll come back a better man.

Standing outside the bungalow, I pause for a second or two. I've thought about this moment over and over since I drove away from here, just a few short days ago, and although I've got a lot to say to Nicki, I need to make sure I get it right. I clench my fists a couple of times and then ring the doorbell, looking down at my feet and taking a breath to calm my nerves.

The door opens and I look up slowly, taking in a pair of fluffy cream socks, tight stonewashed jeans, a pale pink sweater, and finally Nicki's beautiful face, her hair tucked behind her ears, the cut on her forehead healing nicely, with no need for a dressing now, and her eyes wide, gazing up at me.

"Ed?"

"I know you weren't expecting to see me today, but let me say this… please?" She nods her head, waiting. "I—I know what you were asking of me, and I know why… and I'm here to tell you, I'm free." Taking a breath, I hold up my left hand, my ring finger now bare, and she gasps. "I'm completely free, Nicki."

"Where is it?"

"I buried it."

She frowns. "You did what?"

"I buried it at Suzannah's grave. It belongs there, with her. And I belong here, with you. I've drawn a line between then and now. I realised that was what I had to do, to make sense of it all, to separate the past from the present… and the future."

"Oh, my God." She reaches for my hand, but I pull it back and her brow furrows.

"Wait a second. There's something I need to explain… about the guilt."

"What about it?"

"I've said to you a couple of times that it wasn't what you thought."

"I know."

I nod my head. "You thought I felt guilty for betraying Suzannah... for betraying her memory. Is that right?"

"Yes."

"Well... at the beginning, it probably was a bit like that. I felt guilty when you first came back, because I'd realised my feelings for you when we were younger had been a lot stronger than I'd been willing to admit. So, I kept pushing you away, only to pull you back again. I'm sure it was very confusing for you, but it was for me, too. I was torn between denying you and needing you. In the end, needing you won, and that's when everything changed. That's what I was going to tell you before we made love."

"Except I didn't give you the chance."

"I could have taken the chance. I could have stopped you. But I didn't. I wanted you just as much as you wanted me."

"Then why did you react like that? Why did you shut me out?"

"Because the guilt was overwhelming. But it wasn't about betraying Suzannah's memory anymore. It was because I never knew I could feel like that." Her eyes widen. "You were right... I'd only ever been with Suzannah, and I loved every moment with her, but what you did, the way you made me feel... it was beyond anything I'd ever dreamed of. I felt guilty because it was all so different, and yet I couldn't regret it. How could I, when it felt so good? I lost myself in you, and I wanted to do it again, and again... and again." She blushes and I can't help smiling. "I need you, Nicki, like I've never needed anyone before. And before you doubt that, I'll tell you... I loved Suzannah, and a part of me always will, but I don't think I ever needed her. Not like this. My love for you is consuming. I think about you every second of the day, and there isn't a single moment when I don't want you." I close my eyes for a second. "God… I've waited so long to say that. I've fought my past and my guilt just to think it, let alone say it out loud. But I don't feel guilty anymore. The past is the past, and I've accepted that my relationship with Suzannah was different from the relationship I have with you. It wasn't worse, or better… it was just different. I'm sorry for the confusion, and the mess in my head, and for all the times I hurt you. But that's all over now. I'm free of the past, and I need you to say you'll be mine."

I drop to one knee and she gasps as I delve into my coat pocket, pulling out the small square box that's been lying there since I picked it up from the jeweller's the day before yesterday. I pop it open, turning it around so she can see the white gold sapphire ring inside.

"I need you to say you'll marry me, Nicki… please?"

"It's beautiful," she whispers, looking at the ring, with a slight hesitancy to her voice, and although I can't claim to be a mind reader, I'm pretty sure I know exactly what she's thinking.

"Don't read anything into it not being a diamond, will you?"

She shakes her head. "You gave Suzannah a diamond." I was right.

"I said don't read anything into it." I get to my feet again and look down into her glistening eyes.

"Diamonds stand for love," she says.

"Yes, they do. But the thing is, sapphires stand for fidelity. Giving you this ring doesn't mean I love you less than Suzannah. It means I'm yours. I'm all yours, and that I want you to be mine."

A tear falls onto her cheek as she nods her head and I cup her face with my free hand.

"You mean it? You'll marry me?"

"Yes, Ed. I'll marry you."

I release her, pulling the ring from its velvet cushion and dropping the box back into my pocket before I take her left hand and slowly place the ring on her finger.

She looks up at me, her eyes still brimming with tears, despite the smile on her lips. "This is what I've always wanted."

"Then come home with me."

"Now?" Her smile widens to a grin.

"Yes. The new bed hasn't been delivered yet, but I thought we could sleep in the spare room for now." I capture her face between my hands. "To be honest, I decided it wouldn't do either of us any good if we slept together in the bed I used to share with Suzannah. I'm free of the past, Nic, but I think there are always going to be limits."

She nods her head. "That's okay… I understand that."

"If things crop up that are difficult – for either of us – we'll talk them through. Okay? We're in this together…"

"For better or worse?" She smiles up at me.

"Always."

She studies my face for a few seconds, like she's seeing me for the first time, and then, with an excited squeal, she leaps up into my arms. I catch her and she wraps her legs around me, clinging to me. I hold her close, kissing her neck.

"I'm never letting you go again," I whisper and she shudders against me as I walk us into the house, kicking the door closed and lean back against the wall, supporting her with one arm, while my other hand holds her head steady, and I bend my own and kiss her. There's nothing delicate about this. It's frenzied and intense and, within moments, I turn us around, so Nicki's back is against the wall. She's got her arms around my neck, and the wall supporting her, which leaves my hands free to roam up inside her sweater, feeling her breasts through her thin lace bra. She moans and sighs into my mouth, her body writhing against mine.

I break the kiss, leaning back slightly and look down at her. She's breathless, as am I, her lips slightly swollen, her eyes gazing deeply into mine. I still can't be sure, though. Does she want more? Should I ask? Or should I just take her to her bedroom?

I turn my head, looking down the hallway, as though hoping for some inspiration, and my eyes alight on the roses I sent to her, sitting in a vase on top of a side table. I can't help smiling and letting out a half laugh, my hands dropping to my sides, and then coming around behind her, holding her up in my arms again.

"What's funny?" she says and I look back at her, seeing the quizzical expression on her face.

"Nothing…"

"I thought you hated it when people did that."

"I do. And it's not nothing, really. It's just that, when I went to Suzannah's grave this morning, before I came here, Dan had left some flowers there. He always does that whenever he comes home, and he always leaves the same flowers… white and pink carnations. It reminded me of the conversation I'd had with Gemma when I went to order the bouquet for you."

"In what way?"

"I asked her if she knew why he left those flowers in particular. I thought he might have explained it to her, being as they're friends, and he and I haven't been that communicative… until now. She said he hadn't explained it as such, but then she told me that the flowers have a meaning. All flowers do, evidently."

"So what do white and pink carnations mean?"

"The white ones mean remembrance, and the pink ones are for gratitude and love."

Her eyes fill with tears again. "That's lovely," she whispers and then she tilts her head slightly. "Is Dan going to be okay with this?" She holds up her left hand in front of my face, wiggling her fingers.

"Dan's going to be fine with it."

"Does he know? I mean, have you told him yet?"

"No. No-one knows. But I'll call him later and tell him. He'll be thrilled."

"You're sure?"

"I'm positive. He wants this... not as much as I do, but he knows how good you are for me. He's been behind us all the way, ever since Christmas Eve, when you ran out on me, and he gave me that lecture about life being too short to waste on regrets." She smiles. "Of course, his lecture delayed me in coming after you, which meant you were able to leave the hotel and drive away, straight into the path of a drunken idiot... but he meant well."

"He did, and the accident wasn't his fault, any more than it was yours."

"Hmm... well..."

She lets go of my shoulders and clasps my face between her hands, narrowing her eyes at me. "It wasn't your fault, Ed."

"If I'd been quicker..."

She shakes her head. "Stop it. I'm fine now. The cut's even started to itch, so it must be getting better." I glance up at it, and I have to admit, it looks less raw than the last time I saw it. "And in any case," she says with a smile, putting her hands back on my shoulders again. "You still owe me an explanation."

"I do? What for?"

"For the flowers. You've told me about Dan's carnations, but what about these?" She tilts her head towards the roses. "You said you'd explain them to me when you next saw me... and I'm still waiting."

"Oh... I'm sorry. I was busy proposing."

"That's a useless excuse, and you know it."

I chuckle and she does too, our foreheads resting together while I walk a little further down the hallway, stopping by the table and leaning against the wall beside it.

"I wanted to find a way to say 'I love you'. I'd told you over the phone and in text messages, but it didn't feel enough. So I decided to send you flowers. I went to see Gemma at the florist's and when I told her I wanted a bouquet, she asked what the flowers were for… so I told her."

"You told her you wanted to say 'I love you', to me?"

"Yes. I'd already realised by then that I needed to draw a line between the present and the past, so I don't have a problem with the whole village knowing how much I love you. Hell… I don't have a problem with the whole damn world knowing about it. Gemma's like a daughter to me, so telling her was a breeze."

"How did she react?"

"She just smiled, and then explained to me that the best way to declare your love is with tulips… except that's impossible at this time of year, because you can't get them."

"Oh… that's a shame."

"I know. That's what I thought. I was explaining to Gemma that I'd known you since we were children, and she suggested the yellow roses with red tips on the petals… because they stand for friendship and falling in love, which seemed appropriate for us."

"I see. And then you added the red roses because they're all about love?"

"No. I added the red roses because they're all about *passionate* love. And so are we." I look deep into her eyes, closing the gap between us and brushing my lips against hers. What starts as gentle becomes furious within moments and, once again, we're breathless and craving more. I pull back and look down at her. "God, I've missed your lips."

She smiles, leaning forward and kissing me. Hard. Within a few seconds, she breaks the kiss again, tilting her head and says, "There. Better?"

I shake my head. "That wasn't exactly what I had in mind."

It takes no more than the blink of an eye for her to see the light, and she blushes. "Oh... I see."

"Good. Can I just tell you... when you dropped to your knees in front of me that night... when you did what you did... that was a first for me."

Her eyes widen, her blush deepening. "Seriously? You mean Suzannah had never...?"

I shake my head. "She never wanted to, and I never pressured her... and with that in mind, I need to know, was it okay?"

She smiles. "It was better than okay."

"No, you don't understand. What I mean is, I only realised afterwards that I should probably have kept still and let you take things at a pace that worked for you... except I couldn't resist moving."

"I noticed... and I liked it," she says, blushing yet again.

I sigh out my relief. "Okay. I'll bear that in mind."

"Can I ask you something?" She bites on her bottom lip, like she's nervous.

"Of course."

"Did you ever...?" She stops talking. "I don't know how to phrase this... did you ever do it the other way around?"

I smile, loving how cute she looks when she's really embarrassed. "No. I suggested it at the beginning, but she really wasn't interested."

"So you've never done that to anyone?"

"No. I'm not sure I'd even be any good at it."

She leans a little closer. "Would you like to find out?"

"Oh... God, yes."

She smiles and, without saying another word, I push myself off the wall and walk down the hall to her bedroom.

***

"Finally…" Rory says, bringing his speech to a close. "I have one thing to say to Tom as I welcome him to our family." Tom looks over at Rory, his brow furrowing slightly, and Rory stares at his new son-in-law. "Gemma may be your wife now, but she'll always be my little girl… so remember, I can still put you on traffic duty any time I feel like it."

Everyone chuckles, and Tom nods his head as Rory reaches for his glass.

"Ladies and Gentlemen, please raise your glasses to the new bride and groom… Gemma and Tom."

Everyone echoes his toast and Tom turns to Gemma, kissing her. She looks radiant in a long, figure-hugging ivory-coloured dress and she gazes up into Tom's face, the pair of them a picture of happiness.

I glance around the room, just double-checking everything is okay. I might not be working behind the bar today, but I'm hosting this reception, and because it's for Gemma, it matters to me that everything runs smoothly. Dan's in the corner, chatting with Adrian Roskelly. It's the first time I've seen my son in a suit since his mother's funeral, and I have to say, he cleans up well, even if his hair is still too long. Gemma evidently burst into tears when he turned up unannounced at the florist's yesterday morning, surprising her. Dan put it down to her nerves about the wedding, but I knew there was more to it than that. I knew how much it meant to her to have her oldest friend at her wedding… and that he'd made the effort to be here. If I'm honest, it meant a lot to me, too.

Laura is by the bar, chatting with Tom's mum. She's diminutive, especially considering how tall Tom is, and she's also very attractive and quite sophisticated. I'd say she's about ten years older than Rory and myself. The man on her arm, who I'm informed by Rory, is called Neil, and is a former detective inspector, is very attentive. Laura's looking lovely today in a pale blue dress and jacket, the colour of her outfit matching Rory's tie. They keep catching each other's eyes and smiling, and that makes me smile, too.

A peel of laughter sounds from the other side of the bar and I turn to see Gemma's boss, Imelda Duffy, chuckling away in her seat beside Laura's dad. They first met at Rory and Laura's wedding last spring, and got along very well… and it seems their friendship is flourishing, if the expressions on their faces are anything to go by.

At the table beside them are Jack and Rachel, whose pregnancy is showing now. The baby's due in the summer, and they're talking about getting married next year. I worried about introducing Nicki to Rachel, knowing she's pregnant and that for Nicki, that's something that can never be. But Nicki was fine about it and although they talked about the baby for a little while, they spent most of their time recalling stories about Rachel's grandmother, who Nicki remembered from our childhood.

Speaking of Nicki…

She's standing talking to Rory and I smile to myself, recalling my mistaken belief that she liked him… when, in reality, it was me all along. That thought is enough to make any man smile… but not as much as the way things have turned out.

The last few weeks have been full of highs, and I have to say, occasional lows.

Nicki's car was written off by her insurance company, which, according to both Tim Burgess and Rory, wasn't a tremendous surprise. I didn't see it for myself, and neither did Nicki, but evidently the damage was substantial. I don't want to think about what might have happened… although I give thanks every day that it didn't.

The man who caused the accident was charged, and pleaded guilty, to driving while under the influence of alcohol, and possession of a Class A drug. He was banned from driving for eighteen months and fined three thousand pounds, but wasn't imprisoned for the driving offence.

"Are you kidding?" I said to Rory, when he told us the news. Because the man had pleaded guilty, Nicki didn't have to attend court, so Rory had come and broken the news to us afterwards.

"No. I wish I was."

"He could have killed Nicki, and he gets to walk away?"

"Not exactly. He's been given a two-year prison sentence for possession."

Nicki was clinging to me, the court case having brought it all back to her, I think. "Surely," she said, "if he's only been banned for eighteen months, and he's in prison for two years, by the time he comes out, he'll be able to drive again straight away, won't he?"

"No," Rory said. "The ban only starts when he's released from prison."

"That's something, I suppose," she murmured, and I held her in my arms.

I can't deny, we felt let down by the system, but just two days later, Nicki accepted an offer on her mother's bungalow, and that helped take her mind off things.

She also found a job at a school near Truro. She's due to start after the Easter holidays, and Nicki's hoping either the insurance company will have paid up by then, or that the sale of her mother's bungalow will have gone through, because she hates driving my car, and desperately wants to buy one of her own. It transpired her insurance company would only provide a courtesy car if hers was being repaired, not if it was written off, and while the theory of driving my car didn't seem too daunting, the practice has turned out to be completely different. I can still remember peeling her fingers from the steering wheel after that first attempt... and I have to smile.

That's something I've done a lot of lately – despite the occasional low point – and it's all been thanks to Nicki. Waking up beside her every morning in our brand new bed is the best feeling in the world. Well... that's not strictly true. Making love to her is the best, and that's something we've done every single day... starting with that morning in her bedroom.

I can still recall her screams, and then her moans when I kissed her and she tasted herself on my lips. And I'm never going to forget the stupid male pride that filled me to the brim when she told me my skills had been 'exceptional', despite my worries that I might not have been very good. That's the kind of compliment I can take any time.

Of course, I also can't forget how it felt when she returned the favour and fulfilled that particular fantasy to its natural completion. It's something we've done a lot since, but that first time was something else.

We didn't get up for another two hours after that. My recovery time was better than I'd expected... and Nicki was very enticing. When we finally surfaced, though, I somehow found the energy to help Nicki pack her things, and she went to see Shirley and Gerald to explain that she was coming back to Porthgarrion with me. She left them with a set of keys and told them she'd instruct the agents to handle the sale, and that she'd stay in touch... and she has. They've been over here a couple of times for a meal in the pub with us – on the house, of course.

The drive back here that afternoon was filled with anticipation and excitement. I didn't let go of her hand the entire way home, even though she was clutching her 'I love you' flowers in her other arm. She didn't stop looking at me, either. When we arrived and Leanne saw us together, quickly realising the reason for my absence, she insisted I should take the rest of the day off… and I wasn't about to argue. Instead, I took Nicki upstairs, and showed her what I'd meant when I'd told her I wanted to lose myself in her… again, and again… and again.

"I won't ask what you're thinking about." Rory's voice makes me jump and I realise he and Nicki aren't talking anymore, and that my fiancée is now chatting to his wife.

"Hmm… probably best not."

He chuckles, standing beside me. "Thanks for doing all this," he says, looking around the pub. It's decked out with bunting and flowers, and – thank God – there isn't a fairy light in sight.

"You don't have to thank me. Like I said, this was my wedding present to Gemma."

"And like I said, it's a very over-the-top wedding present."

We both look at the bride and groom, standing arm-in-arm, talking to Tom's mother and Neil.

"Is this a proud father moment?" I ask him.

"Absolutely it is."

"And you don't regret Joanne not being here to share it?"

He frowns. "Not in the slightest. Gemma had the option, but Nicki was right. If Joanne had been here, she'd have made the day about herself… and that's not how it should be, so…"

"It's all worked out for the best."

He turns to Laura and I follow his gaze, my eyes settling on Nicki, who's right beside her.

"Yes, it has." He nudges into me. "Do you have any idea how lucky we are?"

"Yes. I lost Suzannah, and I came too close to losing Nicki to forget my good fortune." I pause for a moment. "She saved me, you know?"

"From what?"

"Myself."

He nods his head and then tilts it towards Nicki and Laura. "Shall we?" he says with a smile and I smile back and follow him across the pub and into the arms of the women we love.

The End

Thank you for reading *It Started with Memories*. I hope you enjoyed it, and if you did, I hope you'll take the time to leave a short review.

The characters of Porthgarrion will return soon in *It Started with Songs,* when we'll meet the famous novelist Sean Clayton. He's used to living an independent life in his house up on the cliff, but it's all about to get turned upside down, when he meets the force of nature that is Indigo Nash.

Printed in Great Britain
by Amazon